FLINX'S
FOLLY

By Alan Dean Foster
Published by The Random House Publishing Group

FLINX'S FOLLY

A Pip & Flinx Novel

ALAN DEAN FOSTER

BALLANTINE BOOKS • NEW YORK

This is a work of fiction. Names, characters, places, and incidents are the products of the author's imagination or are used fictitiously.

A Del Rey® Book
Published by The Random House Publishing Group

Copyright © 2003 by Thranx, Inc.
Excerpt from *Sliding Scales* by Alan Dean Foster copyright © 2004 by Alan Dean Foster

www.delreybooks.com

ISBN 0-345-45039-6

Manufactured in the United States of America

OPM 9 8 7 6 5 4 3 2 1

1

He's not dead—but watch out for the winged snake."

As she studied the tall young man lying unconscious on the fast-moving gurney, the alert eyes of the duty physician at Reides Central narrowed. "What winged snake?"

The harried medtech guiding the gurney gestured at the slow rise and fall of the patient's chest. "It's coiled up under his shirt between his left arm and his ribs. Squirmed in there and hid when we arrived to pick him up. Sticks its head out occasionally for a quick look around, but that's all. Won't leave. Hasn't bothered anyone—so far. Almost as if it senses we're trying to help."

The emergency sector physician nodded tersely as she continued to pace the gurney. "I'll be sure and keep my fingers away. Why wasn't it caught and neutralized before the patient was brought in?"

The medtech glanced sideways at her. "Quickref says it's an Alaspinian minidrag. They bond emotionally with their owners. If you'd heard what I was told, you wouldn't get any ideas about trying to separate them."

They rounded a corner, dodged an oncoming stasis chair, and headed up another corridor. "Hell of a way to practice medicine," the doctor muttered to no one in particular. "Like there aren't enough obstacles put in our way." She leaned slightly forward over the motionless form, but she was unable to detect any movement in the indicated area. "It's dangerous, then?"

The medtech smoothly eased the gurney into an empty monitoring chamber. "Apparently only if you try to separate them. Or if it thinks you're trying to harm its master."

"We're trying to help him, just like we're trying to help all the others who were brought in."

As soon as the waiting sensors detected the gurney's presence, a dozen different automated appliances initiated a standard preliminary patient scan. They automatically disregarded the presence of the flying snake just as they ignored the basic but neat and clean clothing in which the patient was dressed. The doctor stepped back from the gurney and examined her pad as one recording after another was made and silently transferred. A duplicate set was simultaneously being entered into the official hospital files.

The medtech looked on thoughtfully. "Want me to stay?"

When the doctor glanced up from her softly glowing pad, it was only to eye the patient. "Up to you. I'll be careful of the snake." Now that she knew where it was, she could see the slight bulge occasionally moving beneath the patient's shirt. "If I have any problems, I'll alert Security."

Nodding, the medtech turned to go. "Suit yourself. They probably need me in Receiving now, anyway."

The doctor continued speaking without looking at him. "How many all together?"

"Twenty-two. All standing, walking, or sitting within a few meters of one another in the same part of the Reides shopping complex. All displayed the same symptoms: a sharp gasp, followed by a rolling back of the eyes, and down they went—out cold. Adults, children, males, females—two thranx, one Tolian, the rest human. No external signs of injury, no indication of stroke or myocardial infarction, nothing. As if they'd all simultaneously been put to sleep. That's what the official witness reports say, anyway. They're pretty consistent throughout."

She gestured absently. "It'll take a minute or two for Processing to finish admitting this one. First thing we'll do is correlate data between patients for indications of other similarities, so we can try and define some parameters. I'd be surprised if there weren't several." Her voice fell slightly. "There'd better be."

Halfway out the portal, the medtech hesitated. "Viral or bacterial infection?"

"Nothing that contradicts it, but it's much too early to say." She looked up from her pad to meet his gaze. Concern was writ large there, and he was clearly looking for some sort of reassurance. "At a guess, I'd say neither one. The zone of influence was too sharply circumscribed. Same goes for a narcoleptic gas. And there are no overt indicators that would indicate an airborne infectious agent—no elevated or reduced blood pressure, no respiratory problems, no dermatological indications, no dilated pupils: not so much as a rash or a reported sneezing fit."

"What then?"

"Again, it's too soon to say. Some kind of area-specific sonic projection, maybe, though there's no evidence of cochlear damage in any of the patients. Delineated flash hallucinogen, cerebroelectrical interrupt—there are numerous possibilities. Based on what I've read and seen so far, I'd say the event was a site-specific one-time event, and that no organic agent is involved. But that's a very preliminary assessment."

With a grateful nod, the medtech departed. As the portal opaqued behind him, the doctor turned back to her patient.

Other than being taller than average and discounting the presence of the alien pet, he appeared no different from others who had been brought in. She knew results were expected fast. Having twenty-two customers suddenly drop unconscious in one's place of business was not good publicity for any enterprise. Fortunately for Reides's management, everything had happened so quickly and the local emergency teams had reacted rapidly enough that the local media had not yet found their way to the hospital. By the time they did, she and her fellow consulting physicians hoped to be ready with some answers.

An attractive young man, she decided, with his red hair and olive-hued skin. Tall, slim, and apparently healthy, if one discounted his current condition. She guessed him to be somewhere in his early twenties. A universal command bracelet encircled one wrist, but there was no sign of whatever specially attuned devices it might control. Probably nothing more elaborate than a vit player, she decided. If it contained usable ident and medical information, the medtech had failed to tap into it. Well, that could come later, following the initial diagnosis. The scanners would tell her everything she needed to know to prescribe treatment. On the bracelet a single telltale glowed softly green, showing that it was active.

Beneath the patient's shirt, a ropy shape shifted position. She did her best not to stare in its direction. She knew nothing about Alaspinian minidrags beyond the little the medtech had just told her. As long as it did not interfere with her work, she had no desire to know more.

She fidgeted, waiting for the scanners to finish. Even though no serious trauma was involved, the sudden influx of unconscious patients had momentarily over-whelmed the hospital's emergency staff. She was already eager to move on to the next patient.

The preliminary readings began appearing on her pad as well as on the main monitor that projected from the wall. Heart rate, hemoglobin content, white cell count, respiration, temperature: everything was well within normal, accepted parameters. If anything, the readings suggested an exceptionally healthy individual. Cerebral scan indicated that the patient was presently engaged in active dreaming. Neural activity levels . . . general brain scan . . .

She frowned, checked her pad again. Her eyes rose to squint at the main monitor. It was already scrolling through a list of possible allergies and finding none. Manually interrupting the process, she used her pad to go back to the readout that had attracted her attention. It now appeared on both her pad and the monitor as a separate insert.

The figures were wrong. They had to be wrong. So was the direct imaging. There had to be something the matter with this room's cerebral scanner. If its results had been a little off, she would have put it down to a calibration error. But the readouts were so far out of line that she was concerned they could potentially compromise patient treatment.

For one thing the patient's parietal lobes—the parts of the brain responsible for handling visual and spatial tasks—appeared grossly swollen. Since according to the steadily lengthening list of benchmarks being provided by the instrumentation there was no neurobiological basis for such enlargement, it had to be a scanner error. However, that did not account for the exceptionally heightened blood flow to all parts of the patient's brain, nor for what appeared to be some completely unrecognizable enzymatic and electrical activity. Furthermore, although the frontal cortex was quite dense, its apparent normality was hardly in keeping with the contrasting readouts for other portions of the cerebellum.

While many neurons were perfectly normal, dense clusters of others scanned in certain parts of the brain were swollen so large and were so inundated with activity as to suggest a potentially fatal ongoing mutation—potentially, because it was patently evident that the patient was still alive. Deeper probing soon discovered additional unnatural distortions, including what appeared to be scattered small tumors of a type and extensive neural integration she had not previously encountered, either in vivo or the medical literature.

She was not prepared to go beyond initial observation to render a formal interpretation of what she was seeing. She was no specialist, and these readings cried out for one capable of properly analyzing them. That, or a technician to repair and recalibrate the scanners. She opted to seek the latter's advice first. Bad scans made more sense than neurobiological impossibilities. Take those distinctive tumors, for example. By rights, intrusive growths of such size and in such locations should have resulted in a serious degeneration of cognitive faculties or even death. Yet all correlating scans indicated normal ongoing physiological activity. Of course, she couldn't be sure the patient was not an idiot until he woke up and started to respond. All she knew was that for a dumb dead man, he appeared to be in excellent shape.

The young man's situation clearly demanded expert scrutiny. But if she went running for help without first having the hospital apparatus checked out, she would be the one considered the idiot. Certainly a respected neurologist like Sherevoeu would think so.

Making sure to lock in and back up the absurd readings on her pad, she forwarded an application for equipment inspection to Engineering and Maintenance. They would notify her when they had concluded the requested check. Then she headed for the next patient-occupied room on her list. If this man's vitals, currently stable and steady, showed any indication of changing for the worse, the machines in the chamber would promptly alert the relevant staff.

In the darkened healing chamber behind her, the figures and readouts on the main monitor grew ever more implausible. Measurement of dream activity increased beyond all established limits. But then, the subject was not exactly dreaming. It was understandable that the instrumentation was confused, because no instruments existed that were capable of measuring what was going on in the mind of the tall young man on the gurney. It was not ROM sleep, REM sleep, or anything else a sleep specialist would have recognized.

Under his shirt a unique, warm-blooded, snakelike creature writhed and twitched with the intensity of the shared empathetic contact.

Flinx had company in the quasi-dream. His perception had been impelled outward before, by the ever enigmatic, ever playful Ulru-Ujurrians. They were not in evidence this time, nor could he recognize what was accompanying him. It was a single mind, but one of a vastness beyond anything he could identify. In some ways it was very childlike. In that respect, it was not unlike the mind of an Ulru-Ujurrian. But this was immeasurably more mature than the brilliant but juvenile inhabitants of that strange world. It bespoke an ancient lineage as complex as it was deliberate.

As it boosted him outward, he felt the presence of other minds watching, observing, unable to participate directly but striving to learn from his experience. They were utterly different from the intelligence that was propelling him through space-time yet in many ways more sympathetic to his situation. Then there was still another type of mind; cold, calculating, observant, utterly indifferent to him yet not to his condition. In his dream he did not shy away from it, but neither could he embrace it, nor it him.

Outward, onward, past stars and through nebulae, the immenseness of space, the conflicting clash of civilizations and galaxies. Gravity washed over him in waves but had no effect on his progress. He was and yet he wasn't. Devoid of control over what was conveying him, he could only go with the glow.

Abruptly, he was in a place of nothingness: no stars, no worlds, no blazing brightness of intelligence burning in the darkness of the void. All was silent and dead. Of burnt-out stars not even cinders were left, the last scraps of helium ash evanesced like table dust on a windy day. He was drifting in a place that defined winter itself: a region where nothing existed. It was as if matter and energy had never been.

What was worse, he had been here before.

In the absence of light and thought and substance there was only evil. From the standpoint of physics—high, low, or meta—it made no sense. In the absence of anything, there should be nothing. Yet *it* was present, and in a form so incalculable that even to begin to try to describe it would have taxed the efforts of theologian and physicist alike. Flinx did not need to quantify it: he *knew* of it, and that was enough. More than enough.

Why show it to him again, now? Was he doomed to dream of it more and more often? As before, he felt that it somehow fell to him to do something about it. But what? How could one tiny bit of short-lived organic matter like himself in any way affect something that could only begin to be measured on an astronomical scale? He was no nearer an answer to that question than he had been when first he had been projected into an encounter with this far-distant phenomenon that lay behind the Great Emptiness.

It was moving. No, that wasn't it. It had always been moving. What was different this time was a sense of acceleration. Throughout the length and breadth of the entire dreadful phenomenon, he sensed a distinct increase in velocity. And something worse.

A palpable feeling of eagerness.

It was coming toward him. Toward his home, the Commonwealth, the entire Milky Way. It had been coming this way for some time but now he had the feeling that it was coming faster. What that translated into in intergalactic terms he did not know. Astrophysicists could tell him, but astrophysicists might not even notice the change. If any did, they would fall to debating fluctuations involving subatomic particles and dark matter and such. Flinx doubted they would attribute the acceleration of something behind the Great Emptiness to a manifestation of ultimate evil.

The phenomenon was expanding and accelerating because it *wanted* to. Could it continue to accelerate, or was its ultimate speed limited by unknown physical constraints? This was a very important question. If it would not threaten his part of the galaxy for ten thousand years, he could relax a little.

Or could he? Was responsibility temporally limited? Could he shrug off that which he had never asked to be burdened with but which he could not deny existed?

The vision of an utterly empty universe confronted him: blackness all around, not a star, not a spark, not a hint of light, life, or intelligence anywhere. Only evil triumphant—omnipresent and omniscient and all-encompassing.

Was the prevention of that his responsibility? The responsibility of someone who worried about whether his teeth were clean or if a pair of passing women happened to be giggling at him? He wanted none of it, wanted nothing to do with it. Yet it had come to him. Certainly others thought so. Other minds he could not entirely identify.

Go away! he thought wildly. Leave me alone! I don't want to be a part of this.

You already are, the vast and somber voice that had boosted him outward informed him.

You already are, a chorus of powerful but smaller and far more individual thoughts declaimed. Immense collective and powerful individual—they were all of one mind on the matter.

And they were all manifestly sympathetic.

An infinitesimal bit of the thing that was the phenomenon behind the Emptiness brushed him. It sent him headlong in retreat—falling, plunging, rushing mindlessly madly away from that unimaginably distant and horrible place. The mind that had thrust him outward fought to cushion his descent, while the other compassionate perceivers looked on empathetically. The third observer remained cold and aloof as always, though not disinterested.

He sat up with a shout. Alarmed, disturbed, and awakened, Pip burst out of his shirt collar to flutter nervously over his head. The young engineering tech finishing up his check of the scanning instruments let out a startled yelp, tripped over his feet, and landed hard on the self-sanitizing floor.

Flinx sensed the man's fear, distress, and uncertainty, and he hastened to reassure him. "Sorry. I didn't mean to alarm you." Reaching upward with one hand, he coaxed Pip into settling down on his shoulder.

Picking himself up off the floor, the tech strove to divide his attention between the unexpectedly conscious patient and his scaly, brightly colored pet. Warily, he resumed packing up his tools.

"Well, you failed." He carefully tucked a sensitive calibrator back into its pouch. "What kind of animal is that?"

Flinx affectionately stroked the back of Pip's head and neck with one finger. "She's an Alaspinian minidrag, or flying snake."

"Cute. Real cute. Me, I'll stick to puppies."

In response to the emotion underlying the tech's reply, Pip thrust her pointed tongue several times in his direction. Then she twisted to eye her master concernedly as Flinx suddenly bent double, both hands holding the sides of his head.

The engineering tech was distressed. "Hey, friend— you all right?"

Little bolts of lightning were shooting through Flinx's skull and invisible demons were squeezing his eyes in heavy wooden vises. He struggled to steady his breathing long enough to respond.

"No, I'm—I'm not." Fighting the pain, he forced himself to look up and meet the other man's gaze. "I'm subject to— I get terrible headaches. I never know when they're going to hit."

The tech made a sympathetic clucking sound. "That's rough." Flinx could sense his concern was genuine. "Migraines, hmm?"

"No, not migraines." Though far from gone, the agonizing pain was starting to subside. "Something else. Nobody really knows what causes them. It's been speculated that the cause of mine may be—inherited."

The tech nodded. Reaching out, he grazed a contact with a fingertip. "I've notified your attending physician. Somebody should be here shortly." He closed his toolkit. It promptly self-sealed, the security strip making a slight bulge around the case's equator. "I hope you feel better. This place has a good reputation. Maybe they can come up with something to fix those headaches." Then he left the room.

There is nothing that can be given for my headaches. Flinx fought back the tears the pain squeezed from his eyes. Maybe a few whacks with a scalpel *would* cure him. Maybe a complete lobotomy. And though thankfully no more frequent, the headaches had been increasing in intensity. He stopped rubbing his temples and let his hands fall to his sides. This last attack made his head feel as if it were going to explode. That it had been triggered by his dream he had no doubt.

A few more like this, he thought, and he wouldn't have to worry about possible future courses of action. A nice, clean, quick cerebral hemorrhage would free him of all obligations, real or perceived.

Lifting her triangular, iridescent green head, a worried Pip began to flick her tongue against his cheek. As always, the slight tickling reminded him of better times, more innocent times. As a child on Drallar, living with the redoubtable Mother Mastiff, he had owned very little. Certainly he had never dreamed of having his own starship. But as a child he'd had freedom, of both body and mind. No longer. Any tincture of innocence had long since been washed away by the experiences of the past ten years.

The AAnn wanted the secrets of his ship. The Commonwealth government wanted to talk to him and perhaps study him. Any surviving remnants of the outlawed eugenicist Meliorare Society would want to make use of him. Several still unidentifiable, vaster somethings seemed to want him to confront a threat on a galactic scale. And all he wanted was to be left alone, to learn who his father was, and to explore a tiny bit of the cosmos in peace and quiet.

Peace and quiet. Two words, two conditions that had never applied to him. For Philip Lynx they remained little more than abstract philosophical concepts. His erratic ability to perceive, to read, and sometimes to influence the emotions of others—often against his will—assured him of that. When his head wasn't full of pain, it was full of the emotions of those around him.

He could sense two of them now, advancing in his direction. They exuded concern mitigated by an underlying coolness. A professional empathy, he decided. Based on what he sensed, he knew Pip would react calmly to the arrival. But he kept a hand on the flying snake anyway, as much to reassure her as to ensure the safety of his visitors.

Seconds later, the opaqued doorway lightened to admit a middle-aged woman and a slightly older man. They smiled, but their emotions reflected a curiosity that went beyond the usual interest in a patient.

"How are you feeling, young man?" The woman's smile widened. A wholly professional expression, Flinx knew. "I'd call you by your name, but your bracelet is locked and you had no other identification on or within you."

"Arthur Davis," Flinx replied without hesitation. "You are . . . ?"

"Your attending physician, Dr. Marinsky." Shifting her illuminated work pad to the other arm, she indicated the white-coated man standing next to her. He was trying hard to keep his attention focused on Flinx and not on the coiled shape resting atop his shoulder. The three red stripes of rank on his right sleeve identified him as a senior surgeon. "This is Dr. Sherevoeu."

Flinx nodded politely. "Where am I, and how did I come to be here?"

Her concern became more personal, less professional. "You don't know? You don't remember anything?" He shook his head. "You are in the postemergency ward of Reides City General Hospital. You are one of a group of twenty-two apparently unrelated and unconnected pedestrians who were in the main city shopping complex when you were knocked unconscious by an as-yet-unidentified agent."

Flinx eyed her uncertainly. "Agent?"

She nodded somberly. "Witnesses report that all of you were going about your respective business. Then, suddenly and without warning, the lot of you collapsed to the floor. Every one of the afflicted, yourself included, was brought here in a comatose state from which you are only recently emerging. No one remembers anything." Her attention shifted to the neurosurgeon. "His reaction is the same as that of the others. No difference," she said to Dr. Sherevoeu. She looked back at the patient. "You don't remember smelling anything, or feeling anything?"

"No, nothing." What he did not tell her was that he had not been unconscious. Not in the medically accepted sense. His body had been stilled, but his mind had been active—elsewhere. "What about the other shoppers? Are they all right?"

"There was some general panic, as you can imagine." Marinsky did her best to sound reassuring. "No one knew what was happening. When it became clear that only you and the other twenty-one were affected, those who had been running away came back to try and help. Some of the afflicted had struck their heads or antennae when they fell—bumps and bruises but nothing serious. There don't appear to be any aftereffects, either. A number have already been discharged to the care of friends and relatives."

He eyed her questioningly. "Then I can go, too?"

"Soon," she assured him soothingly. "We'd just like to check one or two readouts first, maybe ask you a couple of questions. Dr. Sherevoeu is our chief neurologist."

With skill born of long practice, Flinx concealed his initial reaction. He could not hide it from Pip, however. The flying snake stirred uneasily, and he stroked her to calm her.

"A neurologist?" Affecting innocence, he looked from one physician to the other. "Is something wrong? You said that when they fell, some people hit their heads."

"There is no evidence of hematoma or any other immediate damage." The neurosurgeon's tone was meant to be casual and reassuring, but Flinx could clearly sense the eagerness underneath. The man was intensely curious about something, and Flinx didn't think it was the color of his hair. "But in your case there are certain other—anomalies. Scans indicate they are well established and not of recent origin. Very curious, very." He studied the screen of his own pad. Flinx badly wanted to have a look at it. "If even half these readouts are accurate, you ought to be worse than ill. You should be dead. Yet to all appearances you are as healthy as anyone in this building, myself and Dr. Marinsky included. According to your other readings healthier than most, I should say."

"At first I thought some, if not all, of the readings in question might be due to equipment malfunction," Marinsky explained, "but that possibility has been ruled out."

Flinx remembered the engineering tech. Sitting on the

gurney, he struggled to remember what had happened to him. He had been walking in the shopping complex, enjoying the displays, watching the other strollers while trying to mute the torrent of feelings that surged around him. Practice had given him some success at doing so.

Then the headache had come: a sharp, brutal pain. No buildup, no warning, as was sometimes the case. No time for him to use the medication he now always carried with him. The pain had put him down. Then the dream. Whether whatever was responsible for it had triggered the headache by making contact with him or whether the timing was coincidence he did not know. But he did know one thing with a fair degree of certainty. He knew what had happened to the twenty-one innocent and unaware fellow strollers who had gone comatose simultaneously with him.

He had happened to them.

2

This was not the first time his budding ability to project as well as receive emotions had touched those around him, but it was the first time he could remember having unconsciously and unintentionally affected so many uninvolved, utterly innocent bystanders. Assailed by the terrible pain in his head, he had apparently involuntarily emitted a blast of emotion reflective of his condition at that pivotal moment. The output had been restrained—none of those close to him had suffered any serious damage, been killed, or been moved to kill themselves.

This was appalling. Next time, an uncontrolled eruption of his maturing ability might cause permanent brain damage to blameless bystanders, perhaps even children. He had no idea what he was ultimately capable of, and there was no one who could tell him. Controlling his abilities while he was conscious and aware was difficult enough. How was he going to mitigate their consequences when he had no control?

He was losing it. How could he possibly help mysterious, unknown entities combat some monstrous extragalactic threat when he couldn't even control himself?

Guessing at the internal struggle her patient was going through by reading his rapidly changing expressions, a compassionate Marinsky started toward him, only to halt when Pip extended herself several centimeters in the doctor's direction. "Are you still feeling all right, Arthur?"

Flinx nodded. "I was just thinking of all those other poor people. What happened to us?" He kept his attention focused on Marinsky, avoiding the neurosurgeon's intense stare.

"We really have no idea."

If she was telling the truth, and he sensed that she was, it meant that no one had connected the mass blackout to him. They were curious about what they saw inside his head. That was all. No one had any idea he might be responsible for what had happened. Not knowing his true identity, they would have been unable, even if so inclined, to find him by searching the greater Commonwealth box. If he stayed here much longer someone might think to try and match his readings with those on file. But it didn't matter because he had no intention of hanging around.

"We would like to run some tests. With your permission, of course," Sherevoeu added hastily.

Flinx faked interest. "They wouldn't hurt, would they?"

To his credit, the neurosurgeon looked shocked. "Oh, no, no! Absolutely not. They would involve nothing more invasive than what you have already experienced—more external scans, mostly, utilizing more specialized instrumentation capable of greater precision, to acquire information for analysis and evaluation." He smiled. "It's my profession, you know. Wouldn't you like to know if you're in danger from the condition we've already observed and learn if we can help you?"

"Of course. Who wouldn't?" Flinx already knew that surgery for his condition was not an option. The physical changes his brain had undergone were too tightly integrated, too interwoven. Attempting to isolate or re-

move them would kill him as surely as a ceremonial
AAnn skinning blade.

"You really think you can help me?"

The two physicians exchanged a look. It was Marinsky who finally replied. "Dr. Sherevoeu is the finest neurosurgeon on Goldin four. If anyone can do anything for
you, he can."

"But I don't feel sick." The game, he knew, had to be
played to the end.

"As I said before, outwardly you are in excellent
health." Sherevoeu did not want to alarm this potentially fascinating patient. "It's just that in looking inside
your head, we've seen some things, some anomalies,
that we feel would be beneficial to study in more detail."

Apparently indifferent, Flinx shrugged. "Go ahead
and look, then. How long are you going to need me to
stay?"

Greatly relieved at the patient's acquiescence, Sherevoeu consulted his pad. "Just a day or so. Can you do
that?"

Flinx nodded. "I'm on break from work anyway. But
not too much today, okay? I'm pretty tired."

"Yes, of course." Flinx could sense the two doctors
were completely at ease now. Sherevoeu continued, "It
will take time to authorize and prepare the necessary
procedures anyway. If you are willing, we can run one
or two simple preliminaries in a few hours." He smiled
afresh. "If it goes well, perhaps we can even have you
out of here by tomorrow evening."

Flinx flashed a carefully wary expression. "This isn't
going to *cost* me anything, is it?"

Both doctors chuckled softly. "No, Arthur. Since
we're running these tests to satisfy *our* curiosity, any expense will be borne by the facility. You should consider
yourself lucky. You're going to get a very expensive full

cerebral and neural checkup, courtesy of the good folks of Reides General."

How kind of them, Flinx mused silently, as he let the gurney's padded back support cuddle his spine. How utterly altruistic. "Sounds like a good deal to me."

The pair of unsuspicious physicians departed, more than a little pleased with themselves. They were already discussing the nature of the first tests they were going to run before they were completely through the chamber's sound-muting wave portal.

Alone, Flinx took a moment to study his surroundings. Multiple scanners continued to monitor his vitals. If he left the room and passed out of their range, alarms would sound at a central station. Then there was the matter of the hospital ident and tracking chip attached to his right wrist. The longer he waited and debated, the sooner a tech or two would show up to transfer him to another room deeper in the hospital complex, relieve him of Pip and his clothes, and prepare him for the first battery of tests. Tests he had no intention of undergoing. He had spent a good part of his adult life avoiding such tests. He had no intention of letting curious researchers, even on this minor colony world, start poking and probing him now.

Swinging his legs off the gurney, he settled Pip around his upper arm, stood, and walked out of the chamber. A medtech was heading away from him, moving down the corridor. Making no attempt to avoid contact or conceal his presence, he headed in the opposite direction. Within moments he had located the floor's main monitoring station.

"Afternoon," he said politely to the woman seated before the console.

"Hi." She smiled at him. "You're one of the people they brought in from midtown, aren't you? How are you feeling?" She eyed Pip curiously, as did everyone who saw the flying snake.

"Not too bad."

"Funny goings-on." She fiddled with a report, the letters changing on the page as modulated electric charges guided by her fingertips flowed through the malleable writing surface. "We've already discharged more than half the people who were brought in, including the two thranx."

He nodded knowingly, as if he had already been told everything she was saying. "Not me. A couple of the doctors want to run some more tests."

She glanced at his wrist, then at a readout on the console. "You're the one in four-twelve. Yes, I see that they've got you set up for a whole battery of scans. First one at four o'clock." She looked back at him. "We have an excellent pet-holding facility here. While you're being examined we'll take good care of your— What did you call it?"

"Alaspinian minidrag. I'm thinking if I'm going to get any exercise before my tests I'd better get it in now." Turning his head, he nodded up the corridor. "I'm going to take a short walk. Be right back. Is there a cafeteria?"

Her tone was professionally solicitous. "Down on the first floor. Just ask any employee for directions. You weren't told to fast before the tests?"

"Nobody said anything." The ident tab seemed to be burning against his wrist, but in reality only in his mind.

She checked his status file. "Nothing in here says you can't have something to eat and drink," she informed him cheerily. "You don't have to check back in here when you're done. Just go back to your room and wait for them to come for you."

He nodded. He had no intention of checking back in

or waiting for anyone. "See you in a little while," he assured her fallaciously.

Heading for the lift, he knew that in a few minutes she would have put the brief encounter with the tall patient completely out of her mind. Hospitals were like that. If queried later, she'd remember the conversation. And he had no doubt that she would be queried about it. But by that time he expected to have vanished into the depths of Goldin IV's busy capital city.

As he exited the lift on the first floor, he headed not for the cafeteria but for the main hospital entrance, the sleeve of his tunic concealing his ident tag. At the front desk he asked for directions. Not to the cafeteria but to a bathroom. Once inside he pulled back his sleeve to expose the tag. Selecting a remarkably compact and expensive piece of equipment from the row of instrument pouches that lined his belt, he passed it efficiently over the tag. When it buzzed softly, he locked in the reading, transferred it to another device, and then touched the device to the tag. Like a newly metamorphosed butterfly unfolding its wings, it promptly popped free of his wrist.

At the front desk again, he inquired the location of the cafeteria. There, he used his credcard to purchase a drink, a piece of cake, and a large sandwich. Finding an empty, isolated table, he sat down and ate half the sandwich while Pip enjoyed the salty snacks that came with it, stalking the animated bits of food as they bounced around their activating plate. Making sure no one was watching, Flinx then shoved the ident tag into the remainder of the sandwich, rose, and strode calmly through the dining area, past the front desk, and out the main hospital doors. In less than a minute he was on board public transport heading toward downtown Reides. Behind him and receding farther with every second, the ident tag continued to insist to every monitoring device in the hospital that the young male patient from chamber 412 was still in the cafeteria, enjoying a late lunch.

Marinsky did not panic when she arrived at his room later that afternoon to escort the intriguing young man to the first testing session she and Sherevoeu had arranged for him, only to find it empty. Nor was she especially concerned when a search turned up no sign of the patient on the fourth floor. She simply made her way to the central monitoring station and had the operative on duty run the necessary trace. It was hardly surprising that the patient had made his way to the hospital cafeteria, she thought. Since his vitals had been stable at all times and he had emerged cleanly from his coma, he had not been given intravenous nutrition. No doubt he was hungry.

Well, she could meet him there.

She was more puzzled than upset when a walk through the dining area failed to produce any sign of him. Tall as he was, she was certain she had not overlooked him. She checked again, then contacted the fourth floor monitoring station. Perhaps, in the time it had taken her to descend from the fourth floor to ground, he had moved on. She was certain she had not passed him in the corridors.

The tech insisted that the individual in question was in the cafeteria. Coordinating her work pad with the tracer, it led her to an empty table on which were the rapidly drying remains of a quick lunch. Only when she dug the mayonnaise-slathered ident tag out of the center of the sandwich did it strike her how much time had been wasted.

She notified hospital security, then Sherevoeu. Grim-faced, they spent half an hour debating possible procedures with the head of hospital security before a lower-ranking officer of the city police finally responded to their frantic requests in person.

In the security chief's small office, Sherevoeu insisted that the city constabulary immediately issue an all-points for the absent patient. The neurologist's demand was not well received.

"Why am I here?" The officer's displeasure was strong enough to overshadow her otherwise professional demeanor.

The two doctors exchanged a glance. The hospital's chief of security looked as if he wished he was elsewhere. "We just told you," Marinsky finally responded.

"You could have filed a standard missing person's report via the city box. Why did you insist someone be present to take the details in person?" With her head cocked slightly to one side, work pad in hand, the impatient officer looked like an irritated spaniel.

"The matter is somewhat sensitive." Sherevoeu attempted to regain control of the situation. "The patient in question is—a unique individual."

"Unique how?" The officer was not impressed.

Sherevoeu made a mistake. He smiled condescendingly. "It is a question of physiological, specifically neurological, anomalies that demand immediate investigation."

"Too much for a dumb constable to understand, hmm?" The officer straightened in her seat and glared at the neurologist. "What I meant was—see if you can keep up with me here—in what way involving the official constabulary of the city of Reides is this missing individual unique? What crime has he committed? What danger to the citizenry at large does he present? What illegal or antisocial activities has he been involved in? What threats to the hospital or the hospital staff has he made?" Pad at the ready, she sat waiting.

It was a moment before Marinsky finally replied. "Well—none, actually."

The officer made a show of entering this into her pad. "None. I see." She looked up. "Is the patient a danger to anyone, then? Or are you all just upset that someone waltzed out of your hospital without filling out the appropriate eighty pages of paperwork?"

Sherevoeu brightened. "The patient does indeed represent a real danger. To himself. Based on what little information we were able to obtain, we believe that without immediate medical supervision and follow-up treatment, he could very well die."

"Correct me if I'm wrong, Doctor," the officer mused aloud, "but to a certain degree couldn't that diagnosis apply to a good portion of the city's citizenry?" Before Sherevoeu could reply, she raised a hand. "That wasn't a question requiring an answer. Is this patient's condition in any way contagious?"

Marinsky hesitated before being compelled to answer. "We do not think so, no. He needs to be examined so that his unusual condition can be treated. That's all. We just want to help him." One hand rested within the other on her lap. "We have only his best interests at heart."

"Uh-huh. I'm sure you do." Rising, the officer gestured with her pad. "You know, the police in this city have tangible things to do—running down criminals, protecting the public, stopping fights, trying to solve actual crimes. That's why we prefer to receive reports like yours via the box. It conserves manpower and saves money. So far I'm not hearing anything that leads me to believe this to be an especially sensitive matter demanding the immediate allocation of scarce departmental resources."

The head of hospital security, muttering to himself,

led the visiting trio out of his office. "We just feel it's important that this be kept as confidential as possible," Marinsky was telling the officer, "for the patient's sake more than anything else. Information sent through the box is often intercepted by the media. If this were to be splashed all over the tridee, the patient's right to privacy would be seriously compromised."

"*If* anyone in the media was interested," the officer pointed out, "which, given the very general nature of your report, I don't think they would be." She stretched, the lightweight blue-gray material of her tunic lifting with her shoulders. "That's a choice you made, however. Just don't make a habit of this sort of thing. Next time you need the police for something like this, use the box."

"We will," Marinsky assured her, giving her colleague and superior a firm nudge with one forearm to preserve her silence.

The officer sighed. "We'll see if we can find your missing Arthur Davis. His being well above average height should help. But Reides City is a big place. There are a lot of tall human males here." She finally relaxed a little. "I know. I'm regularly on the lookout for them myself."

Thanking the hospital chief of security for his help, the doctors watched him trundle back to his office, still muttering to himself.

"I did not find that officer very responsive." Like his tone, Sherevoeu's expression was pinched. "Nor did I approve of the way you repeatedly truckled to her."

"She was already in a bad mood when she got here," Marinsky sensibly pointed out. "Antagonizing her further would have been a bad way to secure the police department's cooperation." They headed for the central lift.

"I wish we could have made it clear to her how important it is that we get that patient back. He really *is* unique. Of course," Sherevoeu added prudently, "that is only a preliminary finding. Proper verification awaits further investigation."

"There's not much more we can do. Unless," Marinsky added, "we want to go wide with it and involve the very public we told the officer we want to keep on the sidelines."

Sherevoeu nodded. "Alerting the media would certainly locate him faster. But then everyone would know of our interest, and want it explained." Including other doctors and researchers, and that would result in the dilution of whatever renown might be gained from further scientific study of the distinctive and regrettably missing Arthur Davis.

"I see no need to resort to such publicity except as a last option." He eyed his colleague intently. "You follow my meaning?"

"I believe I do, Eli. Surely the police will be able to locate our patient. Reides is a modern municipality, with efficient civil services. The constabulary will do its job." She checked her work pad. "Meanwhile, we must do ours."

"Yes, of course." He checked his work pad. "I have four post-ops to look in on and half a dozen surgeries to program over the next several days. A new piece of capillary dilation software just added to the thrombosis AI needs a final checkout before we can start programming it for work. Whereas you, I believe, have some time off."

"Two days, starting in the morning. I'll be thinking of you, hard at work," she added playfully. In a more serious tone she added, "You'll notify me immediately if there's any sign of our red-headed Mr. Davis? I'll gladly forgo my downtime and get back to town as fast as transport will bring me."

"You'll be the first to know. Tell me something, Neila: do you think he just wandered off, or left intentionally?"

"A patient doesn't remove his ident tag and stick it in a sandwich on the spur of the moment," she replied gravely. "His flight had to have been carefully thought out. We can ask him about it when the police bring him back."

"Yes," he replied absently as he turned toward his own office. "At least by keeping this quiet we can ensure no one else develops an interest in him."

But the neurologist was wrong.

Dr. Neila Marinsky's house backed onto a section of carefully preserved evergreen forest on the outskirts of one of Reides's more exclusive suburbs. From her private transport, encrypted signals were broadcast through the high, camouflaged outer wall of the urb, through the gated fence that surrounded her personal property, and into her garage. From there, it was steps to the interior. She was scanned and processed by additional security before she was admitted inside.

She loved her house. Nestled among the trees and the indigenous wildlife of Goldin IV's southern temperate zone, it was her refuge from the pressures of hospital work and private practice. Though she occasionally shared it with visitors who did not come to discuss matters medical (though physiology was sometimes involved), she was single again, after one marriage made too early and messily terminated four years earlier.

So she was more than a little shocked when she entered the sunken living room to see that despite all the expensive, supposedly state-of-the-art home and urb security, her cherished sanctum had been violated.

The couple waiting there were less than threatening.

They were well dressed according to the fashion of the moment, which usually reflected and ran half a year behind what was currently in style on Earth or New Riviera. The short woman seated on the couch had dark hair and eyes that were active and intelligent. Body in constant motion, eyes often downcast as if he were perpetually looking for something he had dropped, the man was undertall and skinny, his attitude apologetic but determined. They were about as innocuous-looking a pair as one could expect to encounter on the streets of Reides. Except they weren't on the streets of Reides.

They were in her living room, in her home.

Though both wore small satchels slung at their waists, neither of the intruders brandished anything resembling a weapon. The woman smiled. "Good day of those that remain, Dr. Marinsky. You *are* Dr. Neila Marinsky, resident physician at Reides General Hospital?"

Strange greeting, she mused. She saw no reason to deny the query—or for that matter, to respond to it. "Who are you and how did you get into my house?" Reaching into her own bag, she drew out her com unit. While it might take the nearest police ten or fifteen minutes to get here, urb security would arrive in a third of that time.

The man nodded regretfully at the device. "That won't do you any good, I'm afraid." His gaze dipped. "We've cloaked your property in a privacy sphere."

She tried anyway. The intruder was as good as his word. Nothing in the way of electronic communications could get in or out. Putting the com unit back in her bag, she set it down on a table. There were no weapons in the house, but the kitchen contained devices that could cut and bruise. Focusing on the intruders, she wandered slowly in that direction.

"It doesn't matter how we got in," the woman was saying. "What matters is that we are here. Matter is what matters." To this cryptic observation, her companion nodded somberly. "We just want to ask you some questions, then we'll leave." She gestured at the austerely elegant surroundings. "You can see that we haven't disturbed anything. We're not thieves."

Marinsky hesitated. If she could get rid of these two without trouble . . . "What do you want from me?"

"Just some information." The man tried to smile pleasantly, but a quirk of his facial structure rendered it crooked. "You are treating a young man named Philip Lynx?"

Marinsky frowned, wondering if it might be better to make a break for the front door. Outside, it was unlikely anyone would hear her screams, but she might well make it to her vehicle. Once locked inside, she would be safe and could either leave or wait for urb security to arrive. Neither of her unannounced visitors looked particularly athletic.

"I am not. The name is entirely unfamiliar to me."

The man's smile grew more crooked as it widened. "He may have declared himself by another name. As he travels, he often disguises his identity. We know he is on Goldin Four and in Reides. By sheer good fortune we happened to see him, as we were watching the news, being carried, in an apparently unconscious state, onto a hospital transport. The tridee commentator observed that he was among a number of people who had lapsed into a simultaneous and inexplicable comatose state while walking through a local shopping complex. It was announced that all those thus afflicted were taken to Reides Central for treatment."

Marinsky blinked. "I saw the manifest for everyone who was brought in. The name Philip Lynx was not on it. You're tracking this individual?"

The woman spoke up without responding to the ac-

cusation. "He's very easy to identify, our Philip Lynx.
Handsome in a boyish way, red hair, quite tall." Her
tone was confident. "He travels in the constant company of an Alaspinian minidrag. Not a profile that
matches many."

"Arthur Davis," the doctor blurted without thinking.
So their patient had retained enough presence of mind,
even when emerging from his coma, to give a false
name. But why?

The peculiar couple was quietly pleased. "Then it is
him," the woman murmured.

Her companion nodded, the movement terse and jit-
tery like everything else about him.

"What do you want with Mr. Dav— with this Philip
Lynx?"

The man responded quietly, as if what he was saying
was the most natural thing in the world: "We have to
kill him."

Absence of visible weapons or no, a chill trickled
up the doctor's spine. "Kill him?" she echoed dumbly.
"But—why? He seems like a perfectly nice, ordinary
young man." No, not ordinary, she told herself. Which
prompted the sudden thought: Could this somehow
have anything to do with the patient's unusual brain
scan?

The woman replied with perfect calm, "If we don't
kill him, it is remotely possible he may find a way to kill
Death. The Death that is coming for us all."

"The great Cleansing that will remake the universe—
may it hasten on its way." Though softly spoken, there
was no mistaking the messianic undertone in the man's
voice.

Not Qwarm, members of the professional assassin's
guild, an increasingly alarmed Marinsky told herself.
These two didn't dress like Qwarm, they didn't act like

Qwarm, and they didn't look like Qwarm. They especially did not talk like Qwarm, who worked for money. No, the preternaturally polite but still unsettling intruders she found herself confronting were most likely a pair of religious nuts—though representative of what sect or cult she did not know. What was important, she told herself, was not to alarm or upset them. If she could do that and still satisfy them without compromising her personal or professional ethics, they might leave quietly, just as the man had insisted they would. Then she could notify the authorities and have them dealt with appropriately.

"Well, I can't help you with this Lynx person."

"You were identified as the physician in charge," the woman responded. It was not a question.

"Yes, and I did see and treat the individual to whom you refer." Marinsky disliked having to admit to it, but given the emotional volatility that was common to self-confessed fanatics, she knew that the important thing was to get them out of her house without upsetting them. She smiled in what she hoped was an ingratiating manner. "There's no mistaking the flying creature that accompanies him."

The man looked pleased. "What is his condition, and what healing chamber does he occupy now?"

"The last time I saw him," she replied truthfully, "he seemed to be doing fine. As to the latter, he doesn't occupy any room. He skipped out on us earlier today. Left the hospital without authorization." She spread her hands. "I don't know where he is, or even if he's still in Reides. The constabulary is searching for him even as we speak."

"Why would they do that?" Both of them were looking at her with sudden, fresh interest. Had she let something important slip? Reviewing her response, it seemed innocuous enough.

"He left without following proper hospital procedure. There are issues involved. Payment for emergency services rendered, for one thing."

That seemed to satisfy them. "And you have no idea where he might have gone?"

Marinsky's confidence returned. "If I did, the police wouldn't be looking for him. He'd be back in the hospital already." Could she put them more at ease by showing an interest in their bizarre theology, whatever it might be? "What's this about killing death?" Though she had changed her mind about making a break for her transport, she still continued to unobtrusively work her way toward the front door.

The man lifted his eyes ceilingward. "It comes for all of us. For everything. All sin, all inequality, is to be washed away. In its wake, the cosmos will be born anew." He lowered his gaze to meet hers. "What do you know about theoretical high-energy physics and extragalactic astronomics?"

The shift in subject matter startled her. "Not—nothing much, really. They don't exactly impact on my chosen field. What does that have to do with killing death and with Mr. Lynx?"

"Everything." Rising from the couch, the woman eyed her partner. "We'll just have to keep looking."

Now she and Sherevoeu had another reason to bring the young man back to the hospital: for his own protection. Did he even know that certain crazed fanatics were looking for him? When the police located him and brought him back, she would so inform him. He should be properly grateful.

"Was there anything else?" she asked optimistically, hoping to speed her unwanted visitors on their way.

"No, that seems to be, sadly, all you can tell us." The woman preceded her companion in exiting the living room's conversation area. "Thank you for your help."

"We who pave the way thank you," the man added as he strode past. In so doing, he bumped into the nervous doctor. "Sorry."

And then they were gone. Speaking into her command bracelet, Marinsky immediately sealed every entrance to the house. A quick check revealed that the privacy sphere had evaporated along with those who had put it in place. By staying composed, she had disposed of the intruders without harm to her home, to herself, or to them. Feeling relieved and not a little pleased with herself, she was preparing to use her communicator to call urb security when a demanding itch caused her to look down at her left forearm. Where the man had bumped into her, a small red blotch had appeared on the bare skin. It was spreading rapidly. Alarmed, she activated the com unit. When she tried to speak into it she discovered that her vocal cords would not work. The paralysis proliferated with astonishing speed.

When urb security finally arrived she was lying on the floor of her undisturbed living room, the com unit clutched tightly in frozen fingers, eyes open, her mouth parted in preparation of speaking words that had not, and now never would, emerge.

As they sped away from the exclusive development in their rented vehicle, the nondescript visitors discussed the implications of their visit.

"One more killing." As she spoke, the woman's thoughts turned from the physician they had just left to their quarry.

"It does not matter." Her companion was programming the small skimmer to take them to the modest downtown hotel that they had made their center of operations since arriving on Goldin IV. "The Death comes to us all sooner or later."

"May it be sooner." The woman responded automatically in the litany of the Order. "Do you think he is still somewhere in the city?"

"We can only hope." Switching to automatic, the skimmer joined a line of vehicles heading for the city. "If so, we must find him before the local authorities do. We have few associates here."

"The physician knew nothing of his true nature." Sitting back in her seat, the woman pondered the scenery whizzing past outside, scenery that, like everything else, would be obliterated by the same clean slate that would come to dominate all of existence. Though she knew she was personally unlikely to witness that coming, she could anticipate and envision it in her imagination. That was the wonderful thing about nothingness, she knew. It was clean. Pure. So unlike the teeming, festering cosmos of today. It was coming. It was inevitable.

Only one individual might possibly, by means and methods not understood, somehow slow that process. He might do so only because he possessed knowledge of what was coming. Infinitesimal as the possibility of the Forthcoming being diverted or halted might be, it still existed. By dealing with him the Order would ensure that even that minuscule possibility was erased.

It was little enough to do. If others died in the course of seeking him, it meant nothing. If she and her companion died, it meant nothing.

They would find the only one who, besides the members of the Order, knew the full truth of what was coming, and they would kill him. If possible, she wanted to speak to him first, to find out everything that he knew and if he had passed the knowledge along to many others. Because in that event, they would also have to die.

How ironic that if not for him and his knowing, the Order whose members now vigorously sought his demise would not even exist.

3

When Flinx stepped out of the hoverer and into open air he was between two and three thousand meters above the ground. At a command, the feather-light aero-composite wings of the repeller attached to his chest and legs unfolded. He dropped a few hundred meters before the repeller's breatherip intake snagged sufficient air and arrested his plunge. Wraparound goggles snug against his face, hands inserted into the repeller's control mittens, he leveled off and headed for the leading edge of the nearest cloud. It was a big, puffy white cumulus. Ingesting its moisture would top off the repeller's supply of hydrogen. Repeatedly doing so would allow a competent flier to remain aloft for as long as he wished, provided the weather cooperated and he did not get too tired.

He soon left his fellow recreational soarers behind. They had gone east to swoop along the flanks of the mountains where rising air currents would allow them to conserve energy. Flinx preferred solitude. Effortlessly, the repeller carried him westward, high above the gently undulating forest far below. He was looking for company but not of the human kind.

He found it ten minutes later in the form of a flock of kyl-le-kee. Their almost-transparent twenty-meter wings were tinted greenish gold, the better to allow them to

blend in with the surface below and make them difficult
targets for downward-plunging predators. Their torsos
and abdomens were long and slim, flattened and leathery underneath to permit the occasional rare landing
since they had no legs. The kyl-le-kee spent their whole
lives riding the air currents of Goldin IV—eating, mating, living, and dying in the clear blue sky, only rarely
making contact with the ground. They even procreated
aloft, giving birth to live young. Born with inflated air-
sacs attached to their backs, the juvenile kyl-le-kee
floated free until their newly uncurled wings strengthened enough for them to fly on their own. Only then
would a cautious parent bite into the supportive airsac,
whose deflated membrane soon withered away.

Large, protuberant yellow eyes regarded the solo
soarer speculatively. The kyl-le-kee were harmless vege-
tarians, feeding on the plethora of Goldin IV's fascinating bladder-supported plant forms that constituted
a kind of oversized airborne phytoplankton. Moderately curious, exceedingly graceful, they rolled and rose,
dipped and hovered, while the peculiar entity with the
prone human on its back banked and looped among
them. When they grew bored, they gathered into a line
and resumed their course westward. Their thin but
powerful wings accelerated them to a speed Flinx's repeller could not hope to match.

It had been a wonderful encounter. Banking left, he
headed for another cloud mass in search of new companions. When he grew tired, or when the sun began to
set, he would circle back along his route and make for
the landing strip carved from the woods just outside
Memeluc town.

Five thousand k's from Reides City, he felt safe from
the curious eyes of hospital staff and questing authorities. Having read and heard much about Goldin IV's

specialized and beautiful aerial life-forms, he had determined to see at least some of them up close before leaving the prosperous colony world. By the time any search for him reached distant Memeluc, he should long since be leaving the sun of this agreeable system behind.

The cloud cluster he was approaching was smaller than the one where he had topped off the repeller's fuel. A few small, dark, winged shapes flitted below him in its shadows. Erenweth's besketh, perhaps, or maybe the notoriously elusive hakuh-heth. Having seen a vit of a hakuh-heth, he looked forward to the rare opportunity to observe one in person. He put the repeller into a sharp dive, hoping to confront the famously shy flier before it could spot him and flee.

Abruptly, two of the circling shapes whirled upward to meet him. They were not hakuh-heth, he saw quickly, but rather humans lying atop and driving repellers like his own. Fliers from another hoverer, he decided, since none of those he had dropped with had traveled in this direction.

Fortunately, and probably thanks to the steepness of his dive, the first shot missed him. Banking sharply to his left, he headed for the cover of the nearest cloud.

Both pursuers followed. A second shot grazed the left wing of his repeller as he entered the concealing whiteness. Secured around his right forearm, an alarmed Pip stuck her head out and began searching anxiously for the source of her master's sudden distress.

In response to her movement, he drew his arm closer against his body. One of many signals he had developed in working with her over the years, the increased pressure indicated that he wanted the minidrag to stay where she was. Although infinitely more agile than any repeller, she would quickly tire of trying to chase them down. He could not hope to use her against his unknown assailants unless they came very close. And he intended to keep as much distance between him and them as possible.

In the more turbulent depths of the cloud, the lightweight repeller bucked and weaved. Unless they had come equipped with more sophisticated instrumentation than his brief glimpse of them had shown, his pursuers should be flying blind. He was not.

Reaching out with his increasingly maturing ability, he sensed them still following. The excitement of the hunt and the eagerness with which they sought to eradicate their quarry appeared to him as an emotional beacon. In the last few years he had learned how to use his ability to detect and interpret such beacons and also to manipulate them. Knowing, feeling that they planned to kill him the instant the opportunity presented itself allowed him to respond to the threat without hesitation.

Extending himself, he reached out toward them, projecting the fear of death into their minds, striving to overwhelm all other emotions. Having been forced to do it before, he knew the effect such a projection could have. Against his arm, Pip abruptly went motionless, acting like a lens for her master's singular talent.

When he burst out of the opposite side of the cloud, both pursuers were still behind him.

Pushing forward on the controls, he sent the repeller plummeting surfaceward. Landing would not save him. Before he could free himself from the repeller's harness, his pursuers would be on top of him. It wasn't so much that something had gone wrong with his effort as that something was not right about those he sought to influence. He knew now when his talent was working and when it wasn't. He'd pushed confidently against those chasing him, striving hard to upset their emotional balance. It had not worked.

While fighting to take evasive action with the repeller, he struggled once more to read the feelings of his pursuers. What he found both surprised and unsettled him. He knew now why his effort had failed: The people chasing him had absolutely no fear of death. None. Insofar as he could read them, they were totally indifferent to the prospect as a true artist was to boorish criticism.

How could he emotionally affect people who were not afraid of dying?

As another disrupter bolt passed much too close to his head, this became more than an academic question. He couldn't keep this up forever. Sooner or later, a good shot or a lucky one would damage either the repeller or him. Either way, he was too high to risk an uncontrolled fall. And he *did* have strong feelings about dying.

Mightn't he try infusing them with strong feelings about something else? Concentrating harder than ever, he pushed outward with the first thing that seemed to offer some hope.

He didn't know if either of them gasped. Probably they did not scream. But a glance backward showed both pursuing repellers rocketing groundward as fast as their pilots could stand. By the time they finally touched down, safely and to all appearances intact, he was well on his way to the landing site at Memeluc town. They did not try to resume the pursuit. Getting a repeller off the ground was difficult even for professional pilots, which was why casual fliers and tourists were dropped from hoverers. He didn't think they would try—at least, not until the emotions he had planted in their minds had worn off.

Unafraid of death a person might be, but they could still be made to feel an overpowering fear of heights.

As her master relaxed, so did Pip, tucking her head back beneath his rented flying suit. Gradually descending toward Memeluc, Flinx strove to analyze the lingering sensations he had gleaned from his would-be assassins. If only he could read thoughts instead of just emotions. They hadn't been Qwarm. Having caught several glimpses of their attire, he was certain of that. The members of the assassin's guild were quietly proud of their affiliation and lost no opportunity to display it at every opportunity. They would especially want to do so to a prospective target, so that the intended victim would know exactly who was about to do him in.

Constables, whether uniformed or plainclothes, would have announced themselves before shooting. Staff from the hospital would have been told to bring him in alive. While certain elements of the Commonwealth government were more than casually interested in him, subsequent to his most recent hasty departure from Earth, they, too, would want to question him, not bury him. Legally, he was guilty of nothing worse than avoidance. And the one individual who might want him dead and was also strong enough to seriously threaten him was, to the best of his knowledge and perceptive talents, not on this world and knew nothing of his present whereabouts.

Who then? As the rolling forested hills began to give way to the modest conurbation of Memeluc he found he was very tired, and not just from the effort he had expended aloft to avoid being killed. Local authorities, occasionally the Qwarm, and the Commonwealth government all had their reasons for wanting to exert one kind of control or another over him. And now this new element, these new people, whose origins and motives were a complete mystery to him. He sighed heavily. His was not a peaceful life. With every world he stopped at, with every passing year, the tranquillity he sought seemed to fade further into the future. Throw in the occasional encounter with the AAnn, and the only time he ever enjoyed any real peace was when he was traveling alone through space-plus aboard his ship.

Why did these new would-be assassins want him dead? No effort had been made to communicate with him. They had taken shots without first trying to talk. It was not a case of mistaken identity. That much he had been able to divine from their emotions without having to know their exact thoughts. They had not been mentally unsettled, homicidal thrill seekers out to shoot down the first unsuspecting flier who happened to come their way. They had been waiting for *him*.

Even the Qwarm feared death. What philosophical or ethical underpinnings had his pursuers possessed that enabled them to be so indifferent to the possibility of death? Flinx had never encountered anyone sane who had so lacked the basic instinct to survive. And his would-be killers had been sane. That, too, he had perceived.

It didn't matter, he decided firmly. Once he turned the repeller in to the rental agency he would take the first high-speed transport back to Reides. The capital's main shuttleport was located a considerable distance from the outermost urbs. Having been forced more than once to gain access to his grounded shuttlecraft under far more difficult conditions, he had no doubt he would be able to successfully board it at Reides Port.

Still, it was nice to be able to settle back in the private charter vehicle and relax as it left Memeluc, accelerating rapidly toward the capital. There had been no sign of his pursuers while he was turning in the repeller and making arrangements for the transport. Nor had he sensed anything suspicious in his immediate vicinity: no hate directed his way, no bloodlust, no anger or killing frenzy, only the soothing emotional babble of town dwellers and country folk, so much more relaxed and less mentally irksome than the frenetic emotional surge projected by the urbanites.

The transport would deposit him directly at Reides Port. Since he had his own private craft, from there it would take only a few moments to make his way through Emigration. Once aloft, no one could trouble him. If any tried, he had at his disposal a number of means for avoiding interception. So secure did he feel in the privacy of the self-guiding hired transport that he allowed himself to drift into a gentle sleep, the still largely unspoiled landscape of Goldin IV blurring past beyond the single plexalloy window.

It was a mistake.

Not a lethal one. Not by any means. No mysterious, far-ranging sources sent his thoughts racing outward beyond the limits of the galaxy to test his perception and his sanity. Instead, his thoughts churned and dreams roiled as he tossed and twisted uneasily on the padded seat. Helpless as always to calm her master at such times, Pip could only lie coiled nearby, tongue flicking anxiously, eyes staring, her triangular head moving nervously from side to side. Her master's perturbed dreaming was the one persistent adversary she could affect with neither bite nor toxin.

The vehicle's pleasant-voiced arrival announcement woke him. He found himself curled up on the floor of the transport, wet under his arms and on his forehead, his neck damp. His head pounded, though not with one of the terrifying, extreme headaches that made him want to run headfirst into a wall and knock himself unconscious just to make the pain stop. He fumbled with his service belt until he found its integrated medipak. Five minutes after swallowing the appropriate capsule, the throbbing at the front of his head began to recede. Ten minutes later, the transport pulled into the shuttleport commuter station.

The occasions when he unexpectedly and unwillingly found his sleeping consciousness thrust infinitely outward remained infrequent. It was the simpler dreams that had begun to wear on him. More and more often he found it difficult to get a good night's rest. Nightmares that far exceeded anything he had experienced while growing up on Moth plagued him with disquieting regularity. Unable to exorcise the demons that beset him, suffering from more frequent and stronger headaches, the combination of lack of sleep and stabbing head pain was making him tense, irritable, and unable to think clearly. It was the last he feared the most. With assorted folk trying to arrest, examine, or kill him, mental lucidity was the one defense he could not afford to lose.

As if to emphasize that he was even now mentally adrift, even as he contemplated his situation, the transport had to remind him that they had arrived at the programmed destination. And unless he was prepared to pay waiting charges, it was time for him to exit the vehicle.

He did so, making sure both his compact travel satchel and even smaller companion were both with him. Pip remained coiled out of sight, a muscular bulge beneath his tunic, lest the sight of her unsettle other travelers. Highly venomous, she would never have been allowed to travel with passengers on a commercial shuttle. Since Flinx had his own craft, both of them were expeditiously waved through Security. Used to adopting and discarding false identities the way a traditional croupier shuffled cards, one "Sascha Harbonnet," his unusual but complaisant pet, and their one small article of luggage rapidly and efficiently cleared Goldin IV's unpresumptuous departure procedures. Of a certain Philip

Lynx, there was no official sign. As for young "Arthur Davis," formerly a patient at Reides Central Hospital, the small-scale search for him had not yet been extended this far.

As soon as the passenger shifter deposited him at the base of his shuttle, he entered and moved swiftly to settle himself in the pilot's seat. Reciting a by-now familiar series of commands, he secured himself and Pip in the harness while the craft's AI ran through a corresponding sequence of preliftoff checks. When both artificial and organic intelligences were satisfied with each other's responses, Flinx requested and was promptly granted a window for departure by Port Operations.

Waiting alone in his shuttle, snugged tight in the flight harness, he recollected the details of his visit to Goldin IV. One more world cursorily visited, a few more experiences acquired, many more people encountered, another attempt to kill him by still another new set of assailants. With each passing year he seemed to acquire greater knowledge and more enemies. None of which would matter, he knew, if he failed to find a solution to his nightmares, his lack of sleep, his terrible headaches, and the concerns that had dogged him ever since he was old enough to realize that he was seriously different from everyone else. Not to mention his involvement with something unimaginably vast, threatening, and all but beyond human ken.

Just your average boy's life, he mused as the engine roared and he was pressed back into the chair and harness. Only he wasn't a boy anymore, and, except for a brief period on Moth, when he had roamed free and without a care under the casual supervision of the tolerant Mother Mastiff, he was not sure he had ever been one. Time to put away childish things. Trouble was,

Flinx had been more or less forced to do that when he had turned twelve.

Through the shuttle's foreport the sky faded smoothly and rapidly from blue to purple to the familiar endless blackness flecked with stars. One light flashing larger and brighter than the others shot past his field of view to starboard: an incoming shuttle, carrying cargo and passengers preoccupied with the mundanities of normal, everyday lives. An ordinariness, a blissful ignorance he had come to envy. It was a condition that had been denied him for many years now and one that the immediate future held no prospect of his experiencing.

If only all he had to worry about, he reflected, were death and taxes.

"Missed him!"

The woman who had been riding one of the two repellers removed the illegal jack she had used to tap into the shuttleport's box. The faces of her four companions reflected their disappointment.

"What ship?" asked one of the five who had been dispatched by the Order of Null to Goldin IV in an attempt to terminate the potentially unsettling problem that was Philip Lynx.

The woman scanned the information she had downloaded from the port's system. "The only traveler who matches his description was passed by Security and Emigration and left through the private lounge about three hours ago."

"Three hours!" The other woman in the group murmured something under her breath that would have sounded innocuous to most had she voiced it aloud. "He'll be in space-plus by now and untraceable."

"We'll find him." One of her two male companions displayed the quiet confidence that was so characteristic of the members of the Order—or, given their philosophical basis, perhaps *fatalistic* would have been a better description. "Wherever he goes, to whatever world, members of the Order will be waiting and looking for him."

"It would have been better to have concluded this now." The senior member of the group looked resigned. "Though I suppose there is no hurry, as long as he makes no attempt to disseminate what he knows."

"On the contrary," declared his companion encouragingly, "he appears inclined to silence."

"All the better for our ends." The other woman knew their quarry's silence would not keep him from being killed. There were no certainties except death, as members of the Order knew far better than most.

"If he left via the private lounge"—the senior among them was speaking again—"that means he has access to a private starship. I wonder who it belongs to? Given his age, surely it's not his own?"

"On loan from a large Trading House, perhaps. It is evident that he must have powerful friends, to have avoided the Commonwealth authorities for so long."

"It does not matter." The senior man gestured toward the busy main assembly area. "Let's get something to eat. Important friends or not, he has to die. If any others interfere, they may have to share the same fate."

"The fate that is coming to us all," added the woman with satisfaction.

"Strange, is it not," murmured the senior man as he turned to go, "how our colleagues, experienced fliers both, were suddenly overcome by an overwhelming fear of heights?" He contemplated the mystery even as he addressed his companions. "That is a matter that demands deeper examination."

The five strolled in the direction of the port's busiest

area. They were dressed in clean but unspectacular attire, and attracted not the slightest attention. They might have been a group of friends on holiday, members of an extended family setting off to visit far-flung relations, or simply locals out for an afternoon's diversion, intent on sampling the delights of the port's many shops and restaurants.

They certainly did not look like the earnest devotees of ultimate destruction.

4

Drifting in stately procession against the radiant background of stars—separate, apart, and smaller than most of the numerous other vessels in orbit—the *Teacher* awaited his arrival. His ship was unpretentious enough to be innocuous yet large enough for one person to rattle around in in the depths of space for weeks at a time without becoming bored. To anyone who had observed it at its last port of call, it would not have been recognizable.

As always, and as programmed, it welcomed him with music. The undulating opening glissando of Retsoff's *Second Soirée for Orchestra and Bandalon* tickled his ears as he strode purposefully from the shuttle bay to the command and control center. Pip joyfully disengaged from his shoulder and shot forward, glad to be back home. As he passed through the living quarters' relaxation chamber, with its tinkling waterfall, fountains, and aerial displays, the fronds and leaves of some of the decorative foliage from the edicted planet known as Midworld inclined in his direction. The visible motile response no longer surprised him. Plants, he had come to believe, were capable of surprisingly sophisticated responses to external stimuli. It was a personal discovery he intended to delve into in much greater detail one day, when he had the time.

Attuned to his voice, the *Teacher*'s peerless AI welcomed him to the compact bridge. Settling himself into the pilot's seat, he regarded the starfield beyond the curving port. The basso thrumming of Pip's wings ceased as she folded them flat against her sides and took up a comfortable resting position atop one of her favorite instrument panels—one of the few that gave off any heat. Her presence blocked the lens of its heads-up projector, but he had no need of its function at the moment.

"Instructions, O master of a thousand confusions? And how was your sojourn on beautiful, bucolic Goldin Four?"

The sarcasm, like the pleasant feminine voice, was employed at the discretion of the sophisticated AI. It did its best to vary its tone in an attempt to keep him amused. He could have banished it in favor of something banal and less prickly, but decided to let the AI pick its own way. The tenor suited his mood.

More than that, it struck uncomfortably close to home.

"The initial weeks were very pleasant. It's a nice world. But the last couple of days, unknown persons of homicidal bent tried to kill me."

"What, again?" The synthetic voice managed a maternal tut-tut. "You really must find another hobby, Flinx."

"It's not funny," he muttered as he shifted uncomfortably in the chair.

"Sorry." The AI was immediately contrite. "That portion of my humor programming, combined with concurrent library research, suggested that it would be."

He sighed. Debating the roots and timing of human humor with an artificial intelligence, no matter how advanced, was inevitably a dead end. "Another time it probably would be. Not your fault. I appreciate the effort to entertain me."

"It's my job." The voice managed to sound relieved. "You have no idea who these disagreeable persons are or what organization they represent?"

"None. Only that they have no fear of death. I mean, none whatsoever. It's very strange." He straightened. "But hopefully avoidable. I doubt they tracked me here. Head outsystem, please."

A rising hum took the place of the just completed *Soirée*. The chair vibrated ever so slightly. "Destination or vector?"

He had given it no thought. "Just take us a sufficient number of AU's out so the drive can be legally engaged."

Readouts soon showed Goldin IV beginning to recede behind him. Pip dozed atop her chosen panel. Hours later, as they approached the outermost of the system's five gas giants, Flinx had decided on the latest change of appearance. But not for him.

Starships did not molt, but thanks to the skills of the Ulru-Ujurrians who had built this one for him as a gift, the *Teacher* was capable of a few very distinctive tricks besides its unique ability to actually land on a planet—a feat no other KK-drive ship Flinx knew of could duplicate.

Having chosen the new configuration from a standard Commonwealth shipping file, he gave it and the necessary command to the *Teacher*. Within, everything remained the same. But through subtle manipulation of the actual metal, plastic, ceramic, composites, and other materials of which the vessel was fashioned, its exterior began to change.

The ingenious metamorphosis took a couple of hours. During this time the isolated starship was not observed or hailed. Certain false instrument blisters on its hull vanished while others, differing in shape and color, appeared elsewhere. A pair of dummy gun turrets disappeared, to be replaced by concomitant nonfunctional concavities. A large communications array appeared where none had been before, while a brace of maneuvering thrusters rearranged themselves into an entirely new configuration.

Integrated chromatophoric materials in the substance of the *Teacher*'s hull changed its color from stark ivory to a dull blue striped with maroon. Fake scars and pockmarks suggesting frequent in-system collisions with wandering spatial debris appeared on the ship's formerly immaculate epidermis. In less than two hours the *Teacher* changed from looking like a wealthy Trading House's private transport to a battered intrasystem freighter.

Not only could Flinx change his clothes to disguise his appearance; so could his ship. No doubt the Ulru-Ujurrians, who were inordinately fond of elaborate games, had particularly enjoyed integrating that little bit of sleight of ship into the *Teacher*'s abilities.

Satisfied with the alteration, Flinx now contemplated the immense bands of yellow and white that swept across the uninhabitable surface of Goldin XI. By this time, he usually had a destination in mind—yet he hadn't chosen one. His indecision was not caused by a lack of choices. The Commonwealth was a big place, and there were innumerable worlds he had yet to visit. He found himself unable to choose. A meal failed to help his mood. Music and a visit to the relaxation chamber, with its running water, imported greenery, and small wandering life-forms, did not help either.

He didn't fear the unknown individuals who had tried to kill him on Goldin IV. He respected but was not afraid of the Qwarm or the Commonwealth authorities.

He was even prepared to deal with his disturbing dreams. What he was afraid of, and what was contributing so strongly to his present mood of quiet despair, was a realization that he did not know what to do next. Staying alive was a valid objective, as was trying to find his father. But more and more, he found it difficult to justify either as an end in itself.

He badly needed to talk to someone, someone who could understand, sympathize, and offer a different point of view. Across the bridge, Pip sensed her master's distress and raised her head.

"If only you could talk," he murmured affectionately to his constant companion. It was a sentiment he had voiced countless times over the years. But even if Pip could speak, what would she say? That she was hungry, tired, or sorry? She was capable of reading his moods as no one else could, but she was unable to offer advice: only companionship and the occasional tongue caress. Sometimes that was enough. It wasn't now. Tilting his head back, he rested one hand on his forehead as if the gesture could somehow quiet the turmoil within him. Beyond the port, the monstrous gaseous globe of Goldin XI precessed in stately, indifferent silence.

"Ship, I think I'm going crazy."

It was an announcement to give even the responsive AI pause. It hesitated lest it misconstrue the meaning of its owner's words.

Guessing at the reason behind the extended silence, Flinx sighed. "Not literally. At least, I don't think so."

"Is it the headaches?" the ship inquired solicitously.

"It's more than that. These dreams—I hardly ever get a decent sleep anymore. The more I see of people, the more of their emotions I read, the less inclined I am to worry about their eventual fate. And I'm tired of being followed, chased, and being a target for people who want me dead."

"It's nice to be popular," the AI murmured.

I'm definitely going to have to fine-tune the level of programmable sarcasm, he told himself. "It's not amusing. There are only two intelligences who realize even a little of what's going on inside me: Pip and you."

"You are wrong, Flinx," the voice responded softly. "I don't understand anything of what is going on inside you. No AI, no matter how sophisticated or advanced, can truly understand a human being. Logic aside, there are too many aspects of human behavior that do not conform to predictable values. Your individuality precludes general comprehension. I know you as well as it is possible for an artificial intelligence to know a human, and there are too many times when I do not understand you at all."

"That's reassuring." The AI wasn't the only mind on the *Teacher* capable of sarcasm.

"I try." Though he knew it could not be, the AI managed to sound hurt. "Bear in mind, Philip Lynx, that while it is a truism among machine intelligences that no human is entirely comprehensible, you are less comprehensible than most." Then it said something unexpected and surprising. "Perhaps if I could share the dreams that so trouble you."

"I relate them to you." Unlike many people who dealt regularly with AI's, Flinx had not constructed a face to go with the voice.

"No—I mean *share* them. Perhaps then I would understand the confusion and distress they cause you."

"Machines don't dream." He gazed at the ceiling. "Do they?"

"No. In order to dream, an entity must first be able to sleep. AI's do not sleep. Being turned off is different. Hu-

mans sleep. Thranx sleep. Even AAnn sleep. Machines—
when we are turned off we die, and when we are turned
back on we are reborn."

"Sounds exciting," he murmured absently.

"Not really. It's quite straightforward. I wish I could
be more helpful, Flinx. As you know, in the course of
our travels together since I was made, it has been occasionally necessary for me to communicate with other
AI's. It became apparent to me some time ago that you
are an unusual example of your species."

"I know," he replied dryly. "I wish I weren't."

"Wishing. Something else humans can do that is denied to machines. In the course of learning about other
humans, I have become aware of your generally gregari-
ous nature. You usually seek the companionship of your
own kind. Yet you have spent much of the past years
traveling alone in me, with only your flying snake for
company. I believe this may be the source of at least
some of your present discomfort. You need to talk to
other humans, Flinx, and I think also to confide in them
concerning your uncertainties."

It was silent on the bridge for long moments. Either
the *Teacher* knew more about human nature than it
claimed or the AI was being disingenuous. Either way,
the truth of what it had said forced its way into his consciousness and wouldn't let go.

Maybe it was right. Maybe what he needed more than
anything was to talk to someone. But who? There was
no one he could confide in, no one who would understand the nature and gravity of his disturbing dreams as
well as sympathize with his personal problems and the
emptiness that always traveled with him. There was
Mother Mastiff—but she was getting on in years. She
could listen but would not really understand. Empathetic as she was, she did not possess the necessary intel-

lectual referents to comprehend what was going on inside of him. Pip could make him feel warm inside but
could not talk. The *Teacher,* as it had just wisely observed, could provide erudite conversation but not
simple humanity.

Furthermore, not only did he need someone he could
talk to about everything that was going on inside him,
that person also had to be trustworthy. Conversation
and understanding, he had long since learned, were far
easier to find than trust.

Actually, he realized with a start, there was someone.
One someone. Maybe.

Where to go looking? Obviously, the place where they
had last seen each other. He hesitated. Was he doing the
right thing? The possibility of betrayal was always up-
permost in his mind. For many years it had prevented
him from seeking to share intimately of himself. But the
Teacher was right, he knew. He had gone without con-
fiding in another human being for far longer than was
healthy. For better or worse, he had to find a way to un-
burden himself to someone who would not only listen
but also might respond with something deeper and more
emotive than machine logic.

Still uncertain he was doing the right thing but unable to decide what else to do—and desperate to do
something—he raised his voice to finally supply the
Teacher with a destination.

New Riviera was not just a beautiful, accommodating,
and pleasant world. In all of mankind's more than seven
hundred years of exploring and spreading itself through
the Orion Arm of the galaxy, it was still the best place
humans had ever found. Some planets were rated comfortable and others livable. But out of the hundreds that

had been catalogued by humans and thranx alike, only "Nur," as it was often called, was considered even more hospitable than Mother Earth.

It was as if Nature had chosen—in a particularly languid, relaxed, and contented moment—to design a place for human beings to live. Nur was not paradise. It was, for example, home to hostile creatures. Just not very many of them. There were endemic diseases. They just weren't very serious or common. The planet had seasons, but winter, as humans were used to thinking of it, was confined to the far north and south poles. Thanks to a remarkably stable orbit and axis, weather tended to the consistently tropic or temperate over the majority of the planet's surface. In the absence of dramatic mountain ranges, rain tended to fall predictably and in moderate amounts except in the extreme tropics, where it served as a welcome diversion.

The bulk of Nur's indigenous plant and animal life was attractive and harmless. With an abundance of easy-to-catch prey, even the local carnivores were a bit on the lazy side. Imported life-forms tended to thrive in the planet's exceptionally congenial surroundings. Everything from multiwheats imported from Kansastan to tropical fruits from Humus and Eurmet grew almost without effort.

Instead of vast oceans, the waters of Nur were divided into more than forty seas of varying size. Dotted with welcoming islands and archipelagoes, they made for comfortable sailing and cheap water-based transportation. Thousands of rivers supplied fresh water to tens of thousands of sparkling lakes.

It was not surprising that immigration to New Riviera was among the most tightly controlled in the Commonwealth. True, not everyone wanted to live there. There were those who found it too static, even too civilized. There was no edge to this paradise, and many humans and thranx needed an edge to keep them going. But most of those fortunate enough to be citizens could not conceive of living anywhere else, and those that could so conceive did not want to.

The choice of landing sites was extensive. There was Soothal, in the center of one of the eight northern continents, or Nelaxis, on the sandy shore of the Andrama Sea. The shuttleport outside indolent Tharalaia, near the equator, was said to be bedecked with an astonishing variety of tropical flowers whose rainbow of colors changed naturally every week, while Gaudi was the most famous Nurian center for the arts.

Thanks to the singular modifications and advances integrated into its Caplis generator by the Ulru-Ujurrians, the *Teacher* could land on a planetary surface without its drive field interacting lethally with the planet's gravity. Flinx knew it could do so because it had done so—but only on sparsely inhabited or empty worlds. A very few suspected his ship's unique ability and had been actively trying to confirm it and track him down.

So whenever he visited a populated world, he descended and returned via shuttlecraft, in the conventional fashion. Seeking as always to preserve his anonymity he decided to land and pass through Customs and Immigration at Sphene, renowned as the planet's center of commerce. Among traders and manufacturers, businessfolk and apprentices, students and machiavels, he was least likely to draw attention. People who were focused on money and its acquisition, he had learned, had little time for those who were not.

It would also be as good a place as any to begin searching for the person he sought. Whether that individual was still on New Riviera he had no way of knowing. It was the last place they had talked. And if the many kudos to the planet that filled space-minus were to be believed, why would anyone leave Nur for somewhere else? Furthermore, preliminary research had already revealed that the one he sought would easily be able to access appropriate employment opportunities on Nur. That seemed as promising a way and place to start as any.

Metropolitan Sphene was large enough to be served by four shuttleports. Only two handled passengers, the other two being reserved for commercial activities. As the sole occupant of a privately owned shuttle, even one originating from so disreputable-looking a craft as the presently camouflaged *Teacher,* he was directed and guided into the executive landing area. The mild disdain of port control was palpable.

"Use arrival lane four oh three," the voice declared firmly, "and be certain to comply with all fumigation and decontamination procedures prior to disembarkation."

Flinx had to smile as the shuttle slowed and its internal AI guided it to the designated parking slot. The Nurians were a famously fastidious lot.

Customs insisted on running a separate scan on Pip, not only to ensure that she was free of diseases and parasites but also to make certain she was not pregnant. New Riviera was entirely too accommodating to imported species to allow anything out into the wild without official approval, where it would like as not reproduce and thrive like mad. With Flinx close by to keep her calm, the irritated flying snake tolerated the process. It helped that the well-trained personnel assigned to perform the necessary procedures were calm and unafraid. They were shielded by their ignorance, Flinx knew.

As soon as the last of the efficient but extensive landing and arrival procedures had been completed, Flinx shouldered his travel satchel and made his way down the succession of access corridors into the main terminal. The first thing that struck him was the unmistakably high degree of general affluence. That, and the general contentment that filled his mind. The majority of emotions that touched him were happy ones. Not all—the port was full of human beings, after all—but most. It was a refreshing change from places like Goldin IV and Earth, where humanity still struggled harder with itself than against anything else.

First he needed to find a place to stay, someplace comfortable but nondescript, preferably in the busiest part of the city where he would attract the least attention. Then access to the planetary box, to begin his search. The kind of search he planned to undertake would probably veer into the illegal, but that had never slowed or stopped him before.

Breathing in the pleasantly warm, just sufficiently humid air of Nur, he lengthened his already considerable stride. So far, the stories that were told of New Riviera had proven to be true. If he did not feel at home, at least he was comfortable.

It had been a while since Flinx the thief had done any thieving. As always, he was looking forward to resuming what had, after all, been the first and only real profession he had ever mastered.

Barkamp Inn, the hotel where he finally settled, was, like everything else on Nur, clean, comfortable, and accommodating. No one questioned the desire of Alpheus Welles to stay for an indeterminate time until he had concluded his business. No one inquired the reasons for his stay. As usual, any curiosity was directed to the new arrival's unusual pet. Satisfied that it was under the control of its owner, hotel staff flung no further questions in the redheaded Mr. Welles's direction.

For those living and working in a planetary center of commerce and enterprise, the citizens of Sphene exhibited an air of contentment alien to comparable Terran cities like Brisbane and Lala. Not that the conflict was absent. The usual jealousies and hatreds common to humankind were present in abundance. One *could* get mad at one's neighbor, competitor, or spouse as easily here as on any other settled world. It was just harder to stay quite as mad, with the sun beaming down beneficently, the beach so close, and pleasant woods and lakes beckoning at every turn as soon as one left the city behind.

To embark on his search while preserving his anonymity and security, he chose a public access terminal located on the ground floor of a large office building. The structure's architects had made good use of spun fibers, producing a multistory building in the shape of a favorite local fruit tree. The most exclusive offices, he learned, were housed in the "fruits" that hung from woven composite-and-metal branches. On Nur, whimsy as well as technical competence were the hallmarks of a successful architect. Many of the buildings were designed to reflect more than just a prosaic need to house apartments or offices. His favorite was the one topped by a café that was shaped like a pirouetting local quadruped.

Entering the building, he veered left toward the public terminal station and chose a booth as far from the entrance as possible. A transparent wall provided a view of a street outside. Sticking his ident card into a slot activated the booth. The wall opaqued, shielding him from sight. A privacy bubble snapped silently into place. He could now neither be observed nor heard.

Never leaving anything to chance, he pulled a small

device from his service belt that confirmed the security of his present situation. It also assured him that the terminal in front of him was not compromised. He attached two other devices designed to prevent eavesdropping and prove to authorities that he was doing nothing illegal. Finally activating it with a credcard, he proceeded to embark on a legal search.

He found the person he was looking for within a couple of minutes, but since the information given was sparse, he proceeded to dive deep into the box in a scan that quickly became more than slightly illegal. His two devices embedded their systems in the box itself, and prevented the terminal from notifying the relevant authorities that its usage was being unlawfully compromised. Working quickly, Flinx proceeded to acquire as much information as he could.

As it grew steadily more realistic, the prospect of actually seeing the person he sought was generating within him feelings he had not felt in a long time. Along with an unexpected excitement was trepidation. Their final parting had been ambiguous at best. What if his visit were not welcome? What if he were met with hostility instead of the sympathy and understanding he so desperately sought? His nervousness increased in direct proportion to the amount of restricted information he was accessing.

The planetary box provided him with a steady flow of supposedly secure information. He learned that the individual lived in one of Sphene's outer urbs and worked for a large company called Ulricam. His circumspect info thieving reminded him of his happier, more innocent days as a child on Moth when the most extravagant thing he had strived to steal was a used entertainment cube or a child's mutating twinkler—and occasionally, when times were hard, food for himself and Mother Mastiff.

As opposed to such tangibles, mere information was less tactile but in many ways more valuable. If he was discovered, he knew that his action in accessing the restricted personal files of a Nurian citizen could land him in the local rehab for a year or more, possibly sentenced to mind adjustment. At the very least it would certainly be enough to get him deported without any chance of ever returning. Though cautious as always in his activities, he was not too concerned. He had successfully penetrated far more confidential files than this, most recently from the depths of the Terran box itself, and he had slipped away without being caught.

As he continued to search there was still no indication that his incursion had been detected. What limited information there was on his objective flowed freely and without restriction through the tap he had attached to the terminal. The privacy bubble remained intact around him. With each detail, his excitement grew. He noted with unexpected relief one especial bit of demographics that was *not* present.

Why should that matter? It didn't, he tried to tell himself—not very convincingly. Bemused by her master's atypical confusion, Pip stirred uneasily against his neck and shoulder. Flinx always knew what he wanted— or did he? This emotional turmoil was a bit much for a simple minidrag to cope with.

It did not take long for the search to run dry. Carefully shutting down the terminal, Flinx removed his highly illicit attachments, rose, readied himself for anything that might be waiting, switched off the privacy bubble, and stepped out of the cubicle.

No gendarmes stood outside, weapons drawn, to challenge him. No irate official awaited his appearance prepared to itemize the visitor's inventory of outrages against public decorum. Privacy bubbles darkened a couple of the other cubicles. Otherwise, all was as it had been. Feeling more cheerful than he had at any time in recent memory, he strolled out of the building in search of public transport to take him back to his hotel.

5

The flying snake was dozing on its familiar perch, a soft cushion nestled strategically in the office-laboratory's south-facing window. Bathed in Nur's nurturing sunshine, the minidrag's bright colors and muted iridescence formed a wonderful counterpoint to the otherwise humdrum devices that filled the room. So motionless was it that a visitor might easily have taken it for some supernally truthful sculpture and not a real, living creature.

It might as well have been a sculpture for all the attention the two technicians paid to it. They were young, attractive, excruciatingly intelligent, and thoroughly preoccupied with their work. In the center of the room they flanked an oversized holo depicting a number of complex organic molecules. Occasionally, one of them looked away from the large central display to check a readout on one of the several drifting heads-ups that followed each of them around the room like so many flat, rectangular, semitransparent dogs.

By voicing commands or moving their control-gloved fingers within the central display, they could adjust the position and mold the depicted molecular structures to suit their liking. Each new alignment was dutifully recorded, analyzed, and subjected to careful comparison with previous constructions. From time to time, a new configuration was entered into the Euremtalis chemical synthesizer on the far side of the room. Within ten minutes a preproduction sample of the combined organic molecules appeared in a small dish. After a final check and dissection, these samples would find their way to Product Testing in another part of the industrial research complex.

All this work by skilled and highly paid technicians was devoted not to preventing hunger on some primitive world, to curing some exotic disease, or even to making life a little easier for the majority of humankind but dedicated to making human females—and occasionally males—appear slightly younger and more attractive to members of the opposite sex. In that respect, though their methods were as different as their results, the efforts of the two techs mirrored the ancient daubers of henna and streakers of plant sap who had preceded them in the same kind of work by eight or nine thousand years.

The techs did not reflect on this irony as they continued with their work. It was doubtful it had ever occurred to them. They were concerned with tomorrow, not with the past. And in tomorrow's world, rewards came to those who successfully fashioned a new lip sparkle, eye filter, or follicular chromophore.

None of this meant anything to the flying snake. Normally, it spent the day ignoring the efforts of the various techs who shared the lab space. Nor was it unusual for the minidrag to repeatedly shift its position, the better to stretch its longitudinal quick-twitch muscles and soak up still more sun.

So the speed and suddenness with which it abruptly and for no apparent reason raised its iridescent green head was curious indeed.

Immersed in their work, the two techs did not notice the uncharacteristically abrupt gesture. They continued fiddling with their holoed molecules, murmuring to each other in soft, professional voices. Across the room, the flying snake had now raised its head some distance off the cushion and, virtually motionless, was staring in the direction of the privacy curtain that veiled the doorway.

At the soft fanlike snap of leathery wings unfurling in a single movement, both techs turned to look curiously. While one appeared uncertain, the other gave voice to concern.

"That's odd. He usually reacts that way only when I'm threatened." The minidrag's master looked carefully around the room.

A loud thrumming sound, the kind an oversized hummingbird might make, suddenly filled the room. The minidrag was airborne. It hovered for a moment, semitranslucent wings converting the sunlight pouring through the window into pale shades of light blue and pink, before taking off like a rocket through the privacy curtain. The flying snake's master yelled for it to come back. When it didn't, the tech forgot all about work and hurried to pursue.

"I've never had a command ignored before!" The privacy curtain parted for the anxious technician. The other chose to remain behind.

"Better run the thing down before it gets in somebody's face and gives them a coronary." The second tech returned to his work. He had no intention of participating in the chase. There was important research to be completed; the highly venomous nonnative arboreal wasn't his; and, as fond as he was of his colleague, he had never liked the damn thing anyway. Lying there on its window cushion, one slitted eye peeking open sporadically to squint at him, the beast had given the poor tech the willies more than once. Good riddance if it happened to fly out an open window and never return.

Even the confused and concerned emotions the minidrag's owner was experiencing could not persuade it to change its course. Normally, such robust emotional broadcasting would be more than enough to bring the flying snake back to his master. Not this time. Something else had caught its attention and was holding it despite all the frantic, shouted commands that resounded in its wake off impenetrable hallway walls.

A preoccupied administrator turning a corner nearly smacked into the increasingly anxious minidrag. Letting out a startled scream, she threw both hands and everything they had been holding in the direction of the ceiling. The irritated minidrag darted left, right, then finally over the head of the surprised worker. This was not difficult, as she was sliding slowly toward the floor, collapsing like an accordion, eyes closed and paperwork sifting gently to the ground around her.

Rounding the same corner, the tech's apprehension turned to alarm at the sight of the unconscious body. With great relief, the tech quickly realized she had only fainted. Resuming pursuit of the errant minidrag was not difficult. Just follow the successive series of unsettled screams and shouts that drifted back from farther up the corridor.

Then suddenly there were no more cries to trace. The tech slowed. That could mean that the minidrag had finally tired of the game or found whatever had so inexplicably drawn it away from the lab or . . .

It was impossible not to think of the consequences if it had harmed someone. Or if someone had harmed it.

One of the company's domed greeting areas lay just ahead, with a receptionist and comfortable couches. The wayward Alaspinian minidrag was swirling, swooping, and diving in an orgy of exuberance the likes of which could evoke nothing but smiles in anyone fortunate enough to observe the effervescent aerial performance. The receptionist sat with his head tilted slightly back as he gaped at the impromptu aerial ballet that was taking place within the domed space over his head.

Especially since there were now two of the magnificent flying creatures.

The minidrag's owner slowed, mouth opening slightly in astonishment, and tried to comprehend the ramifications of a *second* flying snake. Alaspinian minidrags were not common, not even on their home world. Finding another one inside the company complex carried with it the most singular connotations. Inescapably, so did the voice that quietly broke the silence.

"Hello, Clarity. It's been a while."

She gaped at the speaker, unable to respond. A number of centimeters taller, noticeably older, but otherwise he was still the same Flinx who had brought her to Nur after their encounters on Longtunnel and Gorisa. Was he also the same Flinx who had once been in love with her? Was she still in love with him? She was conscious of the receptionist's stare. Above and indifferent, the two minidrags continued their aerial ballet. No wonder Scrap had gone crazy. What child wouldn't upon sensing the presence of its long-absent mother?

Winged parent and frenetic offspring finally settled down on a nearby couch, repeatedly caressing each other with their pointed tongues. Eyeing them warily, the receptionist returned to his work, politely doing his best to ignore the self-conscious reunion that was taking place in front of his desk.

Flinx stared down at the woman he had come a long way to find again. She seemed little changed from the enthusiastic but naïve gengineer he had first encountered on distant, windswept Longtunnel. Her blond hair had grown out to shoulder length, but she still had a star shaved above each ear. The uniquely hued turquoise eyes gazed back at him. Whereas he had grown more withdrawn and contemplative, she seemed to have become more relaxed amid the comforting balm of Nurian existence. Life here, he reflected, had to be easier than it had been for her on Longtunnel—perhaps not as scientifically stimulating but certainly easier.

She took his arm and guided him down a different corridor, followed by the two minidrags. A short walk found them all in a small service room. One wall was lined with food dispensers. A wide window looked out on one of the thousands of lush little pocket tropical gardens that dotted the city. The flying snakes immediately made themselves comfortable on an empty table half bathed in warm sunshine. This time of day the room was deserted. Sitting him down in a chair next to the window, she took the seat opposite, rested her elbows on the table, interlocked her fingers, and all but spat at him, her voice low and intense.

"*Been a while?* It's been six years, Flinx. *Six years!*"

He couldn't help but smile. "You know, your eyes still sparkle when you're really intent on something."

That took her aback. "Well, *you've* changed. You wouldn't have managed a comeback like that six years ago."

He struggled to find a comfortable place for his longer legs. "Six years ago I was eighteen." He considered where he had been and what he had done since last he'd set eyes on her. "It's been a busy and full six years," he added with prodigious understatement.

"You left me," she reminded him unnecessarily. "I wanted to stay with you. You said you needed time. Time to learn more about yourself, time to try and figure some things out. Then you'd come back for me. One day." She paused. "At the time, I didn't think 'one day' meant six years down the line."

"Neither did I," he replied truthfully. "At the time, I didn't know what it meant or what it would entail."

He smiled hopefully. It was an expression she remembered well: a blend of someone who was simultaneously eight and eighty, a persuasive fusion of childish delight and forlorn hope. She could sense the yearning within him, a yearning that she remembered dominating so much of his character.

How much of that yearning was for her and how much for matters often beyond her ken was as much a mystery to her as it had been when he had bid her good-bye on the tarmac of New Riviera's main shuttleport six years ago.

Uncomfortable at her silence, he nodded in the minidrags' direction. "Scrap recognizes his mother."

Unlocking her fingers, she leaned back in the chair. "Detected her presence all the way from the lab. I'm afraid he startled more than one of my coworkers during his search for her. He wouldn't respond to my verbal commands or my thoughts. I couldn't imagine what was going on." Gazing across the table at him, she shook her head slowly. "I'm not sure I can yet. What are you doing here, Flinx? What do you want?"

He looked out the window, eyeing the spectacular blooms that seemed to flourish like weeds everywhere on Nur. "I told you: I said one day I would come back."

She shook her head more sharply this time. "I know you well enough to know there has to be more to it than that, Philip Lynx. Deity knows I wish it were otherwise, but that's not the reality. You just said hello. You didn't take me in your arms, you didn't hug me, you haven't kissed me."

He started to lean across the table and she flinched. "Oh, no—it doesn't work that way, Flinx. Not after six years."

His confusion communicated itself to Pip, who raised her head to peer in his direction. Scrap was content to doze on.

"I'm sorry," he told her. "I meant to, really, but when I finally saw you, after so long, I—I think I was afraid."

She cocked her head slightly. "Afraid? Philip Lynx, afraid of a little kiss? You forget who you're talking to. I spent a lot of time with you. I've seen what you can do."

"It's the truth," he declared defensively.

"So the man who's not scared of guns, Qwarm, AAnn, or the entire enforcement arm of the Commonwealth is still afraid of personal intimacy." She sighed. "I suppose I shouldn't be surprised. Disappointed, yes, but not surprised. I think I know what that makes you."

"You do? What?"

"A man." Turning toward the food dispensers, she fumbled for her credcard. "I need something to drink. You?"

He let her buy him some local fruit juice mixture. It was tart, cold, and delicious. A container of salty snacks was sufficient to occupy the two minidrags.

"Are you still in love with me?" he asked.

She paused with her drink container halfway to her mouth. "O'Morion, you're still as direct as you always were, anyway. Flinx, it's been six years. I was confused even when I *was* in love with you. What do you expect after six years? Are you in love with *me,* or is everything in your life still subordinate to your endless searching?"

"That's two different questions," he shot back.

"Not for me it isn't. Nor for any woman I know. Well?"

"I don't know." He dropped his gaze, brooding. Emotion washed through him, further alarming Pip. He calmed her somewhat with a familiar hand gesture. This wasn't going the way he had planned. But then, he reminded himself, things rarely did. Could he afford what he was feeling? Did he have time for it? Remember why you're really here, he told himself. Focus on that.

"I needed someone to talk to," he finally replied.

She sat back and her tone changed—and not for the better. "That's *it*? Six years you're out of my life and when you finally show up again it's because you need someone to *talk* to?"

"I didn't mean it like that," he replied hastily. "Not just *someone.* I need someone who knows how to listen and who understands me, who knows *me.*"

She softened slightly. "You told me more than once that nobody understands or knows you, yourself included."

"I'm still working on that," he admitted. "You were the only person I felt I could trust." He waved at the sky outside. "In the whole Commonwealth, you were the only one."

"Well, at least I'm the only one for something." Her voice fell to a mildly incredulous whisper. "Six years." She sighed, and when she spoke again her tone had returned to normal. "What did you want to talk about?"

"Many things. Some involving me, a few concerning

other matters." He rubbed at his forehead, and she was suddenly concerned.

"Your headaches? You still have them?"

"Worse than ever. Deeper and more frequent."

"Have you seen a doctor?"

The twisted smile he felt was not visible on his face. Yeah, I've seen a doctor. Two of them. Just recently. Wanted to run some "tests" on me, they did. So I had to run—again. The difference this time, he reflected, was that for the first time in a long, long while, he had run not to someplace but to somebody.

"They still can't do anything for me." He touched one temple. "Anything that would fix me to the point of eliminating my headaches would probably eliminate me as well. At least, I wouldn't be the same person. There would be—collateral damage."

"If I can help with that—other things aside—you know that I'll try and do so. If it's just conversation you want—"

"Something else right now," he interrupted her gently. "Something less weighty." His smile returned—open, reassuring, encouraging. "Let's talk about you for a while. Are you happy here? How's your life? You're not married?" He already knew she wasn't because he had accessed her confidential files, but he could hardly tell her that.

"No," she told him. "But I have been seeing someone regularly for the better part of a year now," she added, instantly turning the solid ground on which he thought he had been standing to swamp.

His reaction must have been plain to read. "It's been a long time, Flinx. I'm twenty-nine. What did you expect—that when you left me here with no job and no immediate prospects that I'd go live in a hole and wait for you to maybe show up someday?"

"I didn't"—he could not meet her eyes—"I didn't think."

"I'm sorry. I don't have to be, but I am. For someone who can read the emotions of others you never were very good at analyzing or dealing with your own."

"But you never married? Before your current—friend, I mean."

"No." Her tone turned wry. "Apparently, men find me a threatening combination: physical attractiveness *and* intelligence. I'm either too pretty for them or too smart. I intimidate them. Or so I've been told. Even in this day and age it's surprising how many males feel threatened by a woman who's smarter than they are."

"I'm not," he replied quickly.

"Maybe so. But then, I'm not at all sure that I'm smarter than you, Flinx."

"And you're comfortable here?" He changed the subject by indicating their surroundings. "With what you're doing and with life on Nur?"

That was an easier question to answer. "Who wouldn't be? This is New Riviera, the paradise planet, the best of Mother Earth concentrated and then spread like a fine glaze on an entire world instead of just a small part of it."

"I didn't ask for the planetary chamber-of-commerce pitch." His eyes locked on hers. "I asked about *you*."

"And I can't lie about it. Yes, I'm happy here, Flinx." She stared back at him unflinchingly. "It's a lot better than spending the rest of my life inside one small starship, flitting from planet to planet, trying to unearth uncertainties and pin down imperceptibles."

His lips tightened in a knowing grin. "Six years and you sure haven't changed. That attitude is one reason why I finally came back to see you again."

"And what I said is the truth, and why I don't think I could ever be with you again, that way."

He turned his attention to the spectacular flowers outside the window. Midworld in miniature, he found himself thinking. Except something was missing.

"I never said I planned to wander the Commonwealth forever. I'm capable of settling down. Of having a normal life."

She had to smile. "I don't need to be an empathetic telepath to know how much of *that* is true." Reaching out, she took one of his hands in both of hers. "Flinx," she murmured earnestly, "I *am* happy here. I have a good job doing what I like. I'm well respected and well compensated. I've made a home for myself—a real life. It's not extravagant, but it suits me just fine. My life here is—soft. And I've discovered that I'm content with that. It's a better existence than anything I've known before." She let go of his hand. He found that it burned slightly where her fingers had encircled it.

"I've had enough hardship and risking my life on frontier worlds, no matter how exciting the opportunities. I've come to enjoy good restaurants, cutting-edge entertainment venues, and being surrounded by devices that cater to my whims without complaint. I've discovered, Flinx, that I *like* civilization. And when I say that, you know I'm telling the truth."

He did, whether he wanted to or not. The feelings she was projecting suggested nothing but contentment. There might have been a hint of something like dissatisfaction, a twinge of uncertainty—but nothing more. Certainly nothing conclusive.

"So you no longer feel the need to add to the greater store of human knowledge?" he asked her, remembering a discussion they had once had on distant Longtunnel.

"I'm happy in my work. I had years of doing that sort of thing." One perfect brow arched suggestively. "As you know, it didn't work out very well for me. This"—she indicated their immediate surroundings and by inference the convivial world outside the company complex—"is much nicer."

"And this man you're seeing? Is he much nicer, too? Are you in love with him?"

As soon as he put the question to her, he was sorry. She immediately made him sorrier. Without trying, he could sense the sudden, new distance that had opened between them. And a curtain had been lowered by his own crude impulsiveness and impatience.

"That's not for you to know, Flinx. You've come a long way to talk to me, fine. I'll talk to you. But my private life is none of your business." The distance increased, leaving frost in its wake. "You can't show up after six years and expect me to fall into your arms."

He swallowed. "I'm sorry. That was rude. You're right, of course." His gaze wandered to where Pip and Scrap were now lying next to each other, identification complete, greetings concluded, and back to the important business of sleeping in the sun. If only it were that easy for humans.

"I don't know what I expected," he finally continued, "except to hope you'd listen to me."

She laughed softly. "Isn't that what I'm doing? As for anything more . . ."

He could make her love him again, he knew. His ability to manage his unique talents had grown tremendously since the last time he had seen her. On Earth he had made a total stranger, a security guard, fall in love with him. The remembrance of that emotional manipulation had left a sour taste in his memory.

Besides, she had yet to say, or otherwise indicate, that she positively no longer cared for him—that way. He resolved to pursue the matter like anyone else. Like any *normal* human being, he thought bitterly. If she loved someone else now, well, he would just have to accept it and move on. Did he want that kind of love, anyway? Or did he just want help, compassion, and a sympathetic shoulder to cry on?

Despite her initial rejection, he could clearly sense her confusion. She was no more certain how she felt about him than he was about her. The emotions he was picking up were a mélange of affection and fear. It was not the first time he had sensed both projected in his direction. But in the case of Clarity Held, the emotions at both extremes were notably stronger.

He decided to regard this as a positive development, confusion offering more promise than conviction.

Clarity was unsure what to think or believe. The man sitting before her had largely faded from her thoughts some years ago. Now here he was again—taller and more mature and handsomer than ever, and just as infuriatingly unsure of himself. They'd been through much together, during which she had fallen in love with him, lost much of that feeling through fear, and then fallen for him all over again. The last thing she wanted now was to take another ride on that emotional roller coaster.

She stared at him, meeting his eyes, trying to see what lay behind that pleasant, entreating gaze. If only she could read his emotions the way he could read hers, she thought. As soon as she contemplated it, she was glad that she could not. She wasn't sure she wanted to know. In that she suspected they had something else in common. She wasn't sure he wanted to know what he was feeling, either.

Since they'd parted she'd made a good life for herself here on a good world. She'd built something and was on her way to building a good deal more. Visitors from the past could not be allowed to upset that. Especially a genetically altered mutant, no matter how well-intentioned he was today or how helpful he had been in the past.

Like it or not, his unexpected appearance had torn a small rip in the fabric of her comfortable existence. She struggled mentally to repair it and was doing a pretty good job of it, too, when Bill walked in.

The range of emotions Flinx detected in the new arrival was extensive, increasing the moment he took in the pair seated at the table. Curiosity gave way to expectation that was immediately replaced by a mixture of concern, frustration, wariness, uncertainty, and a rising but carefully controlled anger. All natural enough reactions, Flinx supposed, if one assumed the newcomer was in any way emotionally involved with Clarity.

She confirmed his preliminary supposition. Though she did her best to control them, her own emotional reactions were a mixed lot.

"Philip, this is Bill Ormann. Bill, I'd like you to meet an old friend of mine, Philip Lynx."

She smiled. Bill Ormann smiled. Flinx smiled. Without exception, he noted, each smile was present only on the outside. If only everyone had his ability, general conversation would proceed in a far more honest and forthright manner. In the absence of such a development, however, ancient human rituals took precedence.

After a moment's hesitation, Ormann walked over and extended a hand. "Nice to meet you, Philip. Any old friend of Clarity's is a friend of mine," he declared pleasantly. Inside, Flinx sensed, he was seething with curiosity. Before either of them could reply, Ormann noticed the twin serpentines reposing beneath the window. "I was told about your pet's corridor runaway, so I came looking for you to make sure everything was all right. I've only ever seen one Alaspinian flying snake before, and that's Scrap." He glanced back at Flinx. "The other one is yours?"

"Scrap's mother," Clarity informed him before Flinx could say anything. Her inner reaction to Ormann's arrival, Flinx noted with restrained delight, was ambivalent. He chose to take it as a promising sign.

The fact that she and Lynx had something more in common did not sit well with Ormann. Outwardly, he was as cordial as ever. "So, Philip—where do you and Clarity know each other from? She's told me a few things about her past. Did you two do research together on Longtunnel?"

"Something like that," Flinx replied truthfully. Across the room, Pip had raised her head and was looking unblinkingly in their direction, alert to the slightest suggestion of hostility toward her master.

Ormann nodded condescendingly. "When she did mention the names of coworkers, it was always senior administrators, never younger colleagues. What position did you hold?"

"Philip gathered general information," Clarity told him, again speaking before Flinx could respond.

Her explanation appeared to please Ormann. "Fieldworker. Well," he continued expansively, "where would research be without field-workers, eh? Every army needs troops. Where would I, a vice president of Ulricam, be if I didn't have the support of hundreds of line workers? Right, Philip?"

"Absolutely," Flinx agreed, seeing no shame in concurring with an opinion on a matter in which he had not the slightest interest.

"How's the Kerijen project coming, Clarity, darling? You and Armansire continuing to make progress?"

"We're still modifying fragrances, waiting for a new batch of codes to arrive from Mantis. But it's coming along."

"Fine, fine." A bit of a genuine smile replaced the false one. "We still set for dinner tonight? Fragonard's is doing pinkfish in a sepper reduction, I understand."

She hesitated, favoring him with a pleading look. "Could we put it off for a day or two, Bill? Philip and I have a lot of catching up to do."

"Of course you do, of course!" Behind Ormann's crinkled expression, blood boiled. "Take some time to reminisce. In fact, why don't you take the rest of the day off? I'll see that it's cleared with Personnel."

"Thanks, Bill," she replied gratefully. "That's good of you."

"How long's it been, anyway?" he asked conversationally, his attention alternating between her and Flinx. Across the room, Pip was preparing to unfurl her wings. Flinx shot her a calming glance. She settled down but remained wary and alert.

"Six years," Clarity said.

"That's a long time to be out of touch." Ormann felt a little better about her canceling their dinner. "No wonder you have a lot to talk about. I'd join you," he added paternally, "but I'd just be a third wheel. No reference points for the conversation. You two go ahead and catch up, have a good time." He leaned toward Clarity. "The pinkfish will wait."

A raft of conflicting emotions raced through Flinx as

they kissed. It was a polite kiss only, but what else would one expect with a third person present? The shallowness of it did not necessarily translate into a paucity of feeling. Certainly Ormann was deeply in love with Clarity. Nor did it necessarily demand one be an empath to discern the bond. Although he bore William Ormann no ill will, the only thing that mattered was how Clarity felt about the relationship, not him.

"I'll see you later," Ormann told her affectionately. Turning to leave, he smiled amiably down at Flinx. "Where did you say you were from, Philip?"

"Moth," Flinx replied honestly.

The other man frowned. "I don't think I've heard of it. Is it near Eurmet?"

Flinx shook his head. "It's a class five outpost world. Still pretty raw. Circled by gravitationally interrupted rings."

"Oh, now I remember," Ormann said brightly. "The winged planet. I've seen pictures. Raw's the word, I guess. Origins considered, you seem to have turned out well enough."

Flinx smiled back. Across the room, Pip lifted from the table. Drawn by the deep humming noise of her wings, everyone turned to look. Slitted eyes were intent on the company vice president.

"I note the relationship," Ormann commented genially, unaware that he was in imminent danger of being slaughtered. "Perhaps we'll have the chance to talk again, Philip. At more length. But I have work to do, and you two have some ancient history to share." He departed with a last warm smile for Clarity. "See you later, darling."

As he exited he shot a surreptitious glance backward. Her expression as she resumed talking to Lynx was inscrutable. Just a voice from her past, he told himself. Nothing more. As she'd said, an old business acquaintance. Younger than her, too. Also taller, and much too good-looking for Ormann's peace of mind.

He turned up the hallway, heading for his office. Only a field-worker. Surely there could have been nothing between them beyond the kind of professional friendship that inevitably developed between any two people who worked closely together on a distant, undeveloped, uncivilized world. He'd watched with contentment as Clarity had dismissed or dealt with one hopeful office suitor after another before settling on him. She was too clever for them, or her standards were too high.

Not too clever for Bill Ormann, though. He took a certain amount of pardonable pride in their relationship. Though he'd been with his share of women, he'd never met anyone like Clarity Held. Add her compassion and independence into the mix and you had something unique. Someone he fully expected to make, within the year, the third Mrs. William Ormann. His superiors approved, too. And with each passing week, with each pleasant Nurian month, Clarity seemed that much more willing. They got along well together, enjoyed many of the same things.

So an old acquaintance had unexpectedly put in an appearance. From what little he had been able to see, that was all they had in common. Some small, insignificant bit of mutual history. That, and pet Alaspinian minidrags. Hardly a basis for alarm. He lengthened his stride. He hadn't lied to facilitate a graceful exit. He *did* have work to do.

Let Clarity spend the afternoon with this Philip Lynx. Let her spend a day or two with him. What was the harm? His affable compliance, indeed encouragement,

Ormann knew, could only enhance his stature in her eyes.

Yes, he thought as he entered the lift that would take him to the upper floors where the company executives had their nests, he had handled it very well indeed.

6

Though they talked all that afternoon and on through dinner, Flinx deliberately kept the conversation casual. Whenever she tried to probe, he diverted the exchange to her history. She was happy enough to chat about herself, though whenever the subject turned to Bill Ormann she was less forthcoming. That suited Flinx fine. He really did not want to talk about Ormann.

The following morning he met her outside her residential complex. At her insistence, he had dressed for light hiking. She was looking forward, she had explained the previous night, to showing him a little of why the inhabitants of New Riviera were envied by their fellow citizens throughout the Commonwealth.

They took public transportation to a central downtown terminal where they boarded a local transport. In half an hour they were speeding silently down a propulsion rail that wound deep into gentle, rolling hills. Other passengers, young couples from the city, spared the tall redhead and his companion nary a glance. In contrast, the two flying snakes inspired frequent comments and wide-eyed glances from children traveling with their parents. One young girl went so far as to shyly ask permission to pet Scrap. Detecting no threat, the minidrag dozed indifferently on Clarity's shoulder as the fascinated child drew her fingers cautiously down the flying snake's spine, pausing once or twice to feel the pleated wings folded tightly against the scaly body. Raising one eyelid halfway, Pip scrutinized the activity and, sensing nothing inimical, promptly dropped back to sleep.

In twos and family groups, people left the liftcar until only two couples were left. When the transport next slowed Clarity rose, hefted one of the two hiking packs she had brought along, handed the other to Flinx, and headed for the exit.

"End of the line," she announced. "From here we walk."

He followed her outside. The last time he had gone for a hike with a backpack it had been on a world called Pyrassis. His surroundings today were a little more accommodating.

Instead of hostile alien desert he found himself walking through a forest of exotic, colorful blossoms. Instead of sprouting from bushes, the profusion of lavender and cerise, pink and turquoise, white and metallic gold blooms sprouted from the branches of pale-boled trees that twisted their way skyward like spiral bouquets. Whereas on Earth and other worlds he had visited, plants spent much of their time and energy fighting for every scrap of sunlight and ground space, here the trees seemed in competition to see which one could put forth the most spectacular blossoms. Overhead, Pip and Scrap circled and hummed gleefully as they played among the branches.

He had never seen so many flowers in one place. The air was saturated with perfume and his mind grew dizzy trying to assign names to all the colors he saw. The climbing, corkscrewing trunks of one grove of takari they hiked past climbed more than thirty meters into the sky. From the lowermost branch to the topmost sprig, every helical limb and twig was heavy with blooms. It was a flourish of natural beauty beyond anything he had previously encountered. When he remarked on it to Clarity, she only laughed.

"Nur is full of valleys like this one. As many as possible have been left in a wild or semiwild state for the public to enjoy." She paused to point out a miniature carpet of deep blue stem-flowers that hummed whenever they were vibrated by a passing breeze. They were as perfect and delicate as the takari were tall and robust. "This," she informed him, "is why nobody on New Riviera gives flowers to mark an occasion. There's nothing special about them, and anyone who wants some can step outside and pick what they like, even in the middle of a city like Soothal or Nelaxis."

"You flatter them more than they you," he commented.

Her expression turned mischievous. "Now, what book did you pull that out of?" She was not displeased, he believed. That was one thing he had observed about women in the course of his journeys. Where their personal appearance was concerned, there wasn't one who did not prefer to hear a clever artifice as opposed to an unbecoming truth. In this, Clarity was no different.

"It's true," he insisted.

"Bill wouldn't like to hear you say so."

If she was trying to draw him into a reaction by mentioning her paramour, she failed. At least, his expression did not change. He kept his attention focused on the magical landscape, asking the name of this tree and that bush, wanting to know the taxonomy of the variety of small furry things that darted and hopped out of their way whenever they approached. From time to time the pair of flying snakes would dart down to ensure that their respective masters were doing well before resuming their antics in the treetops.

"Where are we going?" He looked over at her. "Do you have some destination in mind or are we just rambling?"

"A little of both," she informed him. "Another hour's walk and we'll be someplace." With one hand, she gestured back the way they had come. "I'd like to get away from the other tourists, wouldn't you?"

Flinx was more than agreeable. The more privacy they had, the better he liked it. If only this sort of thing was as easy for him as it was for her. She could look around and see only forest and flowers, but he could not keep from picking up the nakedly broadcast emotions of every other wilderness hiker within kilometers. It wasn't that he wanted to. He simply had no choice in the matter.

But she was as true as her word. The longer they walked and the farther they were from the transport line terminus, the fewer and fainter were human feelings he was able to perceive. It was not the total emotional silence of free space, but it was mentally much quieter than the emotional pandemonium of a city.

The sun was still rising when they reached the lake. Having tired themselves playing among the blossoms, and somewhat bloated from having tasted more than a few of the sweet-smelling blooms, both minidrags had long since returned to their perches on their masters' shoulders.

Like the forest, the lake and its surroundings appeared so perfect as to have almost been landscaped instead of naturally formed. Set in a depression between rolling hills thickly carpeted with flower trees, the lake was supplied by a pair of small waterfalls rushing downward from opposing gullies.

Clarity pointed northward. "There are three larger lakes off that way. They're closer to the transport terminus and have extensive beaches, so that's where nearly everyone goes." She smiled. "Remembering how you are, I thought you'd prefer privacy to convenience."

"Actually, I like both," he told her. One hand absently stroked the back of Pip's head. "I usually don't find either. Given the choice, though, I do prefer the former."

Predictably, the water was just cool enough to be refreshing. Given the care with which the inhabitants of Nur looked after their environment, he wasn't surprised to find that it was also potable. Lying on his back floating on the surface, he ignored the tiny, questioning touches against his body that were made by curious lake dwellers. None of them were dangerous, Clarity assured him. Pip and Scrap remained on shore, coiled up next to each other in the crook of a blue-boled tree, their forms nearly lost among the blossoms. Minidrags did not much care for swimming.

The sun was just warm enough and the water just cool enough for him to almost relax. He couldn't remember the last time he had done so on the surface of a world. New Riviera was almost obscenely benign. Despite Clarity's assurances, he was convinced it couldn't last. For him, such serenity never did.

Climbing out of the water, they dried themselves and lay down on the compact blankets she had brought along. Though there was no beach, the mosslike ground cover that grew down to the water's edge provided comfortable padding beneath their backs. With the sun warming his face and body, Flinx felt he could fall easily asleep and perhaps even enjoy it.

The subtle sound of branches being pushed aside alerted him to the presence of something larger than the harmless, stingless arthropods who worked tirelessly to keep the flower trees pollinated. Rising on one elbow, he turned to look in the direction of the noise. Next to him, Clarity was staring toward the forest.

"Don't move," she whispered tensely.

He eyed the creature that had emerged from the fragrant brush and was gazing directly toward them. "I thought Nur was a paradise world devoid of dangers."

"Almost." He could feel the apprehension rising in her. "That's a breagar. I'm afraid it falls into the category of *almost*."

The new arrival was the size of a Terran horse but twice as heavy, with massive shoulders that flowed down into stumpy, thick legs, the front ones longer than the hind pair. Its head was huge, with four long jaws that met like pincers. They were lined with rows of teeth designed to cut, with four much longer interlocking teeth tipping the end of each jaw. The breagar's eyes were small, red, and set far back in the skull that comprised almost a third of the animal's length. In place of ears half a dozen coiled, vibration-sensitive hairs protruded stiffly from the top of the skull. They were in constant motion, sampling the air and occasionally curling downward to touch the ground.

"Carnivore?" he whispered to his companion.

"Omnivore," she told him. "Wholly indiscriminate. A breagar will eat anything. I'm told one was once found with half an air scooter in its stomach. The environment department can use only charge-guarded refuse recyclers in areas where they live because they'll eat the recycler along with the garbage. If we keep still, it may very well go away. Probably it just came down for a quick drink."

Sure enough, the scavenger lumbered past them to the water's edge. Bending its front knees, it began to drink noisily. Lacking any sort of tongue, it suctioned water up through the tip of its nearly closed four jaws. Up in the flower trees, alert to their masters' heightened ten-

sion, the two flying snakes were now fully aware of the
potential danger. In the absence of panic on the part of
either Flinx or Clarity, the minidrags remained on their
blossom-bedecked perch. But it was good to know,
Flinx thought, that they were watching.

Having drunk its fill, the breagar turned to leave.
Water dribbling from its complex snout, it suddenly
paused. Maybe it heard something; maybe it smelled
something new and different. In any event, it turned and
without warning broke into a gallop directly toward
Flinx and Clarity. Only a dozen or so meters away, it
had very little ground to cover.

The minidrags, unfurling pink and blue wings,
launched themselves toward their masters. They had no
chance, Flinx saw, of arriving in time. Letting out a
shout that was half scream of fear and half warning,
Clarity scrambled to rise and head for the lake. A breagar could swim but not half as fast as a human. Flinx
saw that she would not make the water in time. Esti-
mating the distance that the minidrags, Clarity, and the
breagar had to travel raced through Flinx's mind in an
instant.

That same mind responded.

As Pip and Scrap sped toward them and a frantic
Clarity threw herself into the water, he let that portion
of himself that was so sensitive to the feelings of others
range outward. The past several years had demonstrated
that his ability to receive and influence the emotions of
other beings was not restricted to the more Byzantine
emotions of sentients but extended to any creature
evolved enough to feel them.

From the breagar he received hatred and hunger. He
responded by projecting the calm that had come over
him ever since he had stepped off the transport earlier
that morning. Concentrating, focusing, he dimly heard

Clarity screaming at him to run for the water. He half closed his eyes, letting the peace of the day flow over him and take complete possession of his inner self.

Of course, if he was wrong, he might end up a mass of broken bone and meat. He would not have tried it if Pip had not been racing to his aid. He was gambling that if his efforts failed, she would arrive in time to stop the breagar. She might not kill it, but a well-placed glob of her highly corrosive venom should be more than sufficient to distract it.

For such a bulky, clumsy-looking creature, the breagar was surprisingly fast. It was almost on top of him when it abruptly slowed, then halted. Shoulder deep in the lake, Clarity stopped yelling and looked on in bewilderment. She shouldn't be bewildered, she knew. This was Philip Lynx. She had seen what he could do. Whatever he had done and might still be doing to the breagar was neither visible nor perceptible.

Slowly, Flinx stood up. The four opposing jaws of the breagar swayed back and forth less than a meter in front of him. The creature was breathing hard from its short, powerful sprint, the immense head turned slightly to allow one red eye to focus on its intended prey. Pip and Scrap hovered anxiously overhead, the loud humming of their wings the only sound.

Reaching out with one hand, Flinx gently and without fear began to stroke the tip of the breagar's long snout.

Arms moving slowly back and forth in the water, hardly daring to breathe for fear of doing something to upset the delicate, unnatural tableau, Clarity stared openmouthed at the scene on shore. Only when the breagar folded its legs beneath its massive torso, lay down, closed its eyes, and went to sleep did she dare emerge slowly from the lake.

Keeping Flinx between her and the snoring omnivore, she picked up a towel and began to dry herself. Lost in contemplation of the breagar, it finally occurred to him that she might have reasons for not speaking, other than inherent non-volubility.

"It's all right," he told her. "It won't bother us now."

"I saw a breagar in a zoo, once. I never expected to get any closer to one than that." Reaching out with a tentative hand, she touched the long snout. The skin felt like warm leather. When the creature let out a contented snort, eyes still shut, she nearly jumped off the blanket.

Flinx had to smile. "I told you it was all right." Tilting his head back slightly, he pointed. "See? Pip and Scrap know we're in no danger." She saw the two minidrags had perched on a sun-warmed rock sticking out of the water.

"You are one very strange man, Philip Lynx."

His smile softened. "That's why I went away, and it's why I came back. If I were normal, I would never have left you in the first place."

"What did you do to the breagar? I thought you could only *detect* the emotions of others."

He nodded. "Originally, that was the case. Over the last few years, I've discovered that I can project them as well. Not always, and the degree of success varies, but I'm getting better at it. When it charged us, I sensed naked hostility mixed with hunger. Animal emotions are far less complex than those of sentients and can often be countered by equal simplicity and directness." One hand caressed a tooth-lined jaw. The breagar snuffled like a giant pig.

"I tried to convince it that we represented no threat and that all was right with the world. Simple emotions. I certainly didn't expect to put it to sleep. No, that's not right. I didn't put it to sleep. I relaxed it to the point where it decided that now might be a good time for a nap."

She shook her head, unable to take her eyes from the dozing monster. "I think you and Nur must be a good match. What happens when it wakes up?"

"Easy to find out," he replied, with a twinkle in his eye. Turning on his knees to face the animal, he smiled at it. He did not shut his eyes, wrinkle his face, or wave his arms. After a couple of moments, the breagar woke up. Clarity started to back away, but Flinx reached out to gently restrain her. Rising onto all fours, the breagar yawned mightily. It was an impressive display, with all four jaws expanding outward in opposite directions before shutting with an authoritative snap. Heedless of the presence of the humans, it turned, shook its head from side to side, and trotted off toward the flowering forest.

Clarity relaxed. "I remember you doing some amazing things, Flinx, but nothing quite so—so bucolic. Can you project like that to any creature?"

"I don't know," he told her honestly. "I haven't had the opportunity to try projecting like this on any creature. But as long as my talents are under my control, I seem to have the ability to do it, yes."

"So," she continued on an utterly unexpected tack, "if you wanted to, you could project ardor on me, and make me love you."

Surprised, he remembered the security guard on Earth to whom he had done precisely that, in order to aid him in his quest to access restricted records within the greater Terran box. He could have lied about it, but chose not to. If he was going to ask for Clarity's help and understanding—and perhaps more—it wouldn't do to try to resurrect a relationship on the back of fresh lies.

"I possibly could, yes. But I wouldn't."

"How would I know that?" Her expression was solemn.

"You might not initially, but you would eventually. To make you, or anyone else, love me month after month, year after year, would require constant effort on my part. Sooner or later I'd forget to project the necessary emotions, and you would realize what had happened, that you were living a lie." He looked apologetic. "After that, you'd never trust me again. Also, I still sometimes completely lose my ability to receive as well as project. There's no predicting when or if that is going to happen. If I was persuading you of my suitability as a partner and my ability to do that suddenly went away, you're smart enough to recognize the results.

"I didn't come here to lie to you, with either words or abilities. I came because you're one of the few people who knows about me and my abilities, who understands, and who I can talk to." He looked at her. "You're the one I *wanted* to talk to. Because you know about me, because you're a gengineer yourself, and—for other reasons."

"Well, I'm flattered." She lay down next to him. The perfect sun of Nur bathed them in its balmy, golden glow. Harpettes fluttered past overhead, describing gossamer crescents between them and the slow-moving clouds. "I'll help if I can, Flinx. What do you want me to do?"

"Just listen. There are things that I've experienced that I can't explain. Or maybe it's just that I don't want to know any more about them than I already do."

She was openly sympathetic—and he felt it gratefully. "This has to be about your talent."

He nodded as well as he could considering his prone position. "That—and other things. Whether they have anything to do with my talent, I don't know. I have suspicions but no more than that." He sighed deeply. "Projecting is always more of a strain than listening. You didn't bring me all the way out here to listen to my troubles. You could have done that in the city." Reaching over, he took her left hand in his right.

She looked down at their entwined fingers, then back up at him. "Bill wouldn't approve." But she did not pull her hand away.

They fell asleep in the sun like that; close but—except for their interlocking hands—not making physical contact. So relaxed was Clarity that she was not even disturbed by the thought that the breagar might come back. If it did, she felt, the remarkable man beside her would somehow make it feel sorry for itself or too content to want to kill anything or something equally non-threatening.

It was a perfect afternoon on a perfect day: perfectly ordinary for Nur. With the organic cushioning of the tiny-flowered ground cover beneath the blanket, the occasional gentle breeze off the lake, and the sun slipping away benignly westward, she was completely at ease. She deliberately chose not to wonder whether that was an honest reaction to the events of the day or an emotional emanation from her companion projected to make her feel as good as possible about her present circumstances. Flinx had said he would not do something like that. She decided to take him at his word.

After all, she mused before she fell asleep, there was nothing she could do about it. If he was lying, it would take time for her to find out.

If he wasn't lying about that, too, she realized, and intended to continue to fool her forever about what she was actually feeling and what was the result of his projecting emotions onto her. Thinking that way, she decided, might very well lead to madness. Or at the least, a knotty succession of thoughts in constant conflict with one another. At least he couldn't read *those*.

She knew how she felt about him, she told herself firmly. That was *not* the result of some ethereal emotional projection. What she didn't know was what she was going to do about it.

If he could project a persuasive answer to *that,* she decided, then Philip Lynx·was far more talented than even he suspected.

7

It was dark within the deep, and deep within the darkness. She didn't know where she was, but it was very, very cold. Wrapping her arms around her upper body did not help. Nothing helped. It was the kind of cold that, instead of penetrating, seems to emerge from the core of one's being and work its way outward to the skin. Not the kind of cold that freezes—the kind that numbs.

Lowering her arms, she touched herself. Even corpses feel like something, but her fingers conveyed nothing to her brain. Though she could sense herself, there was no communication between the nerve endings at the tips of her fingers and whatever part of her body they happened to encounter. Pushing inward against her dull, shadowed flesh generated no sense of pressure. Scraping with fingernails resulted in no pain. Blinking, she found she could not detect the squeezing sensation produced by the small muscles around her eyes. It was too cold.

She was not alone in the blackness.

There was another presence. At once nowhere and simultaneously all around her, she knew it was the source of the cold. It had no outline, no shape, no form. Its existence was defined by the fact that it pulsed. It might have been a waveform, a frigid flush of particles, or a heartbeat. At one stroke she felt that she had always known of it, and an instant later it embodied everything she had never experienced.

Without knowing that it was anything more than the source of the numbing cold, she felt instinctively that she would best be served by not moving and, if possible, not breathing. Her human curiosity extended only so far. At some point, primal common sense kicked in and instructed her to keep silent—not that she was capable of making any sounds—be still—not that she could move anything more than her arms and legs—and watch—not that she could see anything. Be alert, but unobtrusive. Be aware, but invisible. Be conscious, but try not to think too much.

She succeeded at everything except the latter.

She became aware of something moving toward her. It was infinitely small and intolerably vast. Trying not to move, conscious that she must *not* move, she began to shiver uncontrollably. It came nearer. It made contact. A part of it passed through her. She began to scream frenziedly. That no one could hear her and that she made no sound made it only that much worse.

She awoke and sat up sharply, gasping for air as if she had just crossed the finish line of a double marathon. Scrap was in her face, darting anxiously back and forth, his wings driving clean warm air into her nostrils, his tongue flicking out to caress her in a vain attempt to exorcise whatever it was that was tormenting her. She dragged one hand across her eyes, wiping away the residue of the tears she had sobbed in her sleep.

Because that was what she had been doing: dreaming something she desperately hoped never to dream again.

Hearing a moan as she brushed sweat-saturated hair from her forehead, she used both hands to comfort Scrap. Flinx lay where he had fallen asleep beside her, but he was not still. Pip was darting back and forth above him, occasionally making contact with wingtip or tongue, trying her best to comfort her clearly traumatized master.

He, too, was having a nightmare. Was it the same as hers? Wasn't that impossible? People could share many things, but not nightmares. Years before, he had spoken to her about his dreams and his headaches. Surely they weren't contagious?

There was one way to find out. Wake him up.

She started to turn toward him on hands and knees. Recognizing her as a friend, sensing the benevolence inherent in her feelings toward Flinx, Pip darted aside to give her room. That was when Clarity noticed their changed surroundings.

Around her arboreals ought to have been playing in the trees, fliers circling overhead, and small stingless arthropods should be hard at work pollinating the thousands of blossoms. That was the norm for Nur. That was as it should be.

But save for her companion's moaning, all was silent. The inhabitants of the trees had gone. The sky was empty. The steady susurration of pollinating arthropods was absent. It was as if everything living except her, Flinx, and the two minidrags had fled. But from what?

Flinx moaned again, tossing his head from side to side, and the skies of paradise seemed to darken ever so slightly.

Life on the lakeshore had done more than gone away, she saw. Within a radius of half a dozen meters, not a flower remained attached to a branch. The ground was littered with petals, their tips curled, their bright colors already beginning to fade. A little closer, everything had died. Even the mosslike ground cover over which they had spread their blanket was black and shriveled. What she saw now worried her. It was one thing to project a nightmare and something else entirely to broadcast it strongly enough to kill living things in your vicinity.

Having previously experienced what Flinx could do— when he was awake or unconscious—she did not panic. But it was clear that whatever he was dreaming was far from benign. The likelihood that it could have had a serious effect on his surroundings seemed inescapable. She could think of only one way to put a stop to it.

Wake him up.

Moving closer, she reached for his shoulders. Then she hesitated. She had heard that it was dangerous to wake sleepwalkers or people in the throes of a nightmare. Abruptly awakened, they had been known to strike out and injure those attempting to revive them. Though she was not afraid of being struck by an open palm or fist, she wavered. This was Flinx she was dealing with. That he might strike out at her with something more lethal than clenched fingers was a possibility. She vacillated between grabbing and shaking him and waiting.

His moans were piteous like a little boy lost in an endless warren of menacing, unfriendly streets. Though no tears spilled from his eyes, she could see he was suffering as much as she had, if not more. His head arched back and his lips parted to emit a wordless cry for help. It decided her. She gripped his shoulders, closed her eyes, and shook.

"Wake up, Flinx! Come on, wake up!" The two minidrags fanned the air with blurring wings and looked on uneasily.

His moan cut off. He blinked, caught sight of her as she let go, and let his head slump against the blanket. The sun continued to shine, the lake to lap against the shore; her brain did not explode. Somewhere in the forest, a scarlet midrigel peeped querulously.

Staring upward, not meeting her eyes, he murmured, "I was dreaming, wasn't I?"

"You were doing more than that, Flinx." Her tone was grave. "A lot more than that, I think." She gestured with one hand. "Take a look around."

Levering himself up on his elbows, he saw the dead ground cover, the fallen petals. "You think I did that?"

"Who else? It's only you and me here. Your dreams can kill things, Flinx. Like you told me before, you can—project."

"I can, I know that—emotions, feelings. But something like this . . . I've never done anything like this before."

"You said that your headaches are getting worse. I'm going to assume that your nightmares are also getting worse. Maybe you're starting to project the feelings you get from them now—or at least some fractional essence of them." She glanced meaningfully skyward. "If you do that on your ship there's no one to notice and nothing to be affected except Pip. The effect doesn't seem to extend very far."

"Yet," he muttered miserably. "At least if it *was* me that caused this, I didn't hurt you." When she did not reply, he closed his eyes as if in pain. "Please don't tell me I hurt you."

"Not physically, no. Can you describe your dream to me, Flinx?" Before he could reply, she added quickly, "No, let me describe my dream to you."

"You were dreaming, too?" Sitting up now, he was staring at her intently.

"I don't know that it was my dream. I suppose I must have been experiencing your dream." She met his gaze unflinchingly. "You not only projected onto your surroundings, Flinx. You projected on me, too. Or into me."

"Tell me about your dream, Clarity."

When she had finished, he sat in silence for a long moment before replying. "It's different from mine. But not so different that I don't think your experience is related to what I go through."

"Then you *were* projecting." She remembered what it was like to be at once fascinated and frightened of this man. It was no less so now, even though six years had passed.

"Not intentionally." His eyes held a mixture of pleading and concern. "I would never do that. But when I'm asleep I have no control."

And maybe for not much longer when I'm awake, either, he thought as he considered what had taken place on Goldin IV. Clearly, he could no longer play with his talent, let it ebb and flow within his mind subject only to his whims and the circumstances of the moment. Now he was going to have to fight every hour to keep control of it lest he affect or injure others, however unintentionally.

But what could he do when he was asleep? How could he ensure that he would not harm those around him? Clarity had suffered some kind of dream episode that, although not as specific as his, apparently incorporated some of the same effects. He eyed the fallen flowers and dead ground cover. This time it had only been a few plants. This time.

What if next time instead of affecting her dreams, his distorted, errant abilities impinged on her as forcefully as it had on the local vegetation? What if, next time, he woke up next to a twisted, blackened body?

A runaway drive—that's what I am, he berated himself. Or at least, that was what he was in danger of becoming. How many sentients would have to suffer until he gained control of himself? And if he never did gain control, if these involuntary projections continued to increase in intensity and become more widespread, would he at last have the courage to do something permanent about it? The only trouble with suicide, he reminded himself, was that there was no future in it.

"You wanted to talk to me about these dreams, Flinx." He could feel the fear within her, but he remembered her as having courage. Over the intervening years that had not changed. He wondered if he would have had the guts to confront someone like himself.

"You say your dreams are different. Different how?" She peered attentively at him, anxious to learn, keen to understand.

He let his gaze, but not his mind, drift. "You said you had an overwhelming feeling of being in danger, of being threatened." She nodded. "But you never saw anything specific?"

"That's right. There was just an all-encompassing sense of doom. I don't know if that's a strong enough word. It was . . . foul. And when a part of it went through me . . ." Her words failed her, but her emotions did not. What he perceived within her then was far more evocative than any description she could have provided. "It's not just a *feeling* of evil for you?" she continued. "You actually *see* something in these dreams?"

"Some of the time. When the dream begins I'm traveling past stars and systems, past what sometimes seems like everything, only I know it isn't. Though the dream deals with vast spaces the distances involved seem finite." He lowered his gaze from the blue sky. "That's the sense I have of the evil I encounter—distant and vast but finite and drifting in the middle of a vast emptiness."

"It didn't seem very finite to me," she muttered, "but, then, I didn't experience the kind of specifics that you do." A gnawing fear was growing in her. Though she'd heard this story before, she knew she had to pursue it again. "What's it like—this evil?"

He shrugged. "It defines itself by what it is. I'm not trying to be solipsistic. I don't know how else to put it into words." He sighed heavily. "Sometimes I have a sense of it as a natural force, like gravity or a Bose-Einstein condensate. Sometimes I perceive it as a conscious entity. Sometimes as both at once—if that doesn't sound too crazy."

"Not any crazier than this." She indicated the dead flowers, the blackened ground cover around them. A deeper fear shot through her that he sensed immediately. "You're not by any chance channeling this malevolence, Flinx?"

"No!" he snapped back so sharply that she flinched and Pip rose momentarily. "I resist it at every turn. I'm not even sure it's aware of me, in the way we think of awareness. The scale of physical, or maybe metaphysical, values is so different that I'm not sure this whatever it is is even capable of being conventionally aware of me." His voice fell. "And then there are times when I think, when I'm convinced, that it's looking directly at me."

"Looking? It has eyes?"

"Some organ capable of perceiving with, anyway." He regarded her helplessly. "I'm trying hard to find suitable referents for things I don't understand, Clarity."

Her tone was sympathetic. "What happens when it perceives you?"

"I run." Puzzlement and confusion played with his expression. "It's a wholly mental retreat. I have no control over any of this."

"Of course you don't." She tried to sound encouraging. "It's a dream."

"That's what I choose to think. But there are times

when it feels like I'm being guided, or directed, by something else—some other consciousnesses that are forcing me into these dreams and pushing me outward to confront this evil. It doesn't matter anymore. I told you this years ago. Whether all this is taking place of my own volition or under some kind of outside influence, I came to the conclusion that it's up to me to do something about it."

"You still think you can do something about it?" She frowned. "How can you do something about a malevolence you can sense only in dreams? And what difference does it make, anyway?"

"You said you saw nothing in your dream," he said.

"That's right. No light, no color: just darkness."

"That's what there is in the places where this manifestation holds sway. Nothing. No stars, no planets, no life. Nothing. These dreams have convinced me, Clarity, that the nothingness is coming this way. And that's what it will leave in its wake: nothing." He made a sweeping gesture that took in ground, forest, lake, sky, and by inference everything beyond.

"All this will disappear. Life and sentience will vanish from this portion of the cosmos. Everything will become extinct and have its place taken by this evil. Everything." He turned back to her. "Don't you remember before when I told you how I felt about this, in Owngrit, on Gorisa?"

She sat in silence for a while, taking in the flower trees, the lake, the rolling, color-clad hills, because she felt she had to. This talk of vast malevolences and all-encompassing evil had left a growing darkness in her soul that needed pushing back. All the more so because she had indeed heard of it before—six years ago.

"And I thought you just needed to talk about headaches. It's this stupid *purpose* of yours again, isn't

it? The same thing those outlandish Ulru-Ujurrian creatures entangled you with back on Gorisa. I didn't know
you could repeat the experience without them around."

"It's the same thing I felt then, Clarity. I'm sure of it."
He sidled a little closer and was gratified that she didn't
draw away. "As my abilities mature, the headaches in-
tensify and so do these dreams—even without the Ulru-
Ujurrians around to prod and manipulate. And, just like
I told you on Gorisa, I can't escape the impression that
because of my talent, it's incumbent on me to do something about this oncoming darkness. That feeling hasn't
changed, either." He shrugged. "I still see it as my purpose, yes."

She remembered what had happened, on that distant,
highly developed world she had once thought to make
her home. "I was hoping maybe you had gotten over
that. But you're still trying to come to terms with it,
aren't you? Still trying to become a complete human
being. This separated us once before. Why can't you forget about it, Flinx? Tell yourself it's not your responsibility. My God, can't you make that part of it go away?
You said back then that nothing may happen involving
this emptiness, this evil, for a very long time."

He had to correct her. "I said that we may have a *little* time. I couldn't be more specific about it then any
more than I can now."

"Well, can't you leave it at that? I don't understand
how you can give your whole life to trying to combat
something that exists only as a recurring nightmare. It's
just *your* dream, after all."

He looked away from her. "I'm not sure about that,
either, Clarity."

It took a moment for the significance of his reply to
sink in. "Are you trying to tell me that somebody else is

participating in your dreams? *Functioning* in them? That's impossible."

"Is it? Didn't I just project something of what I was experiencing into your dream? If I can do that, who's to say some other entity can't project what it's feeling or dreaming onto me? Remember what I said about feeling that I was being guided, or directed?"

Having to deal with Flinx and his nightmares was difficult enough. That another—or several others—might also be involved opened up a whole range of possibilities, none of them to her liking. "But there's nobody else here, Flinx. Not this time. Nobody but you and me. The Ulru-Ujurrians aren't around to impel you."

He put a comforting hand on her leg. "Just because you had to be close to me to be influenced by my dream doesn't mean that I have to be physically proximate to whatever may be influencing my dreams." He pointed across the lake. "It could be in the hills or back in the city or not even on this world. I don't know. I'm still trying to understand *what's* happening. I haven't had time to try to get to the *how* it's happening."

"You said 'whatever.' Not 'whoever.' Then you do have some sense of what may be influencing you?" She struggled to remember all the confusing details of that singular day so many years ago. "*Is* it the Ulru-Ujurrians again?" She looked around. "Even though they're not present?"

"I do sometimes have the feeling that they're behind at least some of what's happening to me. But I have no proof."

"I thought they were nice, even if they and their world *are* under Commonwealth Edict. If they're the ones making you suffer like this, then I guess I was wrong about them."

"I said it was just a feeling," he corrected her. "There's a sense that other entities are involved as well." His expression tightened. "I keep trying to identify them, but it's difficult. They're only components of dreams, and the evil within the emptiness is so dominant that it's hard to focus on anything else. One source I think I know for sure—it's a device, a very ancient device. The other two are still pretty indistinct. From one I get these constant feelings of warmth—I suppose that *could* be the Ulru-Ujurrians, but I'm not sure—and from the other nothing but the color green. I guess that could be them, also." He put a hand to his head. "Like I said, everything is complicated and imprecise—pretty hard in that context to identify anything for certain."

She eyed him dubiously. "Just a color?"

He nodded. "And sometimes I'm not sure even of that. It's all so maddeningly complex and constantly changing, and my thoughts are never clear. Except for one thing: that these perceptions and I and this oncoming evil are all bound together somehow and that I have no choice but to try to do something about it. That hasn't changed. It's my purpose, my responsibility as a sentient being to contest evil, no matter what form it may take, no matter how extensive its scope." He took one of her hands in his. "And now you're bound up in it, too, because you've shared some of it, if only in the form of a passing contact."

She wanted to pull her hand away, but did not. "That one touch was more than enough for me, thank you very much. I want to help you, Flinx, but I don't want anything to do with some great emptiness and unimaginable evil and some vague, dubious purpose. Life is too short. I'm only a single human being. So are you, if you'll only pull yourself back from these bizarre dreams long enough.

You've already sacrificed most of your life because of it. Don't surrender the rest."

It was a persuasive argument, an appealing argument. One he had already reflected on many, many times before. "Clarity, don't you think I'd like to? Don't you think I want to have a normal life? I'd give anything not to be caught up in this. But I don't have a choice. It's not up to me."

This time she was the one who took his hand in hers. "Of course it is, Flinx. Who else would it be up to? Just set it aside. I know you can't eliminate all thoughts of it completely. It's too strong, too much a part of you. All I'm saying is, let the cosmos find another savior. Live out your life. Let someone else take on this preposterously colossal burden. There's really nothing you or any other individual can do in the face of something so big, anyway. Let all these dream-penetrating, thought-twisting entities, whatever they are, deal with it. Would you try to stop a sun going nova? Could you if you wanted to?" She smiled. "I don't think so."

"Not by myself, no," he murmured thoughtfully, "but I have the inescapable feeling that I'll have a lot of help in this—that I'm a key to it, but not the magnitude. You're right in saying that I'm just one individual. But a very small key can open a very big door."

"Keys are easily damaged." She released his hand. "I say let these interfering entities find themselves another key. I'll listen to you, Flinx. I'll help you if I can. I'd like to see your headaches go away. But you're right about one thing, I think. If you *don't* stop them and the dreams that they make worsen, they *are* going to kill you. I wouldn't want to see that happen."

"Neither would I," he admitted readily. "How do we go about doing that?"

"I don't know." Her lips were set firmly. "But I do

know that we're going to try. Because if we don't make the dreams go away, and you don't die, then you're liable to continue projecting them on me, and I'll do whatever I can to keep from having to go through that experience ever again."

8

William Ormann, vice president of Ulricam Corporation's marketing operations in Sphene, was ostensibly a contented man. In his early thirties, he had risen to hold a position of some importance within a well-respected company whose products were known and appreciated on many worlds. Fortified by modern medicine, he had his health. Assisted by modern surgical technology, he had his looks. Which, to be honest, were once again in need of a little in the way of artificial augmentation. He commanded a substantial salary and bonuses, lived in a beautiful two-bedroom house by the beach, was more or less liked by his colleagues, valued by his superiors, and was all but engaged to the most attractive researcher in the company, if not the entire city. The little matter of his last marriage had ceased to be a complication in his life nearly ten years ago.

If he did not have everything, he certainly was well on his way toward acquiring it. Not only was his job good, but, he enjoyed it. And he had the privilege of doing it on Nur, the most envied world in the humanx Commonwealth.

He and Clarity Held had been going together, dating, romancing, courting, whatever convenient sociological appellation one should choose to append to their ongoing relationship, for about a year now. There had been

113

other men in her life. Ormann had been prepared to hear about them from the time when he had first managed to catch her eye. Given her beauty and intelligence, it would have been irrational to have expected anything else. She had also informed him that she would, if and when it suited her, continue to see other potential partners besides him. That, too, he was prepared to accept. After all, she had without question or comment allowed him the same flexibility.

He did not move too fast, which she clearly appreciated. It was hard to watch her go out with others, though the emotional pain was salved somewhat by his own relationships. Gradually, and especially during the past six months, they had by mutual agreement seen less of others and more of each other. Everything was looking very well indeed. He had the career, he had the income, he had the respect, and with time and patience, he was sure he would have the fitting partner.

Then the redhead showed up.

At first, Ormann found it amusing that some callow youth from Clarity's past should put in so unexpected an appearance. As she had already told him, she was five years older than her visitor. That made Bill Ormann, if not old enough to be this Philip Lynx's father, at least more than old enough to look at the newcomer from a position of complete confidence. Admittedly, the youth was mature beyond his years, but that still could not obviate the age difference.

Furthermore, he was downright weird. The way he looked at other people, at his surroundings, the strange manner he shambled down a corridor in search of Clarity, all pointed to a confused if not disturbed individual. Much of the time he kept his head down and stared at the floor, as if this would somehow lessen his lankiness or diminish his presence. Sometimes when he spoke it was as if he were hesitant to form words, as if his brain were one step behind his tongue.

After their initial meeting, Ormann almost felt sorry for him. All he could see that Lynx and his Clarity had in common was some shared work history from her time on Longtunnel and that both of them possessed identical exotic pets. Observing the two of them on subsequent occasions, the notion that there might be something deeper between them never crossed Ormann's mind.

That was a month ago. Since then, Clarity had been spending more and more of her free time in the tall young man's company. She was apologetic, she was polite, she was never evasive, but she was firm. And each hour, each day she spent with Philip Lynx was one less hour and one less day she spent with Bill Ormann.

At first, he was resigned. Then he began to grow irritated. By the end of the month he was angry and frustrated. Angry, because Clarity continually put him off in favor of Lynx. Frustrated, because for the life of him he could not see what she saw in the guy. He was taller than Ormann but not significantly. He was slimmer, not as muscular, certainly not as handsome. Equivocal about his background and means of support, Lynx said only that he was a student getting by on a family stipend. No brilliant future there, Ormann had assured himself. Clearly Lynx was intelligent, but hardly brilliant. Nor was he entertaining or amusing. If anything, he was downright reticent in the presence of others.

So the question remained: what *did* Clarity see in him? What drew her to him so strongly that she repeatedly kept putting off vice president Ormann's invitations to dinner, to immersion theater, to the beach? For a bad moment he thought that perhaps Lynx was some kind of spectacular lover, but observation and subtle querying of Clarity soon quashed that notion. What then? Ormann decided there was only one way to find out.

He would ask her directly.

She was surprised but not shocked to see him sitting on the couch in her tenth-floor codo when she returned home from work on Friday. To facilitate their relationship, they had swapped habitat security codes several months ago. It had never occurred to her to change hers after Flinx arrived.

At such times Bill could be expected to be waiting for her with cold drinks, a flash-heated supper, a big smile, and a kiss. Tonight there were only the drinks. One did not have to be an emotional telepath like Flinx to sense that he was troubled. His condition was not serious enough to disquiet Scrap, however. As soon as they were through the entrance, the minidrag launched himself from her shoulder and flew to its favorite place atop the decorative aerogel bubbles that lined the back of her lake-view lounge.

"Good evening, Bill." Picking up the drink he had made—it was perfect as always—she sat down in one of the two chairs opposite the couch. That in itself was significant, he felt. Prior to the arrival of this Philip Lynx, she would always have sat down next to him. "You didn't tell me you were coming over tonight."

He fondled his own drink but didn't sip from the self-chilling glass. "I was afraid if I did you'd say you were going to be busy. Out consoling your long-lost friend again. Personally, I think he should be pretty well consoled enough by now. Don't you?"

She smiled. "You're jealous, Bill."

He put the glass down on the swirl of spun silicate filaments that formed the table between them. The small fountain in the center fizzed with tinted energy. "Damn right I'm jealous. Who is this kid, to be taking up so much of your time? Of *our* time. You told me after he got here that the two of you hadn't spent all that much time together on Longtunnel. So why the extended contact now? I'd say you've done more than your share of hand-holding."

She sipped at her drink, the pale liquid redolent of peaches and barru, straight rum and crooked eloqueur. It burned her throat. Not unlike this unexpected and unwanted confrontation. Clearly, she wasn't going to be able to dismiss him with a smile and a kiss tonight. Out of the corner of one eye she kept a watch on Scrap. Whatever Bill Ormann said, the minidrag would let her know what he was actually feeling.

"I've told you, Bill. Philip is just a friend. He's a complicated man who's been through a lot. He needs someone to listen to him, and he doesn't have a lot of friends."

Ormann grunted unsympathetically. "Closemouthed as he is, I'm not surprised." He peered a little harder at her. "Or is he more voluble when he's alone with you, Clarity? What do you do to help loosen his tongue?" He posed the question with a half smile, but beside the big window, Scrap's head lifted and turned in his direction.

"I've told you that, too." She made no effort to conceal her exasperation. "I listen to him. I'm just a sounding board for his problems."

"You sure that's the only kind of board you're being for him?" The now-alert minidrag raised its wings from its flanks but did not unfurl them.

Putting her drink down, Clarity did not even try to fake a smile. "That's not very funny, Bill."

"It was intended as a joke." His expression had turned grim. "This nonsense has been going on for more than a month, Clarity. I think I've been patient. A lot of guys wouldn't just stand aside and let a relationship proliferate between their fiancée and some skinny, eerie stranger from offworld."

"I'm not your fiancée, Bill."

"Not formally, no. I thought what we had between us had progressed past the point of formalities being necessary. Maybe I was wrong. Am I wrong, Clarity?" He was watching her closely.

She sidestepped the question. "Bill, you're not the first man to mistake compassion for passion. He's an old acquaintance who I'm trying to help. When he's said all he came to say, I'm sure he'll leave." Behind her, a drifting chronoture announced the time in soft tones that imitated the call of a particularly melodious local pond dweller.

"Alone?"

That was too much. "I'm an independent woman, Bill. I enjoy talking to Philip and I enjoy talking to you. What I don't like is being interrogated." She pushed her drink toward him. "Maybe this isn't a good time for a talk like this. Maybe you should leave."

"I've been getting the distinct feeling that no time is a good time for us to talk anymore. Or to do anything else." He rose and stepped around the table. But he didn't continue toward the door.

In all the time they had spent together, he had never laid a hand on her. That was not to say they hadn't argued, but their disagreements had always struck her as normal for two people getting to know each other. These occasional disagreements had never involved physical violence. Now that he stood close by, angry and looming over her, she wondered if that record was about to be broken. She wasn't afraid, but she was wary. Ormann was a big man, and despite what self-defense training she'd had, she did not doubt that he could do a lot of damage were he so inclined.

For the moment, however, all the fury bottled up inside him continued to take the form of words and flushed expressions.

"Don't lie to me, Clarity. There's something more between you and this kid than just a desire to listen to his troubles. I've seen the way you look at each other—not all the time, true, but now and again. There's more there than mutual compassion."

"Okay, I admit it, Bill. We had a relationship. It didn't last long and it was six years ago. You didn't have any relationships then, I suppose?"

"We're talking about now, today, not six years ago."

"*He* got rid of *me*," she told him.

That admission took Ormann by surprise. "He dumped *you*? I knew the kid was weird, but I didn't think he was stupid."

"He's twenty-four, Bill. He's not a kid."

"Everything's relative, Clarity." He sat down on the arm of her chair, closer than she wanted. "So, what's his big problem that he had to come all this way just to talk to an old friend?"

Let's see, she thought. Where to begin? Well, for one thing, he's one of the few surviving illegal offspring of a loathsome research project developed by a disgraced bunch of gengineers known as the Meliorare Society, whose biological manipulation of his nervous system has endowed him with capabilities he is still learning about and that may kill him. Oh yes; he also believes he may be the key to saving civilization in this galaxy from an unnamed threat of cosmic proportions, an infinitesimal exposure to which caused my blood to run cold and frightened me so badly it all but stopped my breathing. Furthermore, he thinks he is being manipulated by outside forces he is unable to identify, with the exception of one childlike but absurdly talented sentient species that is so dangerous it has been placed Under Edict by the government. Other than that, he's as carefree as a bidium songfret and there's nothing on his mind—nothing at all.

What she said was, "He doesn't make friends easily. I'm one of the few people he thinks he can confide in."

Ormann made a disgusted noise. "One of the oldest lines in the book: All I need is the love and support of a good woman to help me out of my troubles and misery. Women have fallen for that one since time immemorial. I don't blame you, Clarity." The anger in him had subsided but it had not gone away. "It's maternal instinct, among other things. But I'd prefer that you didn't see him anymore. You insist he's not a kid? Fair enough. Let him work out his own problems like an adult. Or seek counseling. This has been going on for more than a month now. You've done your best. You've done more than your part."

Wishing there were more space between them, she looked up at him unapologetically and without smiling. "He's my friend, Bill. I won't abandon him."

Ormann nodded thoughtfully. "I see. And us?"

"I don't want to abandon that, either."

"But you won't stop seeing him? How about listening to him, talking to him, over the vit?"

She shook her head. "There's no comfort to be found in talking to an electronic image, no matter how realistic."

A hand reached down. It was a large hand, smooth and fine, the nails perfectly manicured, but still very strong. It gripped her shoulder, the fingers digging in.

"You're hurting me, Bill."

He leaned toward her without slackening his grip. "I'm not going to lose you, Clarity. Especially not to some overtall, undermature emotional basket case. I've got too much invested in our relationship."

She reached up but was unable to dislodge his fingers. Her voice was tight and controlled. She knew he knew he was hurting her, but she wasn't about to plead with him. "Let go of me, Bill. *Now.*"

"And if I don't?" His face was suddenly much closer, split by an unpleasant, humorless grin.

She didn't have to reply. The deep humming in his ears was enough to make him release her. Scrap was hovering behind him, less than a meter from his head. Though Ormann's knowledge of the minidrag's capabilities extended no further than what Clarity had told him, he had no reason to doubt her. The slitted eyes were staring unblinkingly back into his own, the scaly mouth was parted, and somewhere within lay the means to render him dead as a doornail in fewer minutes than he had fingers on one hand.

Very slowly, he rose from the arm of the chair. One hand went to the table to pick up the travel pouch that lay there. It contained, among other personal items, a powerful shocker. New Riviera might be the most livable world in the Commonwealth, but it was not devoid of crime. Where there was so much money to be had, there were always those hoping to acquire it without having to work for it.

"I've got personal protection with me." Carefully, making no sudden moves, he clipped the pouch back onto his waist. "One burst would paralyze your damn flying snake for hours, if the charge didn't kill it outright."

She pursed her lips and eyed him pityingly. "You'd never get off a shot. Unless you're better at controlling your emotions than anyone I've met, Scrap would sense your intent before you could get a finger on the firing mechanism. You'd be on the floor, dying and with your eyes melting in their sockets."

His hand cradled the pouch, caressing it slowly. "I've only your word for that, Clarity. I never liked snakes, anyhow—winged or otherwise, terrestrial or alien."

She shrugged diffidently. "I don't want to see you dead, Bill."

"Well, that's something, anyway." His voice dripped sarcasm.

"If you don't believe me about Scrap, you know how to find out for yourself."

Silence filled the room. Then he let his hand slide away from the pouch. In response not to the gesture but to the emotions Ormann was projecting, the minidrag backed off another couple of meters. But Scrap remained airborne with his gaze fixed on the man.

Ormann headed for the front door. "Don't make any rash decisions, Clarity. That's all I'm asking. This kid shows up unannounced after six years—he's likely to disappear again the same way. But I'll still be here when he's gone."

"I know, Bill. I'm keeping that in mind."

It wasn't much to leave with, but it was something, and he clutched at it. The evening hadn't gone at all the way he'd hoped. He was leaving unsatisfied and irate, but at least he hadn't been thrown out. She still cared for him. Genuine affection, he wondered, or hedging her emotional bets?

"I'll see you at the office," he told her by way of good night. She responded pleasantly, if without any great enthusiasm.

He'd made a mistake, he told himself grimly as he took the lift down to the transport level. He'd underestimated everything: this strange guy's appeal, the depth of the relationship he'd had with Clarity, the strength of their lingering attachment, and, yes, even the extent of his own relationship with the beautiful and desirable gengineer.

A few solid whacks might have knocked some sense into her, he mused as he climbed back into his luxury personal transport and activated the autohome. Rising from its charger in the garage, it pivoted and accelerated gently, heading for the exit. But if she was to be believed, any attempt to strike her with anything more edifying than words would result in the intervention of that slimy, leather-winged pet of hers. He needed to do some research, he told himself firmly. Find out how much of what she had told him about the minidrag was the truth and how much embellishment. If things continued to proceed the way they were going, he might need to know.

Meanwhile, he reflected as the transport turned up the guideway, accelerating on automatic, he had no intention of standing politely aside any longer and playing the confident, condescending bystander. Thanks to the arrival of this peculiar specter from her past, his relationship with Clarity was in jeopardy. He would not sit back and watch it be destroyed by some soft-spoken competitor. The kid wasn't even a Nurian, for O'Morion's sake!

There were several things he could do. Some of them would require time and research. At least one he could set in motion immediately. Its outcome would be instructive at the least, highly gratifying at best. Activating the transport's communicator, he spoke a name that would have surprised his superiors as much as it would Clarity. Not everyone he had engaged in business with was an executive or scientist.

Even on a world as civilized as New Riviera, it was sometimes useful to know individuals who were not.

It took a few days. During that time he made an effort to be as affable as possible at the office and as gracious to Clarity as his emotions would allow. His task was made more difficult since she went everywhere with that damn minidrag. It was a struggle not to let his real feelings flow to the fore, even when he was smiling and joking on the outside. He could fool her but not the alien empath. The minidrag would sense the deception, and she in turn would note the reptiloid's reactions.

But he managed. Part of his business success lay in knowing how to massage corporate egos and stroke company personalities. More than once, he caught the minidrag casting a threatening stare in his direction. More often than not, Clarity didn't notice. When she did, he mustered a plausible excuse for the snake's reaction, claiming that he was upset about the way some aspect of business was going or that he'd just banged his knee on the side of the desk.

She was pleasant enough toward him, especially as time passed and he made no mention of the uncomfortable confrontation that had taken place in her codo. Some of her old affection for him returned. Pleased, he did everything possible to encourage her. He even managed a genial word or two when she announced that she would be unable to see him because she would be attending to Lynx's needs. He lied, in short, with consummate skill.

A week later he found himself on the same path through the city park that the two of them had strolled on so often during the past year. This time, he was alone. Clarity was with her psychologically damaged charge.

What they were talking about, he didn't know. What they might be doing, he fought manfully not to imagine.

It was late and the park was no longer crowded. Constrained by municipal regulations, the majority of self-animated drifting advertisements had long since shut down for the night, returning to their camouflaged charging stations like so many diurnal birds. With the return of the sun the following morning they would resume their hard or soft sells, depending on the product they happened to be programmed to hawk. To sleep, perchance to harangue.

Two men sat munching self-warming bags of Frair on the other side of the Tavares-Cellini fountain. Graphic water from the fountain reached toward them with misty tentacles, to moisten slightly without making too much contact. They ignored the aqueous aesthetics in single-minded pursuit of their late-night snacking.

One was almost as tall as Clarity's friend. His thick, muscular torso rested atop a pair of spindly legs. With his equally long, heavy arms and narrow, raptorish face, he looked top-heavy and as if he might topple over if he tried to stand. His companion was nearly as tall and resembled a cartoonist's sketch of a human being: all balloons and circles, as if every part of his body had been puffed up with air. When he moved, however, none of the concentric folds of his great mass rolled or jiggled. The outward appearance of obesity was a sham. The man was buffed up, not puffed up.

It seemed unlikely that any other pair of male visitors to the Tavares-Cellini fountain at this hour would half so well fit the profile of the two men Ormann sought. The nearest glanced challengingly in his direction. The stare was quietly arrogant, designed to fend off a casual approach.

"I'm the oar man for the boat," Bill informed them in

a noncommittal tone. If he was wrong and these two were not the right ones, they would think him no more than a harmless idiot: something even contemporary Commonwealth society had not been able to eliminate.

The muscular man nodded. Neither man made any move to rise from their bench, nor did they make room for him.

Ormann was not offended. So much the better. He had not sought out the services of men like these in the hope they would prove conventionally polite. "Did our mutual friend explain what I need?"

The two men exchanged a glance. Top-heavy replied, "You have a problem with a visitor who's spending too much time with your woman."

Ormann smiled thinly. "She's not mine yet, but things aren't progressing toward that end as smoothly as I'd like."

"Because of this visitor."

Ormann nodded. "I was told you and your friend work quickly and efficiently."

A smile cracked the raptor's visage. "We're not rated by the Nurian Consumer Network, but we know what to do. What you want sounds fairly straightforward."

"It would be." He waited while a meandering couple moved past and out of earshot. "Except that the visitor, like my lady, has an Alaspinian flying snake. They're empathetic telepaths. So if the visitor feels threatened, his pet senses it and reacts accordingly."

The mass of muscle frowned. "It's dangerous then, this flying snake?"

"Lethal," Ormann replied somberly, "and lightning fast. You're dead before you can draw a bead on it with even a lightweight weapon. Or so I'm told. I've never actually seen it in action."

Wiping crumbs from his mouth with the back of his

thick forearm, the big man frowned at his partner. "Don't like this. We were told there was one disrespectful young guy who needed enlightening. Nothing was said about lethal flying creatures."

"I've thought of a way to deal with it."

Raptor face was already thinking of solutions. "Set up and detonate a kill from a distance or by timer."

Ormann shook his head. "Too extreme. No way of being sure about the consequences. And there's always the chance some fool bystander ends up in the wrong place at the wrong time and gets hurt. Then the authorities come into it and things could get awkward. Besides, I don't really want him dead—just scared off." He smiled wolfishly. "He's so relaxed and sure of himself it shouldn't be a problem to bring off what I have in mind. He feels completely secure whenever that minidrag of his is riding his shoulder. Which is, as near as I've been able to determine, constantly."

"Then how do we get to him without getting bit?" raptor face wanted to know.

"The minidrag doesn't bite; it spits venom. But it won't get the chance. I've arranged for the delivery of a special package. It will be addressed from the woman who's involved, so I know the kid will accept it. The package will contain a powerful soporific. Even if he has an unusually strong constitution, it should put both him and his pet out for an hour. You two can move in at your leisure, pack him up, take him someplace quiet and isolated, and finish your job."

Man mountain looked thoughtful. "What if he don't open the package? What if he scans it and sees that the contents are suspicious?"

"The contents won't be suspicious because there won't be anything of consequence." Ormann felt more than a little pleased with himself. "There'll be nothing inside but stuffing. The soporific will be infused into the packaging itself. I managed to obtain a DNA sample from one of his hairs. The packaging material is keyed to him alone. As soon as he touches the package, the wrapping will disintegrate, releasing the soporific. There'll be enough of it and it will be strong enough so that, even if he's faster thinking than I believe he is, he won't have time to do anything. It will be sufficient to saturate the hotel room he's staying in, which means that even if the minidrag isn't on his shoulder but is somewhere else in the room, it will still be rendered unconscious. The agent will dissipate in five minutes, so you'll be able to enter the room almost immediately after he handles the package."

"Better be." The big man shifted on the bench, which groaned beneath his weight. "I'm not dealing with any poisonous offworld pet."

Ormann reassured him. "All you'll have to do is walk in, bag him, and take him to wherever it is you take those who have been consigned to your care. Leave the flying snake behind, blow its malicious little scaly head off, tie its wings to its body and toss it out the nearest window—whatever you want. It's the kid I'm interested in."

Raptor face nodded. "How interested?"

"I told you." After another glance around the park, Ormann leaned toward them. In the pale amber light from the park's glowfloats his expression was as twisted as his words. "Scare him. Frighten him so that when he regains consciousness the first thing he'll want to do is leave Nur and never come back. You don't have to be explicit about the reason. Tell him he's made enemies who don't want him here. Tell him nothing. I leave the details up to you. Mess up his face and anything else you think appropriate for a guy who's trying to steal another man's woman.

"Oh, and one more thing. He's too tall. Break his knees. Both of them." His expression contorted into a smile. "I'll be the first one to convey my outrage and sympathy to him—while he's recovering in the hospital."

Raptor face was neither impressed nor dismissive. This was, after all, part and parcel of the nature of doing his kind of business, and he and his partner had been through it all many times before. Even in paradise, there were parasites.

"Sounds like you went through a lot of trouble to work up that sleep-inducing packaging. Pretty clever. We might hit you up for the formulation."

Ormann nodded agreeably. He was very pleased with the way the meeting had gone. It had all been very businesslike. "I'll be glad to provide you with the necessary information. That's what comes of working for a firm that does a lot of gengineering work. You have access to tools and methods usually denied to the general public. Not that I'm looking to establish some kind of long-term relationship with you two."

"Hey, you never know." It was raptor face's turn to grin suggestively. "Someday you might find someone else hanging on to the rung of the corporate ladder above you. Easy enough to remove the somebody while leaving the rung in place."

Having concluded both their business and their snacks, the two men rose to depart. They stood close to Ormann, who all but disappeared in the larger man's shadow. Suddenly, they did not look quite so businesslike, quite so serene and rational. Conscious of his isolation and the lateness of the hour, he was suddenly anxious to be detached from their company.

"Hope this woman is worth it." Man mountain belched softly and tapped his chest with a fist the size of a ripe melon. As discreetly as he could manage, Ormann turned away from the oral discharge.

"She is."

"When do you want it done?" Ormann noticed raptor face's upper incisors had been replaced with replicants of anodized titanium alloy. He hadn't noticed it before as the man was not prone to smiling.

"As soon as possible," Ormann told him tightly. "Tomorrow."

Man mountain shook his head slowly. "Huh-uh. Tomorrow's my day to visit my ex-wife and kids. How about the day after?"

"Fine." Ormann held his temper. "Like I said, as soon as possible. The package is already made up, and I'll provide you with the location. We'll coordinate the timing."

Raptor shrugged. "At your convenience. You're paying enough."

Ormann nodded and walked away. Halfway around the fountain, he looked back and mouthed the words that had given him more pleasure than anything else he had uttered in a long time: "Remember—*both* knees!"

9

As with every day he was not going to spend with Clarity, Flinx had no idea what to do with himself. She did have to do some actual work once in a while, she had told him with a smile. But tonight they were, as had become an enjoyable habit, having dinner together. He had that much to look forward to.

Not that New Riviera lacked diversions to occupy his body as well as his mind. From the conveniently modest-sized seas to the spackling of clear blue lakes, from rolling hills to dramatic yet easily negotiable mountains and everything in between, there were plenty of natural attractions to keep the interested visitor occupied. Then there were the cultural temptations, from museums and creative displays to theme parks and other amusement venues as sophisticated and enticing as any in the Commonwealth.

None of them interested Flinx. Already in his young life, he had seen and experienced sights that even designers of extreme entertainments could not begin to imagine. He was interested only in Clarity—in her ability to listen to him, to draw him out, to empathize and understand.

That she was beautiful and had once been in love with him had nothing, absolutely nothing, to do with it.

Dinner was hours away. He had a day to kill.

Sphene's famous musiceaum, where, by means of direct cranial induction, composers turned musical inspiration into solid sculpture and painting, still beckoned. Not only did everyone insist it was an interesting place to visit, he was curious to try his hand at the technically sophisticated compositional technique himself. Certainly he had been exposed to a sufficiently wide range of music and natural sounds. What a cerebrally coupled transmogrifier might make of his insights and experiences might make for interesting viewing.

He had dressed and performed his few simple ablutions when the hotel door announced the receipt of a package for him. Knowing that hotel security would automatically have vetted any delivery before transferring it to a guest's room, he did not hesitate to acknowledge receipt. The small box was waiting for him outside his door.

He brought it inside and studied it curiously. Taking no chances, hotel security or no hotel security, he removed a small device from one belt pouch and passed it over the package. The readings were negative. Satisfied, he removed the outer plasticine wrapping to reveal a second casing of paper. To his surprise, it disintegrated on contact with his fingers. Shoddy material, an intentional surprise, or . . . ?

Flinx had survived as long as he had because, among other things, he was exceedingly wary of surprises. But this time he wasn't fast enough. The package's inner wrapping turned into a colorless, odorless gas. He managed a few steps before he collapsed.

Sensing her master's distress, Pip shot across the room. Hovering above Flinx's body, she remained airborne for a few seconds before fluttering down to a rough landing against his back. There she lay, unmoving and silent, eyes closed, tongue retracted.

Five minutes passed. At the sixth, the door clicked several times as its security seal was professionally breached. It swung open to admit two men. Closing the door behind him, raptor face studied the two unconscious forms with professional detachment.

"The salivating stoink was as good as his word." Pushing aside the hotel delivery cart they had brought with them, man mountain knelt to take the unconscious man's pulse. "Sleep mode." He indicated the motionless flying snake. "Looks to be in the same state." Taking an impermeable, acid-resistant sack from the pouch slung over his shoulder, he picked up the flying snake by its tail and dropped it into the bag. "Stoink said we could do whatever we want with the pet. Me, I say sell it. If it's as rare as he claimed, we ought to be able to get a decent few credits for it."

Raptor face wasn't convinced. "Stoink said they bond tightly with their owners."

His companion shrugged his vast shoulders. "Not our problem, is it? That problem belongs to anybody who buys it."

"That's true." Raptor face looked pleased. "Pick him up. The sooner we've finished, the sooner the second half of the payment is credited to our accounts."

Lifting Flinx onto the delivery cart proved no more than a minor inconvenience to the two professionals. Man mountain eased the protective cover back over somnolent man and minidrag.

"Thought about where to take him?"

Raptor face nodded. "Kerwick campground, I think. It's accessible but still enough off the beaten track so that we can let him scream all he wants without having to worry."

His companion nodded tersely. As far as he was concerned, the hard part of the job was already completed.

The rest was mere repetition of work they had done before.

As they guided the cart down the hallway he raised one corner of the cover. "Looks like a nice enough guy."

"They all do." All business, raptor face locked down the delivery cart's cover. "Probably is a nice guy, too. Like you said, not our problem. We'll leave enough of the underlying maxillary structure so it can be reconstructed."

Man mountain adjusted his rented uniform as they directed the cart around a corner and down another hallway, heading for the nearest service lift. "Over a woman, the stoink said. It's always over a woman."

Raptor face sniggered, then added something obscene. "After seeing this guy, I can understand stoink's concern."

"Well, he won't have anything to be concerned about when we've finished." Man mountain took pride in his work.

It was another dream. Strange, Flinx mused, how one could be dreaming and still be aware of the fact. He told himself to wake up but the request was not honored by his nervous system. Pip was nearby, he sensed, so he was not afraid, even though something told him the minidrag was also unconscious.

No, not unconscious, he corrected himself. Asleep. There was a difference.

This time there was no blackness, no all-encompassing, cosmos-spanning evil. After all, when he dreamed, it was not always about that. With his thoughts focused on Clarity Held and not wholly on the serious, carefully thought-out replies she gave to his questions, he felt as if he were floating on a field of flowers. Each delicate petal combined to support a small portion of his weight.

From a physical standpoint it was impossible, of course. This, however, was a dream.

Clarity, Clarity, he thought. How could he have left her all those years ago, even in search of himself? How could he not? Unstable as he was, dangerous even, if he cared deeply for anyone the least he could do was visit them only intermittently. Otherwise, there was no telling what frightful effect he might have on someone's life.

Trouble was, he *wanted* to have an effect on the life of Clarity Held, and for her to affect his. He just wasn't sure how to go about it without harming her. If he could no longer fully control his abilities, he did not have the right to ask anyone to commit herself to him. Who would want to live with a mutated biological time bomb like him? Why, even as he was remembering in this dream the time they had spent by the lake, the sunshine and forest of flower trees and small, inadvertent physical contacts, he might be projecting his feelings, just as he had in the shopping arcade in Reides. If that were so, at least he was not projecting cosmic evil. What he might be projecting instead he did not know and could not imagine, except to realize with slim certainty that it would not be harmful.

In any event, there was nothing he could do about it. That kind of control over his mind was not within his province. He was asleep, dreaming, and he could not wake himself up. He remained calm and quiet, dreaming of blossoms and soft ground cover and what he might feel about Clarity Held.

He awoke on a bench in Sphene's justly famed Crystal Park. Surrounded by reflected light and rainbows, laughing children, and contented parents, he sat up and struggled to recall what had happened to him. He'd been in his hotel room—he remembered that. There had been a delivery. A package. Had he opened it? Yes. Then what? Nothing.

No, that was not quite true. He didn't remember falling asleep, but he did remember dreaming. This one had been positively amorous. A nice change from the frequent and disturbing nightmares. He didn't even have a headache.

Pip lay dozing at one end of the bench, lying on an old sack. Frowning, he moved toward her and inspected her makeshift bed. Though the artificial fibers were unusually tough, a minidrag-sized hole was visible near the bottom. Had she been inside? If so, the experience did not seem to have unsettled her. She lay coiled and composed in the sun, her pleated wings folded flat against her flanks.

How had he ended up here? Was sleepwalking a condition now to be added to the involuntary projection of his thoughts? Even on tranquil New Riviera the authorities still maintained a system of surveillance devices to protect the public safety. Perhaps one of them had recorded some of what had happened to him.

Rising, he called to Pip. With a spread and flutter of blue-and-pink wings, she settled securely around his right shoulder. A couple of children exclaimed and pointed. He had no time to let them ooh and ahh and pet the minidrag. He had a citywide security system to break into.

Ormann sensed something was wrong when there was no message for him, encrypted or otherwise, when he returned home that night. Nor did one arrive the following day. He called Clarity to inquire with forced pleasantries what she might be doing that evening, only to be told that she and her friend were once again having dinner. Concealing his disbelief, he learned that she had talked to him during her lunch break.

So the redheaded bastard was still around and apparently in excellent health. For the rest of that afternoon Ormann brooded in his office, hardly attending to work, wondering what the hell had gone wrong. The two men he had engaged had been recommended to him as the best at their business. If they had failed, who could he try next?

More important, *why* had they failed? And what had happened to them? Clarity had hinted on more than one occasion that there was more to her friend than was apparent. The reference now took on ominous overtones. Had his employees neglected to use proper care in handling the minidrag?

Greater than his shock at learning that Philip Lynx was still functional and healthy was Ormann's response when he learned that raptor face and his companion were unharmed.

He managed to track them down and confront them at an infamous (for Nur) slothzone hangout where he had been told they could usually be found. There they were, in fine fettle and visibly unscathed, sitting in a back booth guzzling fancy concoctions paid for with his money. Perhaps he should have approached with more caution, or addressed them in a more conciliatory tone, but he was too angry.

"Took him apart, did you? Really beat him up? With what? Pillows?"

Raptor face swiveled his narrow, predatory visage around to confront Ormann. It appeared the hired killer was pleasantly intoxicated. "Hello, Bill." He gestured toward the seat opposite. "Won't you join us?"

"I'd rather take any explanations standing, thanks."

"You're too tense, Bill," man mountain murmured

solicitously. "You should get out more, have some fun."
Then he did something that shocked Ormann even more
than the earlier news that his red-headed nemesis had
survived unscathed. Man mountain giggled.

Reaching up with one lethal, steel-corded hand, raptor face patted his immense companion gently on the
cheek. "Now, Emunde, don't tease the poor man. He's
obviously a basket of frustration."

Ormann swallowed. Hard. "You didn't do what you
were paid to do. It doesn't look like you laid a hand on
the kid. What the hell happened? It was the flying snake,
wasn't it? It drove you off. Or," he continued, throwing
caution aside, "it frightened you off."

"We couldn't hurt that nice young man." Man mountain pushed out his plump lower lip. He almost looked
as if he were going to cry. "I feel bad enough about dragging him halfway across town. We left him and his pet
in a nice place, though. I'm sure he's all right."

"Oh, he's just fine." Ormann's tone was tight enough
to crack. "Too fine." He looked from one jovial killer to
the other. "What happened? *What did he do to you?*"

"Do?" For just an instant, a hint of his original murderous character passed over raptor face. "Why, he didn't
do anything, Bill." His smile was beatific. "Emunde and
I, we just suddenly realized that we were wasting our
lives with what we were doing, that we didn't want to
hurt people anymore, and that we were missing out on
so many of the joys of life. And don't worry—we'll refund your fee." He raised his glass. "Sure you won't join
us in a drink?"

Something had happened to these two men. Something strange and inexplicable. In ways unknown, it
was the fault of Clarity's friend. It had to be. Creatures
like these two did not simply go all spineless and silly

overnight. He corrected himself. Something had not happened to them. Something had been *done* to them.

But what? It made no sense. It made even less sense than Clarity's incomprehensible attraction to a man younger than herself whom she hadn't seen in six years.

The evening of wonders was not quite over. Raptor face held up his glass. "Be of good cheer, Bill Ormann. We'll send you an invitation to the wedding." And with that, he put his arm around as much of man mountain's waist as he could encompass and squeezed affectionately.

Ormann stumbled blindly out of the slothzone, seeing nothing. Not the gyrating softiques, nor their human counterparts. Not the spinning silver-eyed ecdysiasts boasting their unnatural virtual accoutrements or the citizens who lapped up the sight of them.

Outside, the cool night air gradually drew him out of his stupor. Heading toward transport, he considered his next step. In Philip Lynx he was clearly confronting something far more subtle and dangerous than he had believed. Before he could devise a method for dealing with him, he had to know more precisely what he was up against. How to go about acquiring that knowledge?

He could try to pry it out of Clarity. Reticent as she was about the young man's background, he didn't think gentle questioning would lead to much information. He could try to force it out of her. While he had little doubt that could be accomplished, by others if not by himself, it might drive her even closer to Lynx. He could challenge Lynx directly, hopefully while not in the presence of his irritable minidrag.

Slow down, he told himself. You've been patient this long. There's still time. She's not running off with him tomorrow. Do some serious research. You set professionals on him too soon, without knowing enough about him. Now enlist the aid of professionals of a different kind.

Whether in business or society, it was always prudent to learn a competitor's weaknesses before attacking. Ormann's jealousy and irritation had caused him to act in haste. That wouldn't happen again, he vowed. The next time he took action, it would be with sufficient information to ensure success.

Meanwhile, he would continue to smile and act the chivalrous, mature protector to Clarity while extending the hand of politeness to her friend. Biding one's time was as vital to the success of any endeavor as moving to accomplish it. It might take more time and effort than he had hoped, but the end was worthwhile. Clarity was too good a catch to surrender to some mumble-voiced postadolescent from . . . from . . .

It occurred to him that he did not even remember from what world his competitor hailed. Just acquiring such personal details might in itself lead to a means for getting rid of him. Ormann began to see possibilities that looked even more promising than simply having his rival beaten to a pulp.

But how had Lynx escaped from the now-outlandishly transformed thugs? Did Clarity know how it had been done? If so, could he obtain at least that information from her? If the redhead was somehow responsible, it would be vital for Ormann to learn what had happened.

Some kind of drug, perhaps. What if Lynx had somehow managed to counteract the effects of the special package? But that didn't explain the sea change that had overwhelmed the two killers.

As he reached his private transport and activated the door, Ormann was convinced he knew the source of the fiasco, if not the actual cause. He would not be denied Clarity. Not after all the work he had put into acquiring her and certainly not by some creepy, attenuated upstart from offworld.

It was just a matter of time.

The woman Ormann was buying dinner for was attractive, slim, dark-eyed and honey-voiced. When he hinted that he might be interested in more than just hiring her to do a little specialized research for him, she put him in his place quickly. "Mr. Ormann—you can drop the false Cavelender name now, I don't work for anyone whose true identity I don't know—you should understand that if you intend to use my services, I prefer to keep my professional and personal interests separate." She smiled around the stimstick that protruded like a small smoking stiletto from her full lips. "You're not my type, anyway."

"No?" Manufacturing a small smile to go with the small talk, he peered at her over his glass. Rainbow-hued liquid swirled within, effervescing Mozart. "Why not?"

"You're underhanded and oily. Nothing personal." The stimstick smoked pungently, redolent of jasmine and byyar.

If calling someone underhanded and oily wasn't personal, he mused as he fought to keep instinctive rising anger under control, what was? He concealed his reaction by taking a long, slow draft of his drink.

"Calling someone underhanded sounds strange coming from a professional prober like you."

She laughed softly. She was without question the most attractive felon he had ever encountered. Doubtless her appearance facilitated her work, which consisted largely of gaining access to information and places that would otherwise have been denied to her. And to her clients, he reminded himself.

"I prefer to think of myself as a subtle seeker after truth. And please—spare me the jokes about penetration. I've heard them all, boredom squared."

"Then if it's all right with you," he said as he set his drink aside, "we'll skip the rest of dinner along with any further informalities and get down to business."

"Down or up." She sounded bored. "It's all the same to me."

He didn't bother to lean toward her; their table had already been privacy-screened. "I'm interested in the background of a recent arrival on Nur. Young man, staying at the Barkamp Inn, room six eighty-three. Has an Alaspinian minidrag for a pet. Never goes anywhere without it. Somehow he managed to dissuade the two men I engaged to teach him a lesson from carrying out their duties. In their own field, they were as reputable and well regarded as yourself."

"Intriguing. What do you know about your man?" A flicker of more than professional interest crossed her smooth, pale features.

"Very little, which is why I'm hiring you, mostly— and most upsettingly—that he and my fiancée had some kind of relationship six years ago."

"And now he's turned up here to complicate your life. What do you want to know about him?"

"Everything." Unable to restrain his anger and frustration, Ormann's voice had gone low and tight. "Where he's from. How old he actually is. What abilities he might possess beyond the inexplicable one of holding the attention of my fiancée. The names and locations of any relatives, close friends, or romantic involvements. His education and social background, resources, homeworld location, politics, religion—everything."

She nodded. A small, dark purple recorder drawn from her purse was pressed against his. Information transferred silently. She preferred it that way; it meant she didn't have to listen to the client as much. Also, machines did not try to hit on her. Generally.

As she rose sinuously from her chair she slipped her recorder back into its holder. "I'll be in touch. When I have something for you."

He gazed moodily into his drink. "Be careful. I don't know what this Lynx did to the two men I hired. I can't prove he did anything, but I doubt the implausible consequences were accidental. You don't want him doing anything to you."

"I'm not going to have any contact with him. If everything goes well, as it usually does, I won't even have to talk to him. And I can take care of myself, Mr. Ormann."

With a short, sharp shove he pushed his glass to one side. Calling for the bill, he glanced at the colorful heads-up, acknowledged the total by waving his hand over it, passed a credcard through the projection, and waited for the receipt.

"You're sure you have to go? You're an interesting lady and I wouldn't mind just talking to you a while longer." His tone was hopeful.

She smiled, checking to ensure that her purse was secured to her waist. " 'Talking'? Why, what would your fiancée say, Mr. Ormann?"

He grinned diffidently. The little-boy pose had served him well before. "She isn't here."

"And in a few seconds, neither am I," she replied as she pivoted on one glidesole and strode purposefully to the exit.

Wholly professional, he thought as he rose from the table and wandered off in her wake. He was in no hurry to go home. An early return to his empty home would give him that much more time to wonder what Clarity and her friend were doing. Just talking, Clarity always insisted. Inwardly, he had begun to doubt her. No male conversationalist was that interesting. Not after this many weeks.

But then, he reflected, he did not know Lynx. In business, he had quickly learned that it was dangerous to generalize. And if Clarity was telling the truth, the young man did not know himself either. Ormann was confident this little bit of self-denigration on Mr. Lynx's part would not impede the work of the very competent woman whose services he had just engaged. He looked forward to finding out all there was to know about his possible rival. Then he would know how to respond the next time.

Which would most certainly be the last time, he assured himself.

10

It didn't happen very often. When it did, Vendra was always grateful. The majority of those she was hired to probe were of normal physical proportions, even if their individual social and moral inclinations were frequently more diverse. This young man was conspicuously tall and had red hair and an exotic flying pet that always rode his shoulder. She was able to follow him easily. Without her being aware of it, the professional indifference she affected in order to blend seamlessly into crowds and scenery also had the effect of removing her from the notice of Flinx's singular ability.

And she was patient. The unpretentious hotel where he was living served as a place for her to begin her work. After alternately cajoling and teasing the desk clerk, she was eventually allowed access to the guest records. Most of these were privacy sealed. That stopped her for about three minutes. Unfortunately, the available portion of her quarry's record was concise and contained no useful information. He had simply registered. In order to satisfy her client she needed to access a lot more than that.

Her patience was rewarded one morning when Flinx unexpectedly entered a branch of a well-regarded chain of jewelry shops. She followed him inside, waving off the eager attendant who offered to assist her. Pretending to examine a display case filled with rings, she allowed her attention to wander in her quarry's direction. With the aid of another salesperson, he was inspecting bracelets and necklaces. Her client would be relieved to learn that the handsome young man was *not* looking at rings.

Buy something, she found herself thinking at him. Buy anything, but preferably something expensive. The more expensive the item, the more carefully the store's in-house security system would check the purchaser's background. The more information it gleaned, the more there would be for her to copy.

She froze. Suddenly, he was looking at her. Before she had time to retreat or react in any suitable way, he was striding directly toward her. The closer he came, the larger the brightly colored winged reptiloid on his shoulder became.

"Excuse me, miss?" He had a nice voice, she decided, pleasant, almost boyishly charming, the voice of someone you instinctively wanted to help. She forced a smile. "Do you mind if—?" He broke off, frowning uncertainly. "You seem upset."

"I do?" She continued to smile, stayed relaxed, her respiration only slightly elevated. How did he know she was upset? She forced herself to remain calm. "I guess expensive jewelry always makes my heart race."

He looked uncertain. Then he shrugged, discounting his initial impression, and held something out for her to see. "I'm buying a present for a lady friend. What do you think of this?" Faceted gemstones sparkled before her eyes. "I'm trying to make a statement but not to overwhelm. I'm afraid this might be too flashy."

She was so relieved she almost laughed aloud. All he

wanted was the opinion of another woman. Making a show of studying the necklace, she inquired with utmost seriousness, "What color is her hair? Her eyes?" He told her, and she nodded. "Needs more green—emerald, tsavorite, celetine. Meteoric peridot is nice, and unfakeable." She handed the necklace back. "Lucky girl."

She almost laughed a second time. This tall, gangly, somehow endearing young man was blushing slightly. "She's not a girl, and I'm not so sure she's all that lucky. Thanks for your suggestions." Turning away from her, he went back to his chair and resumed conferring with the salesman. The creature riding his shoulder had never looked up.

Relieved, she returned to her inspection of the ring case. Expect the worst, she mused, and it's liable to come knocking. Hope for better, and you're often rewarded. Having maintained her self-control throughout, she was convinced he suspected nothing. Why should he? She'd done nothing suspicious.

Her heart raced ever so slightly when he handed a different, greener necklace back to the salesman, who took it into a back room. When the man returned moments later with a small, discreet package, she knew that the purchase had been made. She waited another ten minutes before wandering over in the salesman's direction, to make sure that the customer he had just waited on had indeed left the store.

"Nice young man, that," she said, gazing casually at the rows of fine necklaces in the case.

The salesman nodded agreeably. "Very soft-spoken, very polite. A pleasure to wait on, though when he first walked in he had no idea what he wanted."

"But you managed to find him something." She smiled admiringly.

The salesman shrugged modestly. "Part of the job. You apparently helped some yourself, with your suggestion. He told me."

She nodded back. "The necklace he finally bought. Expensive?"

The salesman's businesslike demeanor was replaced by hesitation. "You saw the piece he showed you. What the gentleman finally purchased was similar in style and execution. A very nice piece. Why do you want to know?"

"Because having seen what he brought over to me, I find I might be interested in something similar myself."

The smile returned. "I'd be delighted to assist you."

She examined more than a dozen examples of the Nurian jewelers' art, fussing over first one and then another. Finally tiring of the masquerade, she settled on one and asked the price. When he told her, she touched a finger to her lower lip and asked, pouting, if he had something in the same design but with slightly larger stones. He did indeed, and would be back in a minute with several to show her. As he retreated to the back room, he left his sales processing unit on the case in front of her. She glanced around hastily. There were two other salespeople on the floor, and both were providentially busy with customers of their own.

Taking the special search unit from her purse, she slipped it over the store processor. The device she favored for such work was small, innocuous in appearance, and preprogrammed with enhanced keying information she had gleaned from her quarry's hotel. Working silently, her device quickly tapped into the processor's program to search for a certain recent sales record. Finding it, the probe then reached out, racing through citywide, planetwide, and ultimately Commonwealthwide data hubs.

Though both the probe and its unique programming were lightning fast, she still found herself urging it on impatiently.

A subtle vibration in the body of the device indicated that results had been achieved. She removed it from the store processor and slipped it back into its carrying pouch just as the salesman was returning with another tray of necklaces to show her. Continuing to play the game, she inspected them for another ten minutes before sending him back for still another tray of samples. Almost as soon as his back was turned, she attached her device to an equally compact expanding recorder drawn from her purse and began to review the results of her stealthy and highly illegal search.

Some of the information she scanned made sense but was decidedly lackluster in content. Some was already known.

Some of it made no sense at all.

Her device insisted the home address given was false. Yet that had not triggered the store's security programming. And nearly everything else except the most recent information provided by the man was provably false. It gave her pause.

Why would such a pleasant, seemingly innocuous young man need to falsify even the most basic and straightforward facts of his background? Only one thing did not ring untrue, and it should have. That was the size of her quarry's bank account. It was much, much too big. Unless he had acquired a truly impressive inheritance from some major Trading House or great family, no one as young as her quarry should properly have access to such extensive credit. And if he *had* inherited, then why all the elaborate subterfuge to conceal everything about his background? The two did not add together.

Then, to her astonishment, wisps of smoke began to rise from her device. Very compact, very efficient, and very expensive, it began to fry before her eyes. Emerging from the back room, the salesman saw what was happening, quickly set the new tray of necklaces aside, and grabbed a small fire extinguisher, whose contents he proceeded to spray onto the smoking machine. She did not object. Clearly, the device was already damaged beyond repair. Nevertheless, she was as careful to pack away the ruined remnants lest its true nature be discovered as she was to thank the salesman and apologize for the incident.

She left the store hurriedly, her thoughts churning. Her probing had begat an unanticipated response; swift, precise, limited, and thorough. It smacked of a warning. She was brave but not foolhardy, courageous but not stupid. Common sense had ruled her dealings and saved her from more than one unpleasant encounter.

What was it Ormann had tried to tell her about the two men he had sent after the tall man? Something had happened to them. Something Ormann had been unable to find an explanation for. From within the depths of her purse she could still feel the lingering warmth of the cooked device. No explanation for that, either. She knew only one thing for certain: whatever defensive programming she had triggered was expensive and sophisticated. She and it had something in common, then.

Every intelligent person realizes it when she falls short of the level of her competition. But only the really smart ones know when to accept that.

Ormann was so surprised to see Vendra in his office that he forgot to be angry. "What are you doing *here*?" he

asked tightly as he entered and made sure the door
sealed tightly behind him. "We're not supposed to meet
here!"

"Why not?" Vendra was clearly more tense than she
had been the last time they had met. "Afraid your fiancée will walk in on us?"

"What do you want?" His tone changed from upset
to one of controlled excitement. "You have something
for me? Information?"

She nodded. "I sure do." She passed him a folded
printout.

"What's this?" Taking a seat behind his desk, he
looked as puzzled as he sounded.

"Confirmation of your refund." Turning, she started
back toward the door. "I'm declining your tender."

"Wait, wait a minute." He moved to intercept her.
"You can't do that."

"It's already done."

"But—but why?" He was genuinely bemused. Then
his expression darkened. "He did something to you,
didn't he? That redheaded bastard did something to you
just like he did something to the two guys I sent after
him before."

She shook her head. "He did nothing to me. I learned
a couple of things I didn't like, that's all."

"So you *did* manage to find something out about him.
Well, tell me, what?"

"No harm in your knowing." She sniffed diffidently.
"I followed him into a store where he bought something
moderately expensive." She smiled in a way he didn't
like. "You'll probably find out about that yourself. Anyway, I had time—not much time but enough—to probe
the store's purchasing system. I use a highly customized
piece of equipment; very small and very efficient. Never

had any trouble with it. It worked long enough for me to learn that your friend has a good deal more credit to his name than would appear at first glance."

Ormann's confusion showed in his reply. "How much more credit?"

She considered how best to explain it to him. "Not enough to buy your company but more than enough to buy the hotel he's staying in. In the absence of any evidence to the contrary, I'm supposing it to be some kind of inheritance."

He nodded. That, at least, dovetailed somewhat with what he knew about Lynx. "What else did you learn?"

"That I don't want to have anything to do with him. Based on years of experience, my professional advice to a client would be to do the same. But, of course, your interest extends beyond simple curiosity.

"Something responded to my device's prying. Not with the usual jamming programming. It actually totally toasted the unit and it's supposed to be able to shield itself against such attacks. It always has defended itself successfully in the past." She shook her head warningly. "To the best of my knowledge, only military countermeasures can do what was done to my device."

"You think the kid is military?"

"I think the *man* is dangerous. What happened to my device tells me that. My instincts tell me that. I don't know what you think he might have done to the muscle you hired to go after him, but I don't want to hang around him long enough to find out. And I don't want him doing anything to me. He's too quiet. Big, loud, boastful antagonists I can deal with. It's the silent, self-possessed ones who make me edgy. Keep your money, Mr. Ormann. And don't call—I won't answer." She unsealed the office door and departed, leaving one bewildered and angry executive in her wake.

What now, Ormann? he asked himself. You hire two of the best to beat Lynx up; they come back all touchy-feely hand in hand without having laid a finger on him. You hire the best investigator in Sphene and she comes back scared. Clarity continues to see and sympathize with him. You can't touch him yourself because that would immediately cause her to move even closer to him—not to mention that you'd have to deal with that minidrag.

Wait a minute, he thought. If this kid is crafty or controlling or powerful enough to do what he's done already, and seemingly without expending any effort, might he have a history of doing such things? If so, there should be some sort of trail. Maybe, Ormann mused silently, he was going about this all wrong. Being subtle, when what was called for was not subtlety but directness. By now he had acquired excellent visual and auditory records of Lynx. It should be a fairly straightforward matter to trace the recent history of his arrival on Nur. Learning how he had arrived and where he had arrived from, however transient, would at least give Ormann something solid to proceed from. Vendra was not the only accomplished investigator on New Riviera. Offering enough money always drew takers, no matter the perceived danger.

His standing in the business community had enabled him to build up an inventory of multiple contacts. It was time to call in some favors.

What he was about to learn would at once surprise and please him far more than anything he had discovered about his nemesis thus far.

"But I don't know how to dance. I've never danced."

Clarity found Philip's embarrassment at his professed

lack of terpsichorean skill almost as amusing as his evident physical discomfort from the suit he was wearing. Going with him to buy it had been an adventure in itself. She had prevailed only because she insisted that if he didn't wear something different she would refuse to see him anymore.

"Don't you even own a formal outfit?" she'd challenged him.

"I have very few personal possessions," he had replied truthfully. Of course, one of those possessions happened to be a starship, but she already knew that.

Now he twisted and twitched like someone afflicted with an irritating skin disease. Having long since given up any hope of retaining even a semi-stable perch, Pip had retired to the retronouveau supports of the table, where she and Scrap blended so well with the sculpted flow of the multiple legs that anyone standing more than a meter away would have had a difficult time telling the living minidrags from the inorganic, flowering metal.

He looked good in the suit, she told herself. Light-traced, body-imaged, patterned, cut, and sealed, it had been composited and tailored on one of Sphene's trendiest shopping promenades in less than an hour. Next week it would be out of fashion, as was the norm. But for one night at least, Flinx looked like something other than a hub-switch repairman. The shimmering maroon material flashed only a minimum sufficiency of highlights. It stood out nicely in contrast to her more subdued forest green, off-the-shoulder casual gown. Sensitized to specific parts of the visible spectrum, significant portions of her attire blinked transparent when encountering anything shifted into the ultraviolet.

Now she discovered that not only couldn't he dress properly, but he also couldn't dance. That did not stop her from rising from her seat, taking one of his hands, and pulling him toward the crowded floor.

"Anyone can dance, Flinx. I've seen you move. You're agile and flexible. I know you can do it."

Feeling like a complete idiot, in which condition he had been preceded by the great majority of the male members of his species, he reluctantly allowed himself to be dragged toward the middle of the softly lit room. The nearer they drew to the dance floor, the more he felt as if his legs were turning completely nonfunctional. The fact that he loomed over nearly everyone else made him feel that much more conspicuous.

Clarity, on the other hand, reveled in the exposure. "Just follow me," she instructed him, her voice rising above the thumping yet melodious music. "Let yourself go."

"I've never been able to let myself go," he confessed frankly.

"Then it's about time you learned." Backing slightly away from him, she began to move, to twirl, and to rise slightly off the reflective surface as the repellers integrated into her silken shoes reacted to the push-pulse of the energized floor.

He would have been happy just to watch her, as several other male patrons of the club were already doing. Without question she was the most uninhibited genginer he had ever met. Struggling with his ingrained inclination to remain unobtrusive, he began, in hesitant fits and jerks, to try and imitate her movements.

"That's it!" Shouting encouragingly above the roar of draums and the graduated timbalon, she moved closer, put her hands on his waist, and began to push and pull as if she were kneading a large, bipedal lump of taffy. He felt himself rising as the shoes she had insisted he purchase responded to the power flow from the floor.

"You smell wonderful," he told her even as he chided himself for the banality of the comment.

She accepted the compliment in the spirit in which it was given. Her smile was radiant. When certain flashes of light caught her phototropically streaked dress and rendered sections of it see-through, he caught his breath. Leaning into her, he inhaled deeply.

"You like the perfume? The test name is Shehwaru. I was one of the principal gengineers on the project."

"You made it?" Strange, he thought. The more one engaged in this tradition called dancing, the easier it became. He was certainly light enough on his feet, even without the aid of the repellers. Growing up as a thief had ingrained that in his movements. Lights flashed around them, sometimes becoming sound. Music metamorphosed into light. Above it all was Clarity, the sight and smell and closeness of her.

"I contributed," she told him. "The fragrance has oxytocin bound into the molecular structure. You know—the 'snuggling' hormone?" She moved away slightly, dervishing gracefully atop ten centimeters of perfumed, tinted air.

Flinx did not know what she was talking about. Pheromonics were not a particular interest of his. But while he was little familiar with the process, he admitted to taking delight in the results. At least, he did until an all-too-familiar pounding began in his forehead.

Clarity was immediately concerned when she saw him wince. She moved close to him, eyeing him with sudden alarm.

"Flinx?" A glance at their table showed the minidrags were moving.

"It's all right, Clarity." Placing the tips of the fingers of one hand against his forehead, he pushed firmly.

Sometimes that helped. The throbbing receded a little. "I never know when they're going to hit. Most of the time it starts up and then just goes away." He mustered a reassuring smile. "I think I'm getting the hang of this dancing. Show me that last move again."

But before she could do so, a bolt of pain razored through his head that made him double over. In an instant, she had one consoling arm around his waist.

"That's it; we're done here. I know you well enough to recognize what's happening, Flinx. You came to me looking for understanding. Well, understand that we're leaving. Now."

That he offered no objection was proof enough of how unwell he was starting to feel. Twice more he bent double, clutching his head, before they could gather up their pets and leave. Maybe getting him away from the lights and music would help, she found herself thinking as she paid the bill.

He did feel a little better once they were outside in the cool night air.

"I don't care," she told him. "I'm still taking you back to your hotel."

Regret filled his reply. "I don't want to spoil your evening."

"We had a good time." Her bracelet was flashing, automatically hailing private transport. "There'll be other evenings. Right now the important thing is to get you to where you can lie down and rest."

The empty, cruising transport sidled up to them and politely asked their destination as it processed Clarity's credcard. Flinx had recovered enough to mouth the name of his hotel. As the transport slid away from the club, humming to itself, he found that Clarity was pressed so tightly against him that Pip and Scrap had to move to opposite sides of their masters to find adequate space in which to perch.

"I had fun." Snuggled into his right side, she let one arm slide across his waist. He twitched. Must be the effects of the Shehwaru, he told himself. Pip looked resigned to coiling up between him and the door.

"When was the last time you had fun, Flinx?"

A ready reply formed on his lips. Trouble was, it was unsupported by memory. For the life of him, he could not recall the last time. Then the answer came to him. "A few minutes ago," he whispered to her. "Tonight."

"I meant before tonight, silly." She gave him a gentle punch on the shoulder.

His neck snapped back, his body arched, and his eyes momentarily gaped wide at the roof of the transport before squeezing tight. Next to him, Pip went rigid. His headache, she knew, had returned with a vengeance.

"Flinx!" She stared apprehensively at the now motionless body. "Is there anything I can do? Do you want me to . . . ?"

Her head wrenched backward, her torso convulsed, and a pain the like of which she had rarely experienced shot through her skull like a hot bullet through fresh meat. Alongside her, Scrap spasmed once before becoming as stiff as a blue-and-pink walking cane.

It is a strange thing to be in a dream and simultaneously be aware that it is a dream. As soon as she became conscious of the unreality in which she found herself, the pain began to go away. It never faded entirely, but it was greatly reduced.

She was in a black place, floating. Expecting to share Flinx's perceptions, half anticipating that she would again encounter the horrible dark thing that had touched her, she was bewildered and relieved when nothing hostile manifested itself. There was no awareness of Flinx, no sense of his proximity.

But there was something else.

Or maybe multiple something elses; she couldn't really tell if the presence she perceived was several or singular. It was not overtly hostile but neither was it welcoming. The impressions she was receiving were more of irritation than anger, as if they found her presence a nuisance. While unable to identify their awarenesses, she was mindful of what Flinx had told her of his own dreams.

There was the mechanism of which he had spoken— ancient beyond belief yet still functional. There was also the greenness, vast yet finite, utterly alien yet curiously maternal. And lastly there was the warmth to which he had alluded; indistinct, indefinable, yet somehow vaguely familiar. These sensations remained indistinct but cohesive, commanding yet accommodating. And in the middle of it all she drifted, astray in a place she did not want to be.

Sensing the disapproval around her, she heard a hazy fraction of herself whisper, "Why?"

"Because you are a distraction," came the reply, "an extraneous diversion from That Which Is Truly Important. You affect his mind. You blur his reasoning. You divert his energies."

She did not have to wonder or ask who it/they were referring to. "What do you want with him? You cause him nothing but panic and pain." The warmth grew slightly more intense around her. Before then, she did not know such a thing could be made visible so that one could not just feel it but see it as well.

"We mean him no harm. But panic and pain advances

on all, and must be countered. It reaches beyond him, and us and everything from white bacteria to red giants. It comes for all and must be resisted by all."

Flinx's nightmares. The blackness that had touched her and left her trembling uncontrollably. "What does such a hostile enormity have to do with poor Flinx?"

"He is the Key," it/they responded without hesitation.

In the nothingness that surrounded her, she felt lost in the multiple, vast presence. She had heard that before, from Flinx. Now she was hearing it again. "How can Flinx be the key to anything? He's just one frightened, lost, confused human."

"He is the Key," she was told again, more forcefully this time. "How, we do not know. When, we do not know. Where, we do not know. But he is the Key. That we *do* know."

"How can you be so certain? You don't sound very certain."

"We are deeply struck by the implausibility of it. There is much we do not know. But him we do know. Everything is changing. Nothing is stable. He is changing, too, in ways even we do not know and cannot predict. In the midst of such immense ignorance the last thing that is needed is a complication."

"Me," she heard herself replying.

"You," the consciousness concurred with infuriating certitude.

"I won't abandon him. You can't make me." This last was said with more determination than confidence. "I'm the only friend he's got. He's as much as told me so. So if you somehow force me to leave him now, then whatever else you are, his friend you're not."

"True," came the somewhat surprising communal response. "We are not his friend. Not in the way you de-

fine such an association. Yet he is needed. This thing
that needs to be done cannot be done without him."

"What thing?"

"We are not certain. Not how, when, or where. Only
that it needs to be done, and that the doing of it needs
him."

"For something vast and powerful you're maddeningly imprecise."

"Do we not wish it were otherwise? Do you think we
are comfortable with this and content with the options?
Do you think we enjoy what we must do to ourselves,
to others, to the human called Flinx? No pleasure is
taken in this. No joy is to be found in it. There are times
in existence when things must be done for the doing of
them, without extraneous considerations. This is one
of them. Now and later. Here and elsewhere."

"I don't care. I won't forsake him. He's my *friend*."
Considering her present condition, she was as defiant as
she could be. "You can't make me." Silently terrified of
having thrown down the gauntlet, she waited for the
threatening contradiction that she was sure would be
forthcoming. It was not.

"We will not." Not, we cannot, but—we will not. "If
you would be a friend to all and not just to one, do not
try to divert him from what must be done."

"But he doesn't know what must be done, and he
doesn't know how to do it. Neither do you."

"Entropy educates. Time tells. With every great pre-
cession, knowledge grows. The moment will come when
we know what is to be done, and how, and where. At
that instant, so will he. If you are present at that time,
you must try to help and not interfere."

"How can I interfere when I don't know what's going
to happen or how it's going to happen?"

"You will know. If you are present at that moment, you will know. We will all know, simultaneously and together." The presence began to diminish. "When that time comes, remember this: you chose your way."

She sat forward with a start. Something small and damp was tickling her face. Reaching up with one hand, she gently nudged the anxious flying snake's head aside. "It's okay, Scrap. I'm okay." Reaching down, she discovered that despite the hired transport's efficient climate control system, she was sopping wet with perspiration.

The vehicle had come to a stop. Peering out, she saw that they were in front of Flinx's hotel. How long they had been sitting there she did not know. It was still night outside, just as it was night within her. But the latter brightened as her awareness strengthened. She directed the transport to display a heads-up chronometer. It was very late.

A piteous moan emerged from the figure slumped in the seat alongside her. Pip was crawling all over her master, desperately trying to wake him. Clarity fumbled in her purse before extracting a scented cloth. As she dabbed his forehead and face with the length of cooling fabric, his eyelids fluttered and eventually rose. Divining her intent, Pip drew back to one side.

For a terrifying instant, Flinx saw something dreadful beyond his ken. Then he recognized her.

"Clarity." Reaching up with one hand, he drew the tips of his slightly trembling fingers down her cheek. Despite his condition and what he had likely just gone through, his voice was strong. "I—I had another bad dream."

Nodding understandingly, she continued to mop his brow. "I know. I did, too."

He sat up straighter. "I projected on you again? Clarity,

I'm so sorry." His other hand absently stroked the back of Pip's head and neck.

"It was different this time. My dream, I mean. I don't think we had the same experience. At least, nothing horrible touched me. It was more in the nature of a conversation." She managed a weak smile. "And my head doesn't hurt."

He stared hard at her. "This isn't possible. What you're describing is nothing like what I dreamed." He looked away. "Mine was the same as usual. Soaring outward, searching, finding, and perceiving, then rushing back into myself and waking up. You said your dream was like a conversation." Seeking answers he searched her face, but found only beauty. "Who were you conversing with?"

"Something doesn't want me to be with you, Flinx." Carefully, she refolded her inadequate cloth and resumed patting him down. "It—they—told me so in no uncertain terms. But they won't try to prevent me from being with you, either. The decision is up to me."

"They?"

"I think it's the same they who keep forcing these dreams on you. It's all bound up with the mysterious phenomenon that's coming this way. You and the ancient device, the green color, and the warmth you told me about. And now, it seems, me too."

Turning in his seat, he grabbed her shoulders and gazed into her eyes. "You can't be involved, Clarity. It's my nightmare, not yours."

She smiled regretfully. "Nightmares, it appears, can be shared, Flinx. Besides, as the voices in head said, the choice is up to me. I told you I would try to help you. I'm not backing away from that because of a bad dream or two." They were rather more than that, she knew, but it made no difference to her. Theirs was a friendship she had determined would endure. One that no ethereal entities would be allowed to rend asunder.

He nodded slowly, gratefully. Then he put his long arms around her and squeezed, holding her tight. Tight enough so that even rampaging galactic horrors, even intrusive dreams, could not fit between them. Enfolded in his strong arms, she found that her fear, like a bad dream, faded away.

11

As on every other developed Commonwealth world he had visited, Flinx was able to order everything he needed to restock the *Teacher* by working his way through the Nurian shell, accessing specific supply hubs as needed while simultaneously maintaining a certain degree of anonymity. Eventually, however, there inevitably came a moment when he had to present himself in person at the port where his shuttle was based. Ordering tens of thousands of credits' worth of goods was one thing; taking possession of them was something else—especially when the goods were intended for shipment offworld. That meant completing export forms.

The functionary standing on the other side of the counter at Sphene's main port was representative of his type: busy, preoccupied, and phlegmatic, with a thin mouth pursed in a perpetual pout—though being a citizen of Nur, his tan was better than most of his ilk. With Pip asleep on his shoulder, Flinx waited patiently for the bureaucrat to finish what he was doing.

"Export codes?" The clerk did not look up from his readout. Flinx responded with a series of numbers that had to be recited in person. He waited while they were slowly checked.

Halfway through inputting the sequence, the port

clerk frowned to himself. He enlarged the readout. "You are Philip Lynx?" he asked, finally looking up.

Flinx had already forwarded his personal ident information. "Want to do a retina scan?" A mind-wave reading would be more definitive, Flinx knew, but he could not allow that. A retina scan had always been sufficient.

"That won't be necessary. I was asking rhetorically." He looked back at his readout. "Quite a load of stores for one man."

"It's not just for me. It's for an entire ship." Of course, he was the only passenger on that ship, but there was no need to volunteer *that* bit of information.

"Oh, a whole ship. Well then, well then," the man muttered, as if that explained everything.

The clerk resumed processing the formalities that would result in the release of Flinx's goods, already warehoused and awaiting transfer to his shuttle.

The clerk hesitated. "I hope you don't mind—I'm just naturally inquisitive—it's part of my job to react to such things as pique my curiosity." He gestured at the readout Flinx could not see. "This one item here. I don't understand it."

At the official's urging, the readout rose and floated over to Flinx, who eyed the manifest warily. "What part do you find confusing?"

"Well—it's this dirt. Compacted aerated high-grade humus mixed with other components but basically—dirt. What do you do with dirt on such a small starship?"

The tall man leaned on the counter and smiled confidingly. "It's all business. There are valuable live plants on the ship. Specialty trade items. I need to do some transplanting."

"You don't strike me as the gardening type."

"I'm not. I told you. They're trade items."

"You didn't perchance try smuggling any of these

trade items onto New Riviera? There are very strict penalties for such things."

"You just said I don't strike you as the gardening type. Do I strike you as the brainless type?" On his shoulder, Pip lifted her head and yawned. In the bright office illumination, her small but sharp teeth glinted like shards of pearls as she stared attentively at the clerk.

The functionary suddenly lost all further interest in such banal items as dirt. Flinx departed with his full clearance approved. Now he could supervise the loading of his supplies. Then it would be time to have a long talk with Clarity Held. One whose subject matter promised to be even more serious than usual.

As he left the building housing Customs, he found himself wondering how he knew that the plants aboard his ship *were* in need of transplanting. Maybe he simply had more of a green thumb than he suspected. Or perhaps he had been emfoling in his sleep. But as the official had pointed out, it only involved dirt.

She awoke to the dulcet *ptwee-ptwerr* of the iridescent-winged *sila languet,* one of the most euphonious of all the inhabitants of New Riviera's takari forests. The cheerful vivacity of the song contrasted forcefully with the murkiness that swathed her thoughts. Not only did she not know where she was, she had no idea how she had come to be there.

She was in some kind of small building with walls made to look like actual wood. Outside, through the air barriers that took the place of old-fashioned windows, she could see blossom-laden trees, a cerulean sky, and the occasional bright yellow-green corkscrew bush. In addition to the arresting song of the sila languet, the crescendoing *mutter-mutter* of colusai climbers filtered in from outside. Neither harmony was particularly reassuring.

Especially since her wrists were secured behind her and her ankles were bound together.

Nothing restrained the rest of her, however. Swinging her legs to her left and pushing with arms and shoulders against the back of the couch on which she lay, she managed to work herself into an upright position. That allowed her to see across the room. Beyond the faux-rustic furniture and particulate-scrubbing fireplace was a kitchen equipped with replicated appliances from humanity's past. Behind the plastic-and-ceramic façades were modern devices, she was sure. On a table sat a large, transparent box perforated with tiny holes.

Inside the box, Scrap moved slowly, as if drugged, while peering anxiously in her direction.

What had happened? The last thing she remembered was going through some recent deliveries. The final item had been a box embossed with the malleable logomot of a famous, elegant perfumery headquartered in the southern city of Quescal. There had been an accompanying letter: something about sampling a new fragrance and hoping to solicit her professional opinion. She remembered opening and reading the letter. She remembered opening the package and . . .

She did not remember anything after that.

Had someone struck her from behind? Nothing hurt, except her bound wrists. They throbbed slightly. She hadn't opened any perfume. Had there been something else in the package? Whatever had put her down and out had apparently done the same or something similar to Scrap. More ominous, the presence of the minidrag-proof container suggested the actions of someone familiar with the flying snake's abilities. As she knew, that information was limited to a small circle of her acquaintances. Which was not to say that someone outside that orbit could not have acquired such information.

She rose from the couch and was hopping toward the kitchen table with an eye toward freeing the minidrag when the front door opened. Most of the doorway was blocked by a familiar figure.

"Bill! Thank Deity you're here!" Hopping around, she fluttered the tips of her fingers. "I don't know what happened. One minute I'm opening packages and the next, I'm waking up on that couch. Where are we?"

Ormann walked over to the kitchen table and sat down on a chair. Inside the transparent container, the flying snake thrust its head in his direction. The emotions it was reading from Ormann were more cautious and hopeful than openly aggressive. It would not have mattered anyway. Ormann had ordered the container constructed from material that was impervious to the minidrag's corrosive poison.

"We're up in the mountains, Clarity. No need to know which mountains. This retro cabin is a loan from an old friend of mine. It's fully equipped, designed to blend harmoniously with its surroundings, and quite isolated. You'll be safe here."

"Safe?" She frowned. "Safe from what? Untie me, Bill."

"In due time. Until then, it can't be comfortable for you, standing like that. Why don't you sit back down?"

She gaped at him, then realized he had no intention of releasing her. Slowly, keeping her eyes on him, she worked her way back to the couch.

"There, that's better, isn't it?" he cooed once she had managed to sit down. She knew that tone well. Or thought she did. Now, she was no longer sure she knew anything at all about William Ormann.

"It depends. Why won't you untie me?"

He moved toward the food storage cabinet. "You might do something foolish. You might hurt yourself. You might hurt me."

"Under the circumstances, I don't think I can deny that. What's going on, Bill?"

"Something to drink?" He poured himself a glass of pale-blue liquid that quickly chilled itself. Humorous faces jelled and dissolved within the fluid, an amusing sales element devised by the drink company's packaging department.

"Maybe later. When I can hold my own glass. Why would you think I might hurt myself? Or do something foolish? You've known me for more than a year, Bill. I'm not one to do foolish things."

"I used to think that, too." He set the half-drained glass aside and eyed her intently. Scrap was beginning to show the first signs of agitation. "Then your old friend arrived, seeking your help, and you began spending more and more of your free time with him. I think I was pretty patient, considering. Then more and more of your free time turned into *all* your free time. We hardly see each other anymore."

She stared at him. As she stared, she struggled with her wrist bonds. "Is *that* what this is all about? Have you lost your mind, Bill?"

"No, but I'm not so sure about you."

Leaning back into the overstuffed couch, a clever reproduction from humankind's primitive past, she rolled her eyes imploringly toward the ceiling. "Bill, I've explained this over and over. Philip has problems and no one to talk them over with. That's why he came here, to see me. Because we're old acquaintances and he trusts me to listen to him. That's what I've been doing: listening." She met his gaze evenly. "That's all."

"I'd like to believe that. I really would, Clarity." His

expression darkened slightly. "Just talk. With this harmless old acquaintance of yours, who still thinks kindly of you even after six years have passed."

"That's right," she replied defiantly. Her wrists and ankles were throbbing. "Just talk."

Walking over to an old-fashioned bookcase filled with facsimiles of ancient tomes, Ormann removed a modern read pad and switched it on. "I've been doing some research, and I've had others helping. Let me tell you a few things about your good old harmless friend Philip Lynx that you may not be aware of, Clarity."

I never said he was harmless, she thought. "I can hardly cover my ears to keep from hearing, Bill."

"Understand, Clarity, that I'm doing this for your own good. For our good."

"If it's for my own good," she snapped back, "then why do my wrists and ankles hurt so much?"

For a moment she thought he was going to free her. However, he turned instead to the pad he was holding. "The enigmatic Mr. Lynx has access to funds whose origins are so far untraceable, though I have people working on it. That, coupled with the fact that he arrived in his own ship, suggests that he derives his income from possibly illegal sources. He claims that he survives on an inheritance but is deliberately evasive about its origin."

"His ship *was* a gift," she muttered.

"Really?" Ormann's tone was mocking. "Somebody just *gave* him a starship."

"It was several somebodies—but, yes."

"Who?"

Sighing heavily, she turned away from his demanding stare. "I can't tell you that."

Lips tightening, he nodded, as if her refusal was explanation enough. "Philip Lynx is also wanted by the Commonwealth for several violations. The list of these is not long, but it is impressive." He glanced at the read-out on his pad. "Violation of shell and box security on Earth. On Earth, no less! Refusal to heed an order to stay in Terran space. Illegal visitation of not one but two worlds Under Edict. Assaulting a female security officer—"

"That's a lie!" She twisted violently on the couch. "He would never hurt anyone unless they attacked him first."

A nasty smirk played over Ormann's face. It made him look less the handsome, successful executive and more like an antique ventriloquist's dummy. "That's not what the deposition of the security guard claims." He shut off the pad. "Even if your friend was as you describe him when you knew him, how do you know he hasn't changed? Six years is a long time. People sour, develop hatreds. Go bad."

"Is that the kind of person you've met?" she challenged him.

He drew himself up slightly. "Actually, I haven't been much interested in getting to know Lynx. If it wasn't for your interest in him—and his obvious interest in you—he would pass completely beneath my notice. Forget the security guard for a moment. What about the other charges? How do they square with the person you claim as an old friend?"

How much could she say? How much could she admit to that would extricate her from her present predicament without compromising Flinx's safety and status on New Riviera? Was Ormann being malicious or simply jealous?

"I know that Flinx has had some run-ins with authority. Given the life he's led, something of the sort was probably inevitable. But I'm sure he had good reasons for everything he did."

Ormann gawked at her—the woman he expected to marry and bear his children. "You *know* about these violations?" Clearly he had expected his revelations of Flinx's wrongdoings to anger or disconcert her. That they had not unsettled him. "And you haven't reported him, have continued to see and counsel him?"

She remained defiant. "He needs help, not incarceration. Whatever he's done, I know there was a valid rationale for it. And despite what your little spy report may claim, I know that he'd never harm so much as a worm without good cause." Outside, the sila langeur sang on, but now its trill was drowned out by Ormann's outrage.

"This is insane! How can you believe that? The man's a fugitive, not an abandoned child!" He took a step toward her and she nearly flinched. "What *is* this, Clarity? What has this man done to you?" His voice fell, became at once more cautious and more compassionate. "That's it, isn't it? He's *done* something to you—affected you with more than just talk."

"Now who's talking crazy?" she argued. Ironically, she knew that had he wished to do so, Flinx could have done exactly what Ormann was hinting at. He had promised her he would not. So he hadn't—had he? The twists and turns in the conversation were starting to make her dizzy.

Ormann took her reaction as confirmation. "Now I understand. And believe me, Clarity, it's a relief to know you're not responsible for what's been happening. All we have to do now is figure out what he's done to you and how, and then reverse the effects." He fell into deep thought. "Some kind of drug, applied subtly enough so that you wouldn't know it was influencing you. Or maybe aural mesmerics. Certainly hypnotics of some kind must be involved."

She didn't know whether to laugh or cry. "Bill, he hasn't done anything to me! I'm the same person. I'm just trying to *help* him."

"Of course you are." Ormann now spoke to her in the soothing tone one would use when addressing an idiot. "That's exactly how he would want you to think. I was proceeding on the assumption that he was evil. Now I see it's much more insidious than that." He smiled reassuringly. "But don't worry. I'll take care of it, Clarity. Once he's been dealt with, whatever he's been using on you, dousing you with, will cease, and you'll recover your senses." The more relieved he looked, the more alarmed Clarity became.

"Bill, all I can tell you is that you've got this whole thing backward. Whatever I'm doing, right or wrong, I'm doing of my own free will. I haven't been mesmerized, drugged, or brainwashed. I'm the same person I was before Philip came here. And I know that Flinx is the same person I knew six years ago. More mature, more knowledgeable but the same person. We just, well, we just connect on a certain level."

"Is that a fact? Something special between the two of you, is it? Naturally he'd want you to think that." He approached to within arm's length and crouched down, so his face was on a level with hers. "Why don't you tell me more about this special connection?"

She searched his face. This was not the William Ormann she had known for over a year, the one whom she had contemplated marrying. The man squatting before her was obsessed. She considered pointing out again that her friendship with Flinx was purely platonic, but she suspected than even an allusion to the possibility of a physical relationship between them would add to Ormann's paranoia. Besides, it wasn't true.

"I—I can't tell you, exactly. It's just a feeling."

"I see. A feeling. You have a *feeling* about this Lynx. A feeling about an accused criminal who—according to what I've been able to learn about him—is capable of extensive and highly sophisticated manipulation of sensitive information and those in charge of it. Not to mention strong individual personalities. And this doesn't trouble you. Because you and he *connect* on a certain level. What level is that, Clarity? Hypnosis? Mind-altering drugs slipped into your drink? That would certainly constitute a connection."

What else could she say? she thought. How could she convince him that he was wrong about Flinx without giving away her friend's secrets? Telling the truth was out of the question. For one thing, it would cause him to realize that Flinx could read his emotions. She knew Bill Ormann well enough to know how he would react to *that*.

The longer she remained silent, the grimmer his expression became. Finally he rose, looming over her. Scrap was now thrashing around violently, beating his wings and tail against the transparent barrier, frantic to get out. Clarity tensed. But Ormann intended her no harm. He loved her. All he wanted to do, since she was so obviously sick, was to make her well again. To remove the poison the interloper had somehow planted in her mind.

"I could simply report him to the local authorities and let them deal with him," he murmured. "I'm sure they'd be delighted to know that there's an important fugitive in their midst."

"What do you mean, important?" Anything, she thought, to get his mind off such a course of action. "Philip has never harmed anyone. He's not a murderer, or an extortionist, or an embezzler."

"Are you sure? You've told me yourself that he bemuses and puzzles you. Who knows what this Philip Lynx may really be or what he may be capable of?"

Not Flinx, she told herself. He's as much in the dark as anyone. That's the reason he's here talking to me.

"Turning him over to the authorities won't help anybody," she insisted desperately. To her surprise, Ormann agreed with her.

"You're absolutely right, my dear. I know from personal experience how our purportedly sophisticated legal system works, and someone with Lynx's resources might easily buy his way out of trouble. Since I would dislike seeing that happen, I've decided *not* to inform the authorities. I'll continue to deal with the situation myself."

She tensed. "What does that mean?"

He frowned as he started for the door. "Why, I'd think it pretty straightforward. Unusual problems require unusual solutions. Rest assured I'll come up with one and that no harm will come to you."

"You don't know what you're getting into, Bill. You don't have any idea what you're dealing with. There's more to Flinx than what you see on the surface."

The door opened, framing her former paramour—and it was now definitely "former," she had already decided—against the blue sky and scudding white clouds.

"Wasn't that what I was just saying? Which is why I've decided to be very, very careful when next I move against him. I didn't get to be where I am, Clarity, without learning how to deal with excessive pride. I'm not afraid to learn from my lessons, and where this Lynx person is concerned, I've already had to absorb a few. I think I know what to do now. I'll deal appropriately with him." His gaze wandered to the container on the kitchen table. "And his lethal pet.

"Don't worry, Clarity. This will all be over soon. And

when it is, you and I can pick up right where we left off. It'll be just like before. I'll be back soon. Meanwhile, just sit tight." He could not resist laughing at his own wit.

"You're going to die, Bill Ormann!" She didn't say how because she didn't know. Though this morning's events had left her emotionally divorced from him, she still didn't want to see him dead. Chastised, maybe, but not dead. Though Ormann was smart, experienced in his own way, ruthless in pursuit of a goal, that would not help him against Flinx.

As she knew, those who went hunting for Flinx all too often found themselves dead.

12

The message that arrived at the hotel was rambling but unambiguous. William Ormann did not like Flinx. He especially did not like what Flinx had done to Ormann's relationship with Clarity Held. She was not to blame, but it had become clear to Ormann that Flinx, through unknown means, had twisted the vulnerable mind of Ormann's beloved. This was a condition that could with time and appropriate therapy doubtless be cured. Meanwhile, the message warned Flinx to keep away from them both and that it would be better for his health if he were to leave New Riviera as quietly and as soon as possible.

As a warning, it had no effect. Flinx had been threatened by and had subsequently dealt with perils rather more extensive than those posed by a single aggravated, jealous executive. Even so, he did not underestimate Ormann. Not after having already found himself abducted once. He never underestimated anyone, or any danger. It was the hallmark of, among other things, a successful thief. His real concern was for Clarity. To Flinx's practiced eye, the tone of Ormann's communication suggested a mind increasingly clouded by envy and fear: a combination that, despite Ormann's protestations of love, could pose as much a danger to her as to him.

Flinx left the hotel in a hurry. Not to flee New Riviera

and Sphene, as the message demanded, but to find Clarity. What might have seemed a daunting task to anyone else proved surprisingly easy for Flinx. Buried in the communication was a supposedly secure electronic signature that identified the location from which it had been sent. One of the clever little devices secured to his belt deciphered it immediately.

The ease with which the trace had been performed only heightened his sense of danger. He made a couple of quick stops at specialized shops around the city. If a man does thee once, it's his fault. If he does thee twice, it's thy fault. Flinx had no intention of being done twice by Bill Ormann.

It took some time for his rented aircar to find the exact spot from which the message had been sent. It was high in another convolution of Nur's beautiful mountains, surrounded by taller takari trees than any Flinx had seen so far. He approached with caution. Just because the message had been sent from here did not mean he would find anyone alive. He relaxed slightly when he drew near enough to sense a flow of anxiety whose source he instantly identified as Clarity. It was accompanied by indications of discomfort, which angered him, but not of pain.

He circled the house from above while Pip fretted on his shoulder. If the place was booby-trapped, neither he nor the instruments on board would be able to detect the method. Despite Ormann's message, Flinx didn't think Ormann wanted to hurt Clarity. He just wanted her, period. It was unlikely that someone else's arrival would trigger an explosion intended to kill them both. Nevertheless, in proceeding, he had to assume a worst-possible-case scenario.

He made several passes over the primitive-looking cabin while bathing it in scans from one of the devices he had purchased in town. Satisfied that nothing explosive lay within, he set down nearby and alighted from the aircar.

"Pip, no!" Ignoring his warning shout, the minidrag immediately winged toward the house. He raced after her. It was entirely possible for traps to be sprung by mechanical means.

But nothing erupted from the building, the purple-and-gold weeded grounds, or the nearby woods to blast the flying snake from the sky. He slowed as he approached the cabin. There was no mistaking who was inside: this close, he could isolate Clarity's emotions as well as his own. Apprehension, unease, discomfort—these were present in abundance. But she was not in pain, nor did she radiate any fear of the threat of imminent physical harm. Most important, insofar as his talent could tell, she was alone.

He became doubly wary.

Accompanied by the dulcet songs of the *puur javil* and a couple of querulous, wide-eyed, long-armed *drolgs* watching from the nearby trees, he approached slowly on the cabin. From the outside it looked like nothing more than a retreat from city work and stress. The faux-wood logs had the advantage over real wood of providing excellent insulation, not leaking, and being impervious to bugs and fire. They were also conveniently easy to penetrate with the small scanner Flinx unlatched from his belt.

The instrument reported two organic life-form signatures to be inside. One was clearly Clarity. Flinx assumed the other was Scrap. Pip's agitation provided confirmation.

He stealthily circled the building, seeing nothing to threaten or impede his entry. He wouldn't, of course. Ormann was jealous, not stupid. Clarity might have been left alone, but he would not have left her un-guarded.

Pausing behind a dense bush whose delicate long leaves curled away from his body heat, he slipped a fil-tering mask over his face. Ormann might assume that what had worked once would work again. The gun he had brought with him drawn and ready, Flinx sprinted toward the cabin.

No one materialized to challenge him as he reached the back of the cabin. No sounds emanated from within. He edged carefully around the building, ducking below first one and then another window as he did. Peering around a corner gave him a good line on the only door. It might be locked or it might not.

He removed and activated a custom-made packet from his belt. The result was an inflated, minimally ar-ticulated replica of himself. For something so light it gave a remarkable impression of solidity. The decoy was capable of only the most limited degree of programmed action, but all he needed was for it to approach the door.

He waited with both hands on his gun. The inflated hand reached out and depressed the control buried in the old-fashioned door handle. The door swung open, and the ground erupted on either side of the decoy.

The ambushing mechanisms were thin, tall, and lethal guns programmed so their deadly cross fire cut the decoy to shreds. Flinx sidled around the corner just far enough to take aim with his own gun. Having adjusted the weapon's targeting settings from Organic to Me-chanical, he fired twice. A neural disruptor makes very little sound—no loud percussive bang, no roar, just a soft crackle, like foil being crumpled.

Each of the weapons at the door twitched as its cir-cuitry was paralyzed, then collapsed. Flinx waited sev-eral minutes to see if they would move, heedful that they might be equipped with diversionary delay backups. When they did not, he advanced and shot them again. Standing over their camouflaged burrows, he methodically fried the subsurface instrumentation that had governed their actions. Only then did he scan the door for additional surprises. Finding none, he fingered the locked handle.

For someone with his experience at breaking and entering, the lock might as well have been made of paper. In barely more than a minute it clicked open. Holding the disruptor, he pushed the door inward.

He saw a great deal all at once: the kitchen to the left, a small den, and a sitting area to his right. On the couch a familiar figure lay on her side, tightly bound and gagged, feet toward him, eyes wide as he started toward her. Simultaneously, Pip soared toward the container on the kitchen table. At her approach, it began to bounce and shake violently. Urgent, excited hisses issued from within.

Every sense alert, he was halfway to Clarity when she managed to spit out enough of the gag to make herself understood. "Flinx, the chair—watch out!"

He whirled just as it began a silent metamorphosis. At once simpler and more sophisticated than the guns outside, it unfolded multiple spiderlike limbs and came for him at astonishing speed. Some of the arms were tipped with blades. Flinx took quick aim at its center and fired.

It dodged smartly. One arm-mounted ceramic blade shot out a meter and with a single low, sicklelike swipe tried to reduce him in height by half a dozen centimeters. He leaped over it, used a stiffened left forearm to parry a second strike from a different cutting edge, and fired again. This time the transformed chair was flailing wildly, striking out in all directions, its circuits destroyed.

While it was fizzing to a stop, the attendant footrest nearly got him. Spotting the padded stool advancing furtively on her master from behind, Pip spat at a vent in its rear. The corrosive minidrag venom wreaked sufficient havoc on the footstool's innards to send it lurching off course toward the kitchen. A burst from Flinx's pistol stilled it permanently.

Clarity was smiling with relief. "Bill thought he could get to you with machines, with something you couldn't hypnotize or drug." She gestured with her bound wrists. "Get me out of this and I'll give you all the details."

He moved toward her but stopped. "So he thinks I hypnotize people or drug them? As you do?"

She nodded. "That's what he believes." She gestured with her hands a second time. "Feels like I'm bleeding. I've been stuck here since this morning. Can't feel my legs, either."

"That's not surprising." With great deliberation, he raised his pistol and pointed it at her torso where the AI cortex would be located.

She gaped at him. "Flinx? What are you doing? It's me, Clarity!"

It looked like Clarity. It acted and talked like Clarity. But it wasn't Clarity. Having made use of self-motivating simulacra of himself on more than one occasion, Flinx was familiar with the sophisticated technology. Anyone else would have assumed this was the real Clarity Held. Certainly William Ormann believed that Flinx would do so. Except that there was one very important thing Ormann did not know. Flinx neither mesmerized nor drugged other people. He simply read their emotions, when his talent was functioning. And it was definitely functioning now.

If it wasn't, he was about to make perhaps the most serious mistake of his life.

The Clarity Held lying bound on the couch was not panicking or projecting fear or anger or uncertainty. It was projecting nothing. As one of its not-so-very-tightly-bound hands started to come around, he squeezed the disruptor's trigger. Shocked by the shot, the hand's three middle fingers fired at the ceiling. Three small explosions left a big hole in the roof as the miniature missiles struck. He raised one arm to ward off the dust and fragments of insulation that snowed down on him. Watching the pop-up guns and the spider-settee convulse in the course of their mechanical death throes had been much easier than standing by while sparks and fluid flew from the humanoid figure on the couch.

He approached cautiously and poked the simulacrum's smoking remnants with the tapered tip of his pistol. The epidermal material gave eerily, like actual flesh, but the illusion was destroyed by the sparking, flaring, failing components within. Ormann was no dummy. If the guns failed, the cabin contained sufficiently murderous backup in the form of the homicidal chair and footstool. If both of them proved unsuccessful, he could rely on the far more stylish and elegant simulacrum of Clarity to fool her would-be rescuer.

Pretty clever, Flinx thought as he moved toward a door at the back of the room, to have the simulacrum deliberately warn him about the chair and thereby put him off his guard. Had Ormann known the truth of Flinx's talent, he no doubt would have engineered an entirely different ploy.

The locked door gave him no trouble. Inside, he found Clarity gagged and bound on a smaller couch. On the floor nearby was a transparent case within which a young minidrag, its frantically beating wings a blaze of color, was banging and snapping like a gigantic dragonfly. Landing atop the container, Pip began hunting for an opening. Within, her offspring's iridescent green head tracked her every movement.

Flinx reassured Clarity with calming words. He had no intention of removing his filtering mask until both of them were safely outside. It was hot in the room and she was sweating profusely. Doubtless she had heard the commotion and wondered what was taking place.

Now her eyes widened as he removed her gag. "He didn't get you."

"No. He didn't get me," Flinx reassured her softly. With a small vibraknife he began to slice through the restraints that bound the rest of her body, starting with her wrists and ankles. "Smarter sentients than William Ormann have tried."

"I know. But I was still worried." With his assistance, she sat up on the couch, rubbing her wrists. "He's gone over the edge, Flinx. Completely lost it—in his quiet, controlled, ice-cold managerial fashion. I told him he wouldn't be able to hurt you." Looking up, her eyes bored into his. "I'm not always right, but this time I'm really glad I was."

"So am I." Slipping his hands under her arms, he helped her to stand, steadying her while sensation returned to her numbed feet and legs. She was surprised at how strong he had become. Perspiration made it difficult for him to maintain a grip that was firm but not impolite. After a minute or two, he started to release her and step back.

"It's all right, Flinx. I can manage now."

He turned to the cage that held Scrap. The seal on the container proved no match for old skills. In a couple of minutes, Scrap was free. The minidrag stretched its wings before taking joyously to the air. Pip pirouetted around him. This aerial ballet continued for a couple of minutes before both flying snakes settled back to the ground, their upper bodies entwining affectionately as they folded their blue-and-pink wings flat against their diamond-patterned sides.

Still walking tentatively, Clarity started toward the outer room. Flinx hastily put a supportive arm around her back.

"Thirsty," she told him. "Water would be nice."

Leaving her, he advanced into the kitchen. Taking a glass from a cabinet, he filled it from the sink, but not until he had first checked the water with the analyzer he always carried with him. There was, it insisted primly, nothing in the glass but plain old dihydrogen oxide.

Taking the glass, she held it in both hands and drank greedily. Pushing past him, she refilled it. Only when she had drained the contents a second time was she able to flash Flinx the familiar smile of which he had grown so fond.

"Better."

He gestured toward the open front door. "I've got an aircar outside. Can you make it?"

"To get out of this place I'd crawl through mud and refuse." She glanced around at the deceptively simple surroundings. "Funny. I used to like this place. But then, I used to like Bill." Starting forward, she noticed that Flinx was hesitating. "Was there something else?"

"I . . ." With a suddenly unsteady hand, he reached up and felt his mask, but the filter was still in place, still sealed against his face. Nothing could get through to him. "Feel strange, all of a sudden." He took a step backward. Alarmed, she moved toward him.

"Flinx? Flinx, what's wrong? You feel all right?"

"I feel fine." Anxiously, she looked all around the room. She could smell, hear, sense nothing out of the ordinary. The front door was open and fresh air was pouring in. What was the matter?

Stumbling again, he managed to sit on the couch at the foot of the simulacrum he had destroyed. He was blinking frequently now and occasionally shaking his head as if trying to clear it. "What's wrong?" she asked him.

"I don't know," he mumbled, his words slurred. "Feel funny. Can't be gas. Don't—understand."

Pip and Scrap rejoined their masters, Pip crawling into her master's lap while apprehensively fluttering her wings. As Flinx started to pass out, Clarity rushed forward to catch him. But he was too heavy for her, and she was forced to ease him down against the back of the couch.

"Flinx. Flinx! Tell me what's happening! I can't do anything if I don't know what's happening!"

"How about *we* tell you?" As she spun around, both flying snakes attacked. The emotions projected by the newcomers were ripe with enmity.

Minidrag venom creased the air. But the three men and one woman who had entered the cabin were clad in full environment suits. The minidrags' poison was ineffective against clothing intended to allow the wearer to function safely in interstellar space.

Fine mesh nets of tough fiber composite ballooned from specialized rifles. Their wings entangled, fluttering futilely, they soon found themselves pinned to the floor.

Two of the men gathered up the frantic, thrashing creatures. They proceeded carefully despite the safety of their suits, and placed both flying snakes in the container that had held Scrap. Another man walked over to confront Clarity. The dumpy, middle-aged woman moved to check on the unconscious Flinx.

"He's out good for now," she reported. "Ormann wasn't sure precisely how long the effect would last."

Clarity could do little more than stare as she once again found her arms being bound behind her.

"Bill—again. Always Bill." The flying snakes safely secured in Scrap's box, the four slipped their protective hoods off.

The men moved to help the woman truss Flinx with the same thin, unbreakable plastic strips they had used on Clarity. Then they removed Flinx's mask and replaced it with a blindfold and gag. Finally, the hood from another environment suit was placed over his head and locked down, together with its accompanying rebreather unit. When the intruders finally stepped back, their subject had not only been rendered immobile but also blind and speechless.

Hypnotism, Clarity thought. Bill still thinks Flinx influences people through some form of hypnotism. She knew that binding, blinding, and gagging him would have no effect on his ability to reach out and affect the emotions of those around him. Of course, he could do nothing while unconscious. When he awoke, his ability would allow him to view those nearby without the need to actually see them. Everything was going to be all right.

Provided, she thought worriedly, their captors didn't shoot them or throw them over one of the many nearby cliffs. She had no idea how much time remained to them. In the interim it might be useful to know what had happened. So she asked.

The woman exchanged a glance with one of the men. "I don't see any harm in telling her. Ormann didn't say anything about keeping quiet." She smiled humorlessly. "Knowing him, I think he'd *want* her to know."

The man shrugged. "Your call, Meru."

"In case you've forgotten, though your boyfriend may hold an important managerial position within your company now, he was originally trained as a gengineer like you. He still knows how to work a lab." She grinned. "Pretty clever, your boyfriend."

"He's not my boyfriend anymore," Clarity muttered.

"You mean you're not enjoying this little drama he whipped up for you? Did you think he was going to rely on mechanicals and deceptions to ensure that a job like this got done? He's been busy, your boyfriend has." The woman turned momentarily reflective. "Shows sufficiently shrewd thinking to get a job in my line of work. But he hired me and the guys to wrap things up. After you took care of your friend first, of course." Her expression was a mask of professional indifference as she studied Flinx. "Nice looking. Too bad."

Confusion swept over Clarity like an ill wind. "After *I* took care of him? I don't understand what you mean. I didn't do anything."

"Oh, but you did, sweetie." Grinning, the older woman ran a gloved finger deliberately along Clarity's bare upper arm. Clarity flinched at a touch that carried with it a hint of something other than professionalism. "Though he doesn't know exactly how your boyfriend does it, Ormann warned us not to get anywhere near him unless he was already unconscious. He had to find a way to make that happen, and he did. Ingeniously, if I do say so, and with your help."

"But I didn't *do* anything," a bewildered Clarity repeated.

The woman continued to trace idle patterns on Clarity's bare skin. Observing this, one of her companions shook his head knowingly as he finished his own work.

"Oh, but you did, sweetie. Passively, but you did. Since you were so busy with your boyfriend here, our Mr. Ormann had a lot of free time. Instead of fuming about the situation, he spent it in one of your company's labs, gengineering the modified molecular structure of an illegal but well-known and widely available epidural narcotizing agent. We were told to avoid contact with it at all costs. Absorbed through the skin, it's supposed to put even a healthy professional athlete under for four to eight hours."

Four hours, Clarity thought apprehensively. Would they leave Flinx alive long enough to regain consciousness and bring his singular talent to bear? Aloud, she said, "I didn't put anything like that on him. I haven't *touched* him."

"I believe you. But sweetie, *he's* touched *you*."

Of course he had. To sit her up on the couch. To remove her bindings. To help her stand. Which meant, the chemical responsible had to be somewhere on her. "Why am *I* still conscious?"

"I told you: Mr. Ormann gengineered the stuff. Did some rearranging of the molecular structure." Her grin returned. "Made the delivery vector site specific, you might say." Again the finger pressed against Clarity's exposed skin, only this time not across her arm. "You're the only one in this room who the agent won't knock out. Why do you think the back room where you were being held was kept so hot?" She peered eagerly into the captive's face, lapping up the hurt and confusion she found there.

To make me sweat, Clarity realized. The dynamic agent that had drugged Flinx had been on her skin all along. Her perspiration had activated it and provided a vector. Driven by his cancerous obsession, Bill Ormann had overlooked nothing.

Regrettably, Flinx hadn't worn gloves.

The heavy-duty environment suits that had protected their captors from the venom of the minidrags had also allowed them to handle Clarity without fear of being contaminated by the agent Ormann had surreptitiously rubbed into her flesh. Once applied, it had plainly traveled throughout her body, to emerge and become actively dangerous when she had begun to sweat. Insidiously and skillfully he had made her, the one agent Flinx was least likely to suspect of posing a threat to him, the instrument of his downfall. She remembered now. Being knocked out by Bill. Being tied up.

It had meant nothing to her at the time, hadn't registered as significant at all. Why should it have? Just because all the time he had been working on her, he had been wearing gloves?

"Sweet, isn't it? You didn't have to do anything. We didn't have to do anything. All that was necessary was for your boyfriend to touch you, which our friend Ormann was certain he'd do at the first opportunity without thinking about it too much." The woman's tone reflected a calm, practiced admiration for the method that had been employed.

"He's promised to help me and the boys out in the future, in case we need the compound rejiggered to work for another client. The beginning of a fruitful business relationship. You'll be around to enjoy it. Apparently, he doesn't want you harmed." The gloved finger moved. "I can see why."

Clarity's bindings prevented her from flinching from the lugubrious caress. "What about Flinx? What are you going to do to him?" As much as she didn't want to know the answer, she had to ask.

Her captor turned to eye the long-legged figure on the couch. Nearly mummified by his bindings, Flinx lay unmoving, his face hidden. For the first time since she had known him he appeared to be completely helpless, mentally as well as physically.

"We were told that when we reached this point we

should ask for final instructions. Thanks for reminding me."

The last was unnecessary, Clarity knew. The woman would not have forgotten how to proceed. It was simply a deliberately sadistic fillip to the conversation. As the immobilized Clarity looked on, the woman chatted briefly with her companions before pulling out a com unit.

She and Flinx didn't have the balance of four hours left; Clarity saw. They hardly had any time at all.

Get up, Flinx! she thought furiously. Wake up! Can you feel my fear? You have to wake up.

The body on the couch did not move. Within their minidrag-proof container, Pip and Scrap were growing even more agitated. Did they sense something about to happen, and were they reacting more vigorously because they were unable to influence it? Did she and Flinx have even an hour left?

He might be dreaming, he might be traveling, but the tall redhead was definitely not perceiving her emotions. She did not have to try to falsify them in her silent efforts to bring him around.

She was truly scared.

13

Ormann did not have to wonder at the source of the incoming call even though he was at work. It was on his private com line, encrypted and untappable. All he had to do to unscramble what anyone else receiving the call would hear as mindless gibberish was to answer it. He let it chime for his attention a few extra times. The anticipation was delicious. Because anyone calling him on that line would only be doing so if certain objectives had been successfully met, and he wanted the warm feeling to last as long as possible.

When he finally did answer it, the voice he expected to hear was on the other end. For security reasons, there was no video. The words spoken were calm and assured. Though he had embarked on the project with confidence, and with much greater care and preparation than on similar previous attempts, he had learned the hard way not to take anything for granted where Lynx was concerned.

It was with great pleasure that he heard the woman on the other end inform him that everything had gone as planned. Yes, the target had made his way past the outer defenses and survived attack by the chair and footstool. Yes, he had somehow solved the puzzle posed by the simulacrum and defeated it, only to be ensnared by Ormann's sublest ploy: the gengineered soporific applied to Clarity Held's skin.

"What's he doing now?" Ormann asked. At last he could relax a little. It seemed that the redoubtable Philip Lynx's baffling bag of tricks was not bottomless after all. He did not ask about the flying snakes. If they had not been dealt with successfully, he knew he would not be receiving this call.

"Sleeping. Maybe not like a baby, but sleeping. Looks like he went out exactly as you predicted. My compliments, Mr. Or—"

"No names," Ormann snapped. Secure line or no, he was taking no chances.

"Sorry. Listen, my associates and I are sufficiently impressed that we might like to engage your cooperation at some future time. We might even work out some kind of mutually beneficial barter agreement. Cost you a lot less."

"I'll think about it." Ormann was flattered but preoccupied. "Let me pay you for this job first. I'll consider your offer later."

"As you wish." She sounded disappointed. "You still want us to turn him over to the authorities?"

"I've been thinking about that." Outside his office, the day was even more beautiful than usual. "You know how the court system can be. Even truth sensors can be deceived. After having gone to all this trouble to see justice done, it would displease me greatly to see the individual in question walk away subject to only some minor penalty."

"And maybe come back to bother your girlfriend again? Not to mention tossing a few uncomfortable questions your way."

"Exactly." He allowed the woman to reach her own conclusion. She did so with admirable promptness.

"How do you want it done?"

"Efficiently. I'm not vindictive. I just want it done. Make certain any evidence is eliminated as thoroughly as him. If she asks, tell Clarity you're going to have him boxed and shipped offworld unharmed."

"We can do that, too, if you wish," the voice assured him.

"Excellent." Ormann felt he was lingering. "Just make sure you seal airtight whatever container you use. I want nothing left for anyone to find."

"It will be taken care of. We can . . ." There was a pause.

Ormann waited impatiently. "What?"

When it finally responded, the voice on the other end sounded less assured than before. "Not sure. One of the guys thought he heard something." Her assurance returned. "I'll get back to you when it's done."

"Fine. Final payment will be made in the usual manner. If you have anything else to—"

A loud crash echoed over the communicator. It was followed by several sharp crackling sounds, as if something carrying a lot of voltage had suddenly violently shorted out. Ormann frowned.

"Hello?" He forgot his own admonition against using names. "Serale? Are you still there? Hello?"

Another crackling, underscored by faint voices, as of people shouting in the distance. The woman's voice returned, breathy and with an underlying tension. "It's nothing. A minor disturbance. Nothing my people can't handle. We—"

Ormann stared at the communicator. "What kind of disturbance? What are you talking about? What's going on there? Serale?"

But Serale was busy. In fact, it sounded like everyone on the other end was busy. Ormann tried to activate the communicator's visual component. It responded immediately but with a blank screen. Either the Send on the other end still wasn't activated, or . . .

No, he could still hear plenty of noise from the unit. Something was happening at the cabin.

As time passed without either the line going dead or any response from Serale or anyone else, he grew increasingly agitated. The "nothing my people can't handle" was rapidly becoming, in his mind, a very real something that was giving them trouble. Did Lynx have friends on Nur he had neglected to mention, even to Clarity? Did he have associates on his ship who now had arrived to try to rescue him? The longer nothing but confused noise issued from the com unit, the greater became the executive's anxiety.

Finally there was a response. "William Ormann? Am I speaking to William Ormann?" The query ended in a curious yet somehow familiar whistle.

He said nothing, just stared at the com unit in his hand. It lay there, cool and inorganic. He started to formulate a reply but was having difficulty remembering his name.

"I am going to assume I am speaking to William Ormann, a minor middle-level employee of Ulricam. Mr. Ormann, it has come to the attention of others that you intended to do Philip Lynx grievous bodily harm. We will not permit this."

"*You* won't permit it?" Ormann finally found his voice. "Who—who are you? Are you crew from his ship?"

A different, deeper whistling, distinctively modulated, emanated from the com. It might have been the wind or something else. "His crew. I find that amusing. Flinx would find that amusing. Although I'm sure your intention was anything but to amuse. It's not for you to wonder who we are nor is it necessary for us to inform you. From what this young female has been telling me, you've done some very bad things lately, Mr. Ormann. Bad business. Unhappily, steps must be taken."

The com unit beeped once, indicating the transmission had ceased. Try as he might, Ormann could not raise the cabin again. The voice that had spoken to him presented unforeseen complications. It had not been Serale's voice. He suspected it was not that of one of her associates. It had certainly not been Clarity's voice or that of the thrice-damned Lynx.

It had not even been human.

Clarity had not been able to do anything to help Flinx. He remained unconscious as two of the men swathed him in enough police-grade plastic fetters to restrain an elephant. Serale, the woman who appeared to be in charge, was talking to Bill on a com unit. Pip and Scrap in their cage were unable to help.

It was then that a figure had stepped through the open front door. The new arrival was well, even elegantly, ornamented, and, despite its evident age, carried itself with confidence. Looking around the room, gleaming golden compound eyes had taken in the seated figure of Clarity, the woman Serale standing nearby, the rattling cage on the kitchen table, and the tall young man being mummified on the couch. She thought she heard the visitor emit a small, resigned sigh. A trace of perfume emanated from him; she inhaled hints of ginger and frangipani. The two men binding Flinx halted. Serale looked over her com at the intruder.

"You will let him go. Now." The arrival punctuated this command by reaching up with a truhand to preen his left antenna. The other truhand and right foothand cradled a sonic rifle, while the left foothand held a pistol.

The fourth member of Serale's group, who had stepped outside a few moments earlier to attend to a call of nature, came in and leaped at the much smaller and lighter thranx from behind.

The four-foot-tall insectoid sprang to his left, both sets of vestigial wingcases snapping out to knock the human aside. The chitinous coverings were, Clarity noted even as she began struggling to try to free herself from her bonds, the dark, deep purple of advanced age.

Old or not, the agility and speed with which the thranx maneuvered himself on his four trulegs was wonderful to see. As Serale lowered her communicator and gaped at the intruder, two of her colleagues reached for their weapons. Firing pistol and rifle simultaneously, and without hesitation or fear of hitting Lynx, the multilimbed intruder shot them both.

That gave the third man time to dodge and recover and Serale long enough to swap her com unit for a handgun. Both their first shots missed the rapidly dodging thranx, who ducked behind the kitchen counter. The two humans fired again, but since the counter was constructed of composite material designed to only look like wood, holes appeared in its front, but the shots did not penetrate.

Serale directed her fire at the same spot on the counter in an attempt to punch a hole through. The noise of the small but powerful explosive charges she and her associate were firing was deafening.

No answering fire came from behind the counter. Had the thranx been hit? Clarity wondered. Or was he biding his time, preparing a counterattack?

Then Clarity noticed that the impervious container holding the two minidrags was inching its way backward. A moment later it fell behind the counter. Concentrating on breaking down the counter that was sheltering their adversary, neither Serale nor her associate noticed.

"Look out!" Serale cried when two fast and very angry minidrags shot directly toward them.

Serale pointed her weapon at the flying snakes. Her companion hesitated briefly, then dashed out the open door. A second later, the thranx's compound eyes and antennae appeared over the edge of the counter, followed by the muzzles of two weapons.

Serale did not even have a chance to get off a shot at the minidrags before she was cut down by a burst from the thranx's sonic rifle. The shaped acoustic charge punched a sizable hole in her neck, nearly decapitating her. Not even the spurting blood could make Clarity avert her eyes. There was still the one remaining gunman.

His scream was indistinct, showing that he had managed to run some distance. But not, clearly, far enough. Scrap returned moments later to rejoin his mother in inspecting the corpse of the woman who had been in charge. On the couch, Flinx slept on, oblivious to everything happening around him, and because of him.

Working to steady her own breathing, Clarity watched intently as the four-legged thranx ambled around the ruined end of the kitchen counter and advanced on the limp, ragdoll body of Serale. Picking up her com unit, he spoke briefly into it, then set it aside and came to Clarity. As the elderly thranx drew near, its flowery natural perfume helped to mitigate the stink of dead and dying bodies. The visitor stopped only when very close. Both antennae dipped forward to lightly stroke her forehead. It was as if she had been caressed by a pair of feathers.

"Who—who *are* you?" she finally stammered in symbospeech. Her eyes roved over the blue-green limbs and joints, took in the exquisitely embroidered thorax pouch and backpack. "I don't see any peaceforcer insignia."

"Me, a peaceforcer?" the thranx replied in perfect, remarkably unaccented terranglo. An amused fusion of clicks and whistles issued from behind the mandibles that formed the hard edges of its insectoid mouth. "What an amusing notion." He set rifle and pistol aside. "I dislike guns. I would rather win a disagreement through debate."

She nodded in the direction of three of her tormentors. "You certainly won your disagreement with them." He wasn't listening, she noticed. Instead, he had moved to stand over Flinx, and then he reached down to place a delicate truhand against the side of the unconscious human's neck.

"Respiration and heart rate have slowed. Two hearts would have allowed him to recover faster, but he will be fine." The lustrous, valentine-shaped head turned toward her. "What happened to him? I fear I was almost too late."

"How did you know he was here?" She, apparently, was something of an afterthought to the thranx.

"All will be explained, when Flinx has awakened and can also hear and understand. Causation?"

"Oh." She looked away, embarrassed. "My exboyfriend gengineered some kind of soporific that he applied to my skin but it's activated only when I perspire. When Flinx touched me, he absorbed it through his pores."

"Clever. It won't affect me, of course." The thranx took a small cutter from his thorax pouch and went to work on her bonds. "Our exoskeletons seal us against such dangerous invasions, we don't perspire, and I'm sure the relevant chemical formulation is specific to human physiology anyway. There," he declared a moment later.

Freed from her bonds, she rose shakily. Though of average height, she loomed over the thranx. "You still haven't told me who you are. If not a peaceforcer, then what?"

"I am by avocation a Philosoph. My title is not peaceforcer or soldier but Eint. I am an old friend of this most interesting human. My name is Truzenzuzex. You may call me Tru."

"True enough?" She smiled. He looked up at her but could not smile back, as his physiognomy was not designed for it. But she had the feeling he recognized the expression.

"I assure you I've heard all the wordplay on my name that you could possibly imagine. But if it amuses you to do so, please indulge yourself."

"That's all right." This was a thranx Philosoph, she reminded herself, and one holding the exalted rank of Eint. Until she knew him better, it might be wise to confine herself to sensible speech and forgo any further jejune attempts at witticism.

She sat down beside Flinx on the couch and began to run her fingers through his hair. Wings humming, Scrap came to wrap himself around her neck. Pip settled down on her master's hip and curled up, but remained watchful.

"How long have you known Flinx, Truzez—Tru?" Flinx's hair, she noted not for the first time, was thick but remarkably soft, his skin still smooth and deeply tanned.

Looking around the room, the thranx stepped indifferently over the body of one of Serale's fallen associates.

"Ever since he was an interesting boy. He's not a boy anymore. That's one reason we've spent some time trying to find him."

"*We?*" Clarity frowned, glancing at the doorway behind the tranquil thranx. "You're not alone?"

"Well, *crrskk,*" Truzenzuzex replied thoughtfully, "yes and no."

Still staring in bewildered disbelief at the communicator in his hand, Ormann set it down on the desk. Up in the distant mountains, in that cabin, something had gone very, very wrong. But how? This time he had thought of everything.

At that moment, something else he had not thought of walked into his office. His visitor was taller than average, though not quite so tall as Flinx. Slim and dignified, he advanced into the room with the grace of a dancer. Very black eyes shining with intelligence peered out from beneath bushy brows in a face that was all sharp angles. Like a jumble of knives that had been overlaid with deeply tanned skin that was then pulled tight over the blades. The lips were thin, the mouth small. It was a visage that bespoke an Oriental, probably Mongolian ancestry. His hair was graying, with one streak of white running from front to back. Ormann guessed him, correctly, to be in his early eighties.

"How did you get in here?" Smiling pleasantly, Ormann's right hand drifted toward the drawer that held a small pistol.

"Walked."

A comedian, Ormann found himself thinking. An old comedian. "You know what I mean." He furtively slid open the drawer. The gun lay flat in its charger. It was not a big gun. But then, given the charge it carried, it didn't have to be.

"Your office manager let me in."

"That will cost her. She knows not to let anyone in without first contacting me."

"Don't be too hard on her. She was very nice, and I can be very persuasive."

"Can you, now?" Ormann tried not to look in the direction of the pistol. "Then maybe you can convince me why I shouldn't have you thrown out."

"First, because you couldn't." This was stated with such assurance and finality that Ormann was half tempted to believe it. "Second, because I've come a long way to deliver a short message."

"Is that all?" Some of the tension in Ormann's gut eased. "Well then, say your piece and leave. I'm very busy."

"I know you are. My name is Bran Tse-Mallory. I am an old friend of Philip Lynx, the man you are trying very hard to get rid of. Stop." He smiled thinly. "I told you it was a short message."

Ormann's brows drew together as he stared at the man who, though lean, appeared to be in excellent physical condition. He kept his hands in full view and his distance from the desk. A valet of some sort? Ormann wondered. Lynx had money, so why not a human servitor or two? However, something in the man suggested otherwise.

"I'm a sociologist." The voice was dry, professorial. "I'm interested in all aspects of sentient behavior. Right now I'm concentrating on yours." His voice fell. "Don't disappoint me. Hatred hovers in the air of this room like rotting meat."

"Not hatred," Ormann corrected him, "determination. You say that you're an old friend of Lynx. If that's the case, then maybe you also know that he's wanted by the authorities." His fingers crept closer to the concealed pistol. "Maybe you're even responsible for helping him in his illegal activities."

"It's been nearly seven years since my friend and I last saw Flinx. We came here to have a talk with him about an issue of considerable importance. A matter whose import far exceeds any personal concerns: his, mine, or yours. Leave him alone."

"The argument between the young redhead and me is personal. It has nothing to do with you." Fingers slowly closed around the pistol's grip.

"It has everything to do with me. And with you, too, believe it or not."

"I choose not to believe it." The visitor's empty hands were still in plain view. "I choose to believe that your friend Philip Lynx has somehow drugged or hypnotized my fiancée and that he plans on spiriting her away with him."

For the first time, the visitor looked surprised. "The woman Clarity Held is your fiancée? I didn't know that. There's no record of an official engagement."

"It hasn't exactly been formalized. That is, I haven't proposed a . . . No record of—you've been prying into my private life! Who are you, really? And who is this Philip Lynx, who the Commonwealth authorities want to talk to and who has strange friends who go around prying into things that are none of their business?"

Tse-Mallory was so still he hardly seemed to be breathing. "He was a very interesting boy who has grown into a very interesting man. He's also very hard to track down. I'm not so sure he intends to run off with your fiancée. If you'd just let things settle down, they might take a course to your liking."

"I've been letting things take their course." Ormann's tone was tense, threatening. "The result is that Clarity continues to see more and more of this Flinx and less and less of me. It's reached the point where I feel I have no choice. I've decided that nothing is going to be allowed to come between us. Not Philip Lynx, not anything or anyone. Especially not uninvited visitors." In a swift move he drew the gun from the drawer and pointed it at Tse-Mallory.

"Get out of my office. You can leave the way you came in or horizontally. The choice is up to you."

"It frequently is," Tse-Mallory murmured. "So many times I wish that it weren't." Tse-Mallory dodged with astounding speed as he reached into a breast pocket and threw something that struck Ormann before he could pull the trigger. The small device contained a large electric charge that noiselessly discharged in a single burst.

Ormann convulsed and fell onto his desk, his eyes open, his gun still clenched in his hand, electrocuted. Calmly, Bran Tse-Mallory walked over to the collapsed form. Slipping on gloves, he gently removed the pistol from Ormann's paralyzed fingers, placed the weapon back in its charger, and quietly closed the drawer. After a moment's thought, he folded the executive's hands on the desk in front of him, lifted the limp head, and rested it on the hands. To anyone entering the room, it would appear as if Ormann had fallen asleep at his desk. To anyone examining the body, it would seem that he had suffered a massive heart attack.

Tse-Mallory pocketed his now-harmless voltchuk and left the office. The office manager asked him how the important meeting had gone.

"We came to an understanding," he informed her kindly. She replied that she was glad it had gone well.

It did not go well, Tse-Mallory thought as he headed for the nearest exit from the Ulricam complex. But we did come to an understanding.

He disliked having to kill. Discussion and debate were

always better. His killing days were well behind him, back when he and Tru had formed the two halves of a stingship fighting team. But sometimes, sadly, logic and reason were not enough. Besides, Tse-Mallory had reason to believe that Ormann might have shot him in the back if he'd simply turned to leave.

Aim arguments at a man and he reacts one way, Tse-Mallory ruminated. Aim a gun at him and he is forced to react in another. He wondered how Truzenzuzex was getting along. No doubt his old friend and companion had enjoyed an easy time of it, sauntering in to greet a surprised Flinx and his female friend. Thranx had all the luck.

14

"High metamorphosis to you, Flinx."

Awakening from a surprisingly invigorating sleep, Flinx found himself staring up at a trio of faces—a quintet if one counted Pip and Scrap. Two of the other faces were human. The one from which the greeting had emerged was anything but. Flinx sat up too sharply in the bed, and the resultant wooziness momentarily blurred his vision, but not so seriously as to prevent his throwing both arms around the thranx's upper body.

"Truzenzuzex!"

"You always were competent at incontestable identification," the thranx replied dryly. "Yes, it's me. Now please remove your upper limbs from my b-thorax so that I can breathe." A grinning Flinx complied. "That's better. You know, I'm currently reading your writer Kafka's *The Metamorphosis*. It's about a human who thinks he's an insect. Fascinating. The details are all wrong, of course."

"I'll remember." Flinx turned his attention to the tall man standing near the bed. "And you too, Bran. Here, on New Riviera." Flinx shook his head in disbelief.

Standing near the head of the bed, Clarity Held reached down to give him a gentle punch on the shoulder. "Hey, I'm here too, you know."

"Oh, right. Sorry, Clarity. It's just that I haven't seen either of these two disreputable nomads in—six years, isn't it, Tru?"

"Nearly seven," the Philosoph corrected him. "You've grown, Flinx. And changed, I think, in other ways as well."

"Well, you two haven't. You look exactly as I remember you. This is my friend, Clarity Held. Clarity and I know each other from—we know each other pretty well, that's all." His old friends, Flinx knew, would not pry. "Clarity, this is the Eint Truzenzuzex."

"We've already met." Reaching out, she playfully teased the tip of one of the aged thranx's feathery antennae. It twitched away from the touch. "Tru is responsible for rescuing us both." Her expression fell. "Once Bill finds out he's failed again to get rid of you, Flinx, he's liable to try something even more drastic the next time."

"I don't think so," Tse-Mallory commented quietly.

"Oh, and this is Bran Tse-Mallory," Flinx informed her. "In their youth, Bran and Tru were a stingship team." He grinned. "Now they just sit around and pontificate."

"Pontificate," Tse-Mallory admitted, "and other things. Like looking up old acquaintances."

"How can you be so certain Bill Ormann won't try to hurt Flinx anymore?"

Wise, dark eyes peered at her from beneath those explosive eyebrows. "Because he's not going to hurt anyone anymore, Clarity Held."

She hesitated. The silence persisted for a long moment before she murmured, "Oh," and said nothing more on the matter of William Ormann because she suspected, quite correctly, that there was nothing else that needed to be said.

With Clarity's help, Flinx eased himself off the bed and moved slowly toward his hotel room's refreshment unit. Pip and Scrap ignored everyone in the room, from whom only benign emotions emanated.

Flinx's head throbbed but this time not, thankfully, from one of his headaches. The last thing he remembered was trying to free Clarity from her bonds. The important thing was that Clarity was all right. So were he and Pip. And now, to top it all off, to see Bran Tse-Mallory and Truzenzuzex again! What a wonderful coincidence.

Except that he knew it wasn't. It couldn't be. The Commonwealth was too big. Something specific had drawn the wise man and the sage thranx to New Riviera. Flinx had the feeling it was not the climate.

Still, he remained cheerful as he drew not one but two cold tumblers of fruit drink to slake his thirst. Clarity helped herself and offered refreshment for their visitors. Both man and thranx declined.

"It's wonderful to see you both again. What are you doing here? Do you still serve 'only your own philosophies'?" Ascetics, she wondered, or just not thirsty? Fully in keeping with the persona she had come to know better than ever, Flinx certainly had interesting friends.

Truzenzuzex clicked his mandibles at the remembered comment. Flinx had a fine memory. That was far from the only aspect of his mind that was exceptional, the Philosoph knew.

"Since leaving the United Church, we have pursued our own interests. As you know, Flinx, among them is our study of extinct sentient races such as the Tar-Aiym."

"The who?" Clarity looked from thranx to Flinx. "I never heard of them."

"As their history is somewhat obscure, they are not as well known as they should be," Truzenzuzex continued. "This is a characteristic they share with a number of other intelligences who have also passed from the galactic scene, among whom historic interconnections are still being established.

"Though Bran and I have preferred to carry out our work independent of any institution, governmental or scholarly, we still retain a considerable number of useful contacts within both the United Church and the Commonwealth government. Occasionally, though not often, one of these contacts has a query for *us*. I recently received one such myself." The head turned so that compound eyes could focus on Flinx.

"It came from Counselor Second of Science Druvenmaquez."

Flinx said nothing. There was no point in volunteering information that Truzenzuzex already had. But he was intensely curious to see how much his old mentor knew, as well as how he had come by it.

The thranx did not disappoint him. "It seems that the good counselor touched antennae with you in a proscribed place, a world that is only now beginning to appear on highly restricted Commonwealth charts as the straightforwardly named Midworld. He went there in search of you in the course of following up on a tale you had told a certain Padre Bateleur on Samstead."

"Yes, I remember," Flinx murmured. Bran Tse-Mallory was watching him closely, he noted.

"While thrown together on this formerly lost, accidental colony world, you inquired of the counselor if he knew me. He told you that he did not. However, when you took your leave and Druvenmaquez returned to his work, he remembered your query and managed to make

contact with me. We engaged via space-minus in a most
interesting exchange, part of which involved the counselor graciously allowing us to view the transcript of
your conversation with Padre Bateleur, the same conversation that moved the counselor to go looking for you
himself. A number of things you said to that padre
intrigued Bran and myself as thoroughly as they had
Druvenmaquez, especially in light of our past mutual
encounters with Tar-Aiym and Hur'rikku artifacts.
Furthermore, they coincided with work we were already
doing. Strange, is it not, how the three of us continue
our fascination with ancient races and the artifacts they
have left behind?"

"So we decided to come looking for you, Flinx." Tse-
Mallory smiled reassuringly. "We would have wanted to
see you again even if we three did not share a common
interest in a certain distant region of the cosmos."

Up until now, Clarity had felt that the conversation
was leaving her further and further behind. But Tse-
Mallory's mention of a shared interest in a distant region of space immediately caught her attention.

"Flinx, are they talking about the place you visit in
your nightmares?"

Truzenzuzex's head shifted from one human to another. "So, Flinx, you continue to experience the visions
of which you spoke to Padre Bateleur? You feel that you
have mentally somehow visited this distant region of
space and encountered something there?"

"Something very unpleasant," Tse-Mallory chimed
in. Arms crossed over his chest, he was leaning against
the wall beside the bedroom door. He might have been
guarding it or simply relaxing.

Flinx sighed. He had never intended the substance
of his dreams—or mental projections or whatever they

were—to become common knowledge. Or even uncommon knowledge. But in a needy moment while on the run he had confided in and briefly discussed what he had seen and felt with a representative of the United Church.

He was glad to see his old friends again. He only wished their motivation for seeking him out had been otherwise.

"I've experienced it, too," Clarity piped up before he could think to warn her to keep quiet.

Tse-Mallory was instantly alert. "You? But how?"

Noticing Flinx's expression, she wondered if she might have said something wrong. But weren't these old friends of Flinx's? Wise fellow travelers? Hadn't they saved them both from Bill Ormann's maniacal scheming? "Apparently, if someone is close enough to Flinx when he's having one of these experiences—close enough emotionally as well as physically—she can sometimes share them."

"Remarkable." Truzenzuzex's antennae waggled back and forth with excitement. "Truly remarkable. And what did you experience during this sharing, my dear?"

She looked at Flinx, who shrugged. Schrödinger's cat was out of the galactic bag. "Might as well tell them, Clarity. If anyone can make sense of it, it's Bran and Tru. Besides," he added with a glance in the thranx's direction, "most of the people I trust in the entire Commonwealth are in this room right now." Tse-Mallory smiled slightly, while Truzenzuzex made a meaningful gesture with both truhands.

The visitors listened intently while Clarity described her experience. When she had finished, they pondered her words for long moments before Truzenzuzex broke the silence.

"It certainly coincides with what Flinx told Padre Bateleur. You have these experiences frequently, Flinx?"

He shook his head. "Not frequently, no. But more often than when I was younger. They're entirely unpredictable. What I do have more often are skull-splitting, brain-rattling, mind-numbing headaches. Not only are they increasing in intensity, but I also have reason to believe that they sometimes can affect others who happen to be in my vicinity."

"Thanks for the warning." Tse-Mallory's response was devoid of irony or humor. He had experienced firsthand the volatile potential of the young man's capricious mind.

"So you can now not only read the feelings of others," Truzenzuzex was saying, "but you can also project emotions." The Philosoph seemed remarkably unconcerned for his own safety. "Is this ability as erratic as the original always was, or have you learned how to control it?"

"It's still erratic, but I am getting better at it. I don't know how to describe what's happening. Both processes are becoming more fluid. But as they do so, my headaches grow worse."

"We must try to find a cure, or at least a palliative, for that. According to your conversation with Padre Bateleur, you believe something existing within or behind the astronomical phenomenon known to us as the Great Void to be a great evil—evil existing in an actual physical sense and not merely as a moral judgment or a quantum probability."

Flinx nodded somberly while Clarity added vigorously, "That's certainly how it felt to me." Remembering, she all but shuddered. "It—it *touched* me."

"Most intriguingly strange." With a foothand, the thranx scratched idly at a joint in his carapace. "All this is clearly somehow linked to your unique neurological gift."

"I don't think I'd call it a gift." There was more than a hint of bitterness in Flinx's reply. "You still haven't said how you found me."

Tse-Mallory nodded and stepped away from the wall. "After we determined to try and do so, we began by paying a visit to Midworld. At Counselor Druven-maquez's urging and with the aid of the first colonists' intriguingly adapted descendants, a small scientific station is in the process of being established there. Apparently, there are some—difficulties."

Flinx repressed a smile. He knew Midworld. "I'm not surprised."

"It became quickly apparent that you were not there. No unauthorized vessels were in orbit, nor could any be detected elsewhere in the system. So—well, Tru and I put out the word, as it were. We have our own extensive network of contacts, many time-honored and long-established, others that might best be described as non-traditional."

"It took a while." Truzenzuzex took up the tale. "The Commonwealth is a big place." Compound eyes glistened at Flinx. "And you tend to move around a lot."

That's because I'm equally comfortable everywhere, Flinx thought, and because I'm completely comfortable nowhere.

"On the other feeler," the thranx continued, "there aren't many young men walking around with Alaspinian minidrags. After following up numerous false leads, our search eventually brought us to New Riviera." He eyed the man on the bed. "As I remarked earlier: in the interim, you've grown."

In more ways than you know, Flinx thought.

"In addition to researching the Tar-Aiym," Tse-Mallory explained, "we have also been striving to delve into the history of their ancient enemy, the Hur'rikku."

"And that somehow ties into my experiences?"

"Not directly, no. You see, in the years that Tru and I have spent digging into what little is known about pre-Commonwealth sentients, we occasionally came across information about extinct species other than the Tar-Aiym and the Hur'rikku. We made careful note of these on the chance that they might tie in to the history of one or both of those two long-gone races." He smiled. "Remember that I mentioned our interest in interconnections. One of these involves a singular discovery that was made on the world of Horseye, known to its inhabitants as Tslamaina."

Flinx gave a twitch of recognition. The ever-observant Truzenzuzex took note but said nothing.

Tse-Mallory continued. "The discovery in question was made several hundred years ago, in 106 A.A. to be exact, by a husband-and-wife team of researchers named Etienne and Lyra Redowl. Concluding their tour on that world they prepared an extensive report of their findings. Like so many such reports, it was filed away for peer review only to vanish into the bowels of Commonwealth Science Central on Earth."

Truzenzuzex concluded for him. "We read the report because we thought the technology described might connect with either the Tar-Aiym or the Hur'rikku. When it was apparent that it did not, we set it aside." Both of the thranx's feathery antennae were inclined in Flinx's direction. "We immediately recalled this particular information when we gained access to the details of the report Padre Bateleur filed concerning his meeting with you on Samstead. Can you imagine why?"

Flinx noticed that Clarity was staring at him intently. It made him uncomfortable and he tried to focus his attention on his old friends. "I'm sure you're going to tell me."

"It seems that there is a still-functioning, incredibly ancient device on Horseye whose origin and purpose are unknown and unfamiliar to the three native sentient species of that planet. Locked in ancient glacial ice and powered, remarkably, by the planet's own internal tidal forces, it is at the center of a kind of uniquely unified network of widely scattered smaller devices that appear to be monitoring two corners of the cosmos. These functions have since been identified and isolated by a research team from Hivehom. What particularly intrigued Bran and myself and sent us looking for you again is that one of these cosmic locales is the same as the one you specifically identified for the somewhat bemused but dutiful Padre Bateleur. To the best of our knowledge, you have no access to a similar alien device."

"You understand, Flinx," Tse-Mallory added softly, "how certain people such as Tru and myself might find this an intriguing coincidence. One worthy of investigating."

"And all this time I thought you'd come looking for me just to say hello and reminisce about old times." Flinx sighed heavily. "Actually, I do happen to know about the device on Horseye."

The two scholars exchanged confounded glances. "How?" Tse-Mallory demanded. He did not say "You couldn't possibly" because he and Truzenzuzex knew Flinx too well.

"I'd rather not say. But I don't have *access* to the device, or to anything similar." He was reluctant to identify his friends the Ulru-Ujurrians as the source of the information. For one thing, their world was still strictly Under Edict.

Much to his relief, Truzenzuzex and Tse-Mallory did not force the question. Both knew that Flinx had "ways" of finding things out. For now, it was enough that he had confessed to familiarity with the discovery.

"Very well. We can discuss the particulars at a future time. What do you know about the workings of the device?" Truzenzuzex asked.

"Not much," Flinx responded truthfully. "Only that it may be all or part of some kind of warning system related to the spatial phenomenon I've encountered in my dream—the one I spoke of to Padre Bateleur."

Truzenzuzex acknowledged Flinx's response with a slight gesture of one foothand while murmuring to his companion, "That much correlates with what we know." Louder, he resumed explaining to Flinx. "The Redowls were informed by the Mutable responsible for watching over the mechanism that it had been constructed by a race called the Xunca. Our research indicates that these Xunca dominated this portion of the galaxy before the rise of the Tar-Aiym and the Hur'rikku, so the device is incredibly ancient indeed."

"Wait a minute." Clarity put in. "There's no such thing as Mutables. Rumors of such things occasionally crop up in the gengineering community, but that's all they are—rumors."

Tse-Mallory turned his deep black eyes on her. "Apparently, my dear, there is something more to such creatures than inventive anecdote. In their report, the Redowls claim to have met one. I can say with confidence that that aspect of their report has been confirmed. Tru and I have been to Horseye and seen the proof for ourselves.

Or at least, we have viewed the meager remnants of what purports to be that same thing."

Flinx was immediately intrigued. "You actually saw a Mutable? Did you talk to it? Did it remember the Red-owls? Did you ask it about the device and the specifics of what it was intended to warn against?" Responding to her master's excitement, Pip opened her eyes, raised her head—and promptly returned to her nap, since the source of the perceived stimulation was not visible.

"Sadly," Tse-Mallory explained, "we were unable to do any of those things, since by all reliable estimates the Mutable had lain dead and frozen in the ice for at least a hundred years. Or so we were told. As Tru stated, we were able only to view the remains. They were very, *very* ancient. According to the official report, great care was taken when removing the creature from its icy tomb in order that a proper autopsy might be run on it. In spite of the team from Hivehom taking every precaution, the remains swiftly disintegrated. The researchers assigned to the task never were able to decide if it had been a living creature or some kind of organic appliance that had been constructed from basic molecules on up."

Truzenzuzex continued, "The system itself employs subspace wave communications and is at once much more powerful and yet simpler in design and execution than anything known to Commonwealth science. Not only is it monitoring two areas simultaneously, but the most recent report on the device claims that it also occasionally emits a spurt of modulated wave indications via a still-not-understood variant of space-minus toward a location different from those it is monitoring. The scientific team on site hasn't been able to find out how the device is doing this, far less where it is sending to or what might be on the receiving end. Work on these enig-mas continues even as we speak."

So the Xunca device could send as well as receive, Flinx thought. Could it still be trying to carry out its original function of warning its builders of a threat? And if that was the case, would the unknown, enig-matic, ancient Xunca be in a position to receive it?

"You said that the system is monitoring *two* different locations in space." He eyed Truzenzuzex absorbedly. "I'm only aware of one."

"Yes, the one you spoke of to Padre Bateleur," the Philosoph noted. "The site of perceived evil that you visit in your dreams, or whatever peculiar state of mind you enter into when performing such observations."

Flinx nodded. "Whatever it is, I have a feeling it must be what the system centered on Horseye was designed to warn the Xunca about."

This time Truzenzuzex gestured with both truhands. "Except there are no more Xunca to interpret the read-ings or receive a warning or anything else."

"No," Tse-Mallory added somberly. "There is only us." He peered steadily at Flinx. "The phenomenon we are discussing lies behind the Great Emptiness, a region of space called by the thranx the Great Void, in the di-rection of the constellation Boötes as seen from Earth. It is some three hundred million light-years across, en-compassing a volume of approximately one hundred million cubic megaparsecs, and appears to be moving in the general direction of our galaxy. What this something is or might consist of is blocked by a vast gravitational lens composed of dark matter that prevents anyone from seeing behind it or into it. Through means we do not yet fully understand, the Xunca system centered on Horseye can peer beyond the distorting effects of the lens. While we do not yet understand the physics involved, we have been able to decipher some of the data." Clasping his hands behind his back, he strolled over to the window to gaze thoughtfully down at the busy street outside.

"One thing is clear. Where this unidentified something passes, everything else vanishes. Virtually nothing is left behind, only a little free hydrogen gas, not even the dark matter composed largely of CHAMPS particles. Incredibly, the phenomenon may even violate the law of the conservation of energy by neither converting energy into mass or mass into energy, but by utterly eliminating both." He looked to Truzenzuzex to continue.

"Calculation of the eventual consequences to us is not particularly complex," the thranx informed them. "One day in an undetermined future, depending on an as-yet-unspecified rate of acceleration, this phenomenon will reach the Milky Way. And possibly consume it."

It was quiet in the room. Outside, the happy and contented citizens of the accommodating world of New Riviera went about their daily concerns, unaware that in an ordinary hotel room not far from where they were walking and talking, a most unusual quartet was calmly discussing Armageddon.

"What about the other place?" a subdued Clarity finally thought to ask. "The other phenomenon this Xunca device is monitoring? Is it anything like the—like what you just described?"

"On the contrary, it is everything the Great Void is not," Truzenzuzex informed her. "The other area of the cosmos that the system on Horseye is monitoring is known to your kind as the Great Attractor. This is a region of space that all the galaxies in the local group are moving toward. Whatever it is—and both your astrophysicists and ours have been studying it for hundreds of years—it possesses the energy of ten thousand trillion suns. Current cosmological theory still can't explain it." He turned from Clarity back to Flinx, who looked surprised.

"Well, don't look at me, Tru—*I* certainly can't explain it."

The thranx chittered softly. "I didn't mean to suggest that you could, Flinx. No one can."

"If the Xunca system is monitoring both what's behind the Great Emptiness and this Great Attractor," Flinx hypothesized, "then it follows that there may be a correlation of some kind between the two phenomena." Visions of swirling galaxies filled his head, among which he and his friends and the Commonwealth entire were so insignificant as to constitute little but nihility.

"So one would suppose," the Philosoph commented. "To make such a connection one would almost have to be intoxicated with physics. Or with metaphysics."

"Go ahead and tell them, Tru," Tse-Mallory urged his friend.

Truzenzuzex tried to wave his companion off. "It's too absurd, Bran. Too fantastic to share. I feel a complete fool for wasting the thought-time even to do the envisioning."

"Tell us, Tru." Flinx was as encouraging as a former acolyte could be. "Nothing you could imagine could be more fantastic than what I've already experienced and encountered in my dreams."

"You think not?" The thranx cocked his head. "Contemplate this, then: imagine a sentient species, perhaps our mysterious Xunca, who have advanced so far beyond contemporary intellect and science that they can conceive of trying to save not merely themselves but an entire galaxy from a threat of the magnitude posed by whatever lies behind the Great Void—by moving it out of harm's way. How to accomplish such an impossible feat? By somehow creating something like the Great Attractor. Something with sufficient gravitational strength to draw an entire galaxy out of the path of the oncoming Great Emptiness."

From his position near the door, Bran murmured tersely, "Just call Galaxy Movers, Inc."

Truzenzuzex nodded somberly, effortlessly employing the human gesture of which his kind had become quite fond. "We are speaking here of technologies beyond imagination. But if that's the case, if there's any truth to the outrageous hypothesis, it doesn't matter. Because it's not working. The Great Emptiness and whatever it hides has begun to accelerate even faster toward the Milky Way. Whether this is a coincidental phenomenon or a direct—I hesitate to say *conscious*—reaction to the pulling of our galaxy out of its path and toward the Great Attractor we have no way of knowing."

Clarity swallowed hard. "So—how much time do we, do the peoples of the Commonwealth—have?"

Tse-Mallory eyed her compassionately. "We are still talking sometime in the far future before the first congruency occurs. But when it does, unless some kind of solution can be found, it will mean the end of everything. Not just of humanxkind, the AAnn, and every other sentient race but of planets and stars and nebulae and—everything. With nothing left behind to re-form or re-create what has gone before."

"Apparently," Truzenzuzex added, "other solutions to the threat have been pondered, though not by us."

"What other solutions?" Remembering his few but always terrifying mental encounters with whatever lay beyond the Great Emptiness, Flinx was hardly sanguine. "If moving the whole galaxy doesn't have a chance of working, what else possibly could?" He did not mention that he had come to feel that he himself might somehow be a part of, be one of the keys, to such a solution.

Vast, shimmering golden eyes regarded him thoughtfully. "Flinx, have you ever heard of a world called Comagrave?"

15

Flinx and Clarity exchanged a glance before admitting that neither of them was familiar with that world.

"No need to be self-conscious of your mutual ignorance," the Philosoph assured them. "It's a minor Class Eight colony world located in a distant reach of the Commonwealth, in the general direction of the AAnn empire. The nearest settled world of any consequence is Burley. That alone tells you how far the place is from the centers of civilization. Though inhabitable, the surface is mostly desert to semidesert. Needless to say, it is not high on the list of places where I, or any other thranx, would choose to spend time, though humans seem to find it agreeable enough."

"So do the AAnn, which led to some unpleasant business many years ago," Tse-Mallory put in.

Truzenzuzex gestured concurrence. "What raises Comagrave above the level of casual interest are the fascinating, sometimes immense monuments left behind by the world's dominant sentients, a race known as the Sauun. For a long time it was believed that they were extinct. It was later discovered that this is not the case."

Clarity's expression twisted. "Seems to me I've read or seen something about them. Aren't a lot of them buried in a special mausoleum, or something?"

"Or something," the thranx agreed. "During the past

fifty years, millions of them have been found at several similar but widely separated sites. They are not dead, but suspended in stasis, their metabolisms slowed almost to a standstill. Thus far, no attempt has been made to revive any of them, since a technique for safely doing so has yet to be discovered. Various theories have been advanced to explain why an entire intelligent species would choose to abandon what by all evidence was a thriving, successful society to consign itself to a condition so close to mass death." Truzenzuzex looked over at Tse-Mallory, who took up the refrain.

"Drawing on our work with ancient civilizations, and particularly the recent revelations from Horseye, Tru and I think we might have stumbled on one possible explanation. The substance of your dreams, Flinx, as related to Padre Bateleur only serve to strengthen our hypothesis." He cleared his throat.

"Tru and I surmise that, whether by means of tapping into the Xunca system or via some other methodology, long ago the Sauun, too, became aware of the approaching danger that lies behind the Great Emptiness. Ascertaining its magnitude indicated to them that their technology was neither sufficient to counter this threat nor to allow them to flee from it."

"So they chose to bury their heads in the sand," Clarity murmured.

Tse-Mallory offered a thin smile. "Not exactly. Your analogy implies an attempt to ignore a problem in the hope that it will go away. In contrast, the Sauun chose mass racial stasis in the faint hope that they would not be revived until the danger had passed or until another intelligent species had found a way to overcome it. Through their vast, collective racial effort they may hope not to ignore the crisis but to sidestep it."

"Cowards?" Flinx muttered uncertainly.

"No, clever," Tse-Mallory corrected him.

"Not so clever if they think a species like ourselves is likely to come up with a solution."

"Speak for yourself, Flinx," countered Truzenzuzex. "Of course, *chu!!k,* it's true that we do not yet even understand the exact nature of the danger. As to that, you may know more than anyone else alive."

"I only know that it's malevolent and aware," Flinx mumbled. "I couldn't tell you its size, shape, color, or anything else."

"It may possess none of those characteristics." The thranx's tone was calming if not reassuring. "It may not be necessary to know them in order to find a way to deal with the threat being posed. The important thing is that your dreams confirm not only the report filed by the Redowls but also our theory about the Sauun. We will continue to add pieces to the puzzle."

"I don't think I like the picture you're putting together, Tru."

"None of us do, Flinx." Still staring out the window, Tse-Mallory spoke without turning. Raising one hand, he gestured out toward Sphene's busy thoroughfares. "All these people, of many diverse species, are blissfully unaware of the danger that threatens not them but their descendants." He looked back into the room. "It is left to such as us—those who seek knowledge, such as Tru and me and to those upon whom knowledge is thrust, perhaps unwanted, such as you—to make a beginning, to try to do something about it, assuming something *can* be done. It isn't the first time."

Flinx felt himself drowning in the brutal, inexorable truth of Tse-Mallory's words. Like all other truths, it was inescapable. But Flinx could no more flee from what he knew than he could from what he was.

Clarity interrupted his inner turmoil. "Do you think

that's what the Xunca did also—put themselves in suspended animation in the hope the danger will pass them by or be averted by others?"

The two scholars exchanged a glance. "No such place has yet been found," Truzenzuzex told her, "which, of course, doesn't mean one does not exist. Yet it strikes both Bran and me as odd that a species would put in place such an elaborate warning system as is centered on Horseye—one designed and built to last through eons—if they did not expect to be conscious to receive its transmissions. Then there is the matter of the subspace wave indications the system sometimes emits. Is anyone, or anything, receiving them? Or are they simply being beamed outward to a location from which the intended recipients have long since departed?"

Flinx asked, "Then you think that, instead of putting themselves into extended suspension like the Sauun, the Xunca may simply have fled elsewhere?"

The thranx responded with a gesture of overriding significance that required the simultaneous use of all four hands. "Who can say what a race like the Xunca may have done? Any species capable of bringing into existence an astronomical phenomenon like the Great Attractor in an attempt to shift the position of an entire galaxy, if indeed they did so, might be accounted capable of anything. We are dealing with technologies here, my young friend, that are as far beyond anything we can imagine as the KK-drive is to the first human wheel or the thranx talk-stick."

"The Xunca *may* be asleep somewhere," Tse-Mallory added, "or they may have gone somewhere or they may have tried to escape by engaging in some distortion of physical reality we do not even have sufficient terminology or mathematics to describe. We simply don't know."

"What we do know," Truzenzuzex asserted, "is that there is something vast and disagreeable concealed behind the Great Emptiness and that it is coming this way. The Xunca warning system affirms it, the condition of the Sauun underscores it, and your dreams, Flinx, provide us with the best depiction of it that we have so far been able to obtain."

Uncomfortable, Flinx looked away. Through inference, Truzenzuzex had yet again placed on him the sense of responsibility he had been feeling for years. Had been feeling and was unable to escape.

Clarity saw it in his expression and moved instinctively to comfort him. So did Pip, who offered no objection to the ministrations another human was offering to her master. "Flinx, it's nothing you can do anything about." Clarity placed a warm palm against his cheek. "I know that you feel otherwise, but listening to your friends"—she glanced back to where the two scholars were looking on—"it's pretty obvious there's nothing you or anyone else can do about this phenomenon, whatever it is. I mean, if one advanced race elects to put itself to sleep and another to run away, what can one sentient of any species hope to do?"

What indeed? he mused as he put his hand over hers and pressed it more tightly against his face. What, except try to run away from what he felt and what he knew. That wouldn't work. He'd tried it on several occasions, only to fail each time. He knew what he knew and was what he was.

Whatever that was.

"Yes, I've dreamed of this thing—or seen it or perceived it or however you want to describe what I've experienced. So what? What can I do about it? What can anyone do? Seeing isn't stopping."

Tse-Mallory nodded gravely, while Truzenzuzex's antennae dipped forward and slightly to opposite sides.

"What you say is true enough, Flinx," the thranx readily admitted. Delicate truhands described small arcs that were as meaningful as they were graceful. "But remember that Bran and I have seen you do other things besides *see*—activate and make use of a machine built by the Tar-Aiym, for example." Air whistled from his spicules. "If only the Tar-Aiym or the Hur'rikku had built a device capable of projecting a singularity intense enough to adversely impact this malevolence that is coming toward us. But there was only the one anti-collapsar weapon, and it has been used, and only the one Krang."

Flinx cleared his throat. "I don't know about any other Hur'rikku anticollapsar mechanisms, but I do know that there is more than one Krang."

"How do you know that, Flinx?" Tse-Mallory asked.

Clarity stared at Flinx. The automaton in his dream? she found herself wondering. Did it have anything to do with the device of which they were speaking? Or was that mechanism something else? What was a "Krang," anyway? Hadn't Truzenzuzex just referred to it as a weapon? And what was all this talk of anticollapsars and intense singularities?

What had happened to the two of them just taking in an evening's entertainment or going for strolls in the countryside?

"Because I've seen them," Flinx answered, "on an artificial world disguised as a brown dwarf that was formerly the second outermost planet of the Pyrassis system."

"Pyrassis lies within the AAnn area of influence." Tse-Mallory frowned uncertainly.

"Yes, *clr!rk*," Truzenzuzex added thoughtfully. "And what exactly do you mean by *formerly*?"

"It's not there anymore," Flinx explained flatly. "It moved itself. Through circumstances too involved and complicated to relate here—"

"Yet more discussion for later," the thranx clicked under his breath.

"—I found myself there in the middle of an altercation involving humans and AAnn. As the disagreement developed, the true nature of this construct made itself known. I . . . made contact with it, in much the same way I did with the Krang on Booster. This disguised world ship was dotted with Krangs—I don't know how many."

"Exciting," the thranx commented. "I wonder. If the projections from such devices could be combined and appropriately focused, would it be sufficient to make an impression on a menace of astronomical dimensions?"

"It certainly sounds more promising than anything we've been able to come up with," Tse-Mallory agreed. Black eyes bored into Flinx's own. "You said it moved itself, Flinx. To where? Where did this world-size weapons platform go, and where is it now?"

"To your questions, Bran: yes and I don't know." Flinx spread his hands helplessly. "It entered space-plus and vanished from the Pyrassian system. I can't imagine where something that big and that ancient might want to go after being unexpectedly revived from the stasis in which it had been placed. I have no idea if it's even still functional."

"If it is intact, it will still be functioning. Tar-Aiym technology was built to last."

"Perhaps it entered the Blight," Truzenzuzex proposed, "in search of long-dead masters and additional instructions. Perhaps it never came back out of space-plus. Perhaps it emerged from space-plus inside a sun and was annihilated. We'll never know if we don't try to find out."

"And how do you propose to do something like that?" Clarity could not keep herself from asking.

Both man and thranx gazed silently at Flinx. When he did not comment, Tse-Mallory prodded him. "You are our best hope for finding this potentially valuable artifact, Flinx. You've experienced that which is coming toward us, whatever it is, and you've engaged previously with Tar-Aiym weapons technology. Help us find it again."

Flinx would have fled, but a wall blocked his retreat. "Forget it! I want to get away from these things, not go looking for them." Clarity put both arms around him and glared at the two scientists.

"Ah." Truzenzuzex dipped his head, the better to preen one antenna. "An unexpected element is added to the equation."

"It doesn't matter." Tse-Mallory continued to force the issue. "Nothing here matters, Flinx. Not you, I, or anyone else in this room. Infinitely greater issues are at stake."

"What do you expect me to do," Flinx snapped, "jump in a ship and go look for a massive object that by now could be anywhere in the cosmos?"

"Not exactly look." Truzenzuzex was less insistent than his companion. "You have at your disposal a unique means of perceiving, Flinx. Could it not be put to use in such a search?"

"No!" Flinx shot back with sufficient vehemence to surprise even himself. Pip looked up but only briefly. "I am capable of sensing *emotions* in others, and sometimes projecting them. That's all."

Not quite all, Clarity knew—but she was not about to volunteer such information.

"You might be able to contact the device again, under the right circumstances." Dripping with honeyed clicks and whistles, Truzenzuzex's tone was annoyingly persuasive. "Bran and I could help you."

"Oh, really?" Flinx did not try to hide his disdain. "And exactly how might you do that?"

"With training and advice," Tse-Mallory told him without missing a beat. "Tru and I were both struck from the moment we first met you, Flinx, that your special potential was only partly realized. Clearly, that's changed somewhat. With proper guidance, it might be changed significantly more."

Truzenzuzex rested his left truhand and foothand on Flinx's leg. "No one knows what you are ultimately capable of, Flinx. Not Bran, not me, and certainly not you. Perhaps even something as improbable as becoming able to perceive the emotional state, and therefore the location, of a machine."

His words gave Flinx a jolt. He had discussed the same issue with the AI that controlled the functions of the *Teacher*.

"If nothing else, Flinx," Tse-Mallory continued compellingly, "you can help us physically search for something that only you have encountered and that only you may be capable of recognizing."

"At least, this appears to be our best hope for possibly countering this threat," Truzenzuzex said, staring at him. Or at least, Flinx had the impression the thranx was staring. With those compound eyes it was always hard to tell. "Should something more efficacious come along, rest assured we will pursue it as a potential solution with equivalent vigor."

"You really intend to try and fight whatever's coming." Flinx's gaze shifted back and forth between his two old friends.

Truzenzuzex made a gesture indicative of unavoidable promise. "We will not put ourselves in stasis, as did the Sauun, and we will not run as the Xunca might have done, because we don't know how to do either." Four hands gestured meaningfully. "What else can we do but fight?"

"Who else knows of the danger?" Flinx heard himself asking.

"A few individuals who work in Commonwealth Science Central. Perhaps some others who may have come across the original report. It will not be more widely distributed. It would do no good to do so. Only panic and fear would ensue. Without reason, since the threat will not become imminent for several generations at the earliest."

"Though we can't be sure of that," Bran put in. "The phenomenon continues to accelerate."

"True," the thranx admitted. "Bran and I will organize and initiate a search for this perambulating Tar-Aiym weapons platform because it offers the best chance for countering the approaching danger that has thus far been made known to us. Will you help us, Flinx? In return, we will attempt to tutor you, to edify you. To enlarge your knowledge of yourself. Isn't that what you want? What you've always wanted?"

Yes, yes! But *not* at the expense of any chance of real happiness. Not at the risk of losing what little serenity and joy he'd managed to scrape together from the shattered detritus of a damaged life. Though he'd spoken not a word, an alarmed Pip lifted her upper body to peer anxiously into his face and caress it with her tongue.

He found he wanted to scream.

For the first time in many years he had succeeded in

talking about and sharing the particulars of his troubled inner self with someone else, shared them far more effusively than he had intended, but shared nonetheless. Did that mean that he loved Clarity Held? He loved Mother Mastiff; he knew that. And he loved Pip (at which thought the flying snake coiled in upon herself in a small paroxysm of delight). But did he love Clarity, or was he simply grateful for her sympathy and understanding? It would make a difference to know.

More important, did she love him and could he trust such feelings? The older he grew, the more chary he became of human emotions. Better than most—perhaps better than anyone before or since, save for, possibly, certain poets—he knew how fleeting they could be. Could he build a life on such an insubstantial human ephemera? Did he want to try?

What was the alternative? To continue his search for his father, since he now knew the disagreeable history of his mother. To travel and learn—to what end? Bran and Tru were offering instruction and training—perhaps the best he could hope to find anywhere. But at a price. Not much of a price, he reflected. They only wanted his help in trying to save the Commonwealth. No, not the Commonwealth, he corrected himself, the *galaxy*. Save the galaxy: it sounded like an ecologist's bad slogan.

Why should he? What did he owe the galaxy or the Commonwealth? Both had dealt him a raw deal. Let both disappear, smothered by whatever was advancing from behind the Great Emptiness. Let everything start over fresh and new and clean.

Except, if the astronomers were right, there was nothing behind the Great Emptiness. No material to make new stars and new planets, much less new civilizations. There would be no fresh start in this corner of the cosmos. He cringed inwardly.

Some people were anxious about bills. Some fretted about their marriages, their kids, or the career promotion that might never come. Some were concerned for their health. Me, he thought, I'm expected to worry about the fate of a couple hundred million stars and a few civilizations. That, he reminded himself, and what to do about Clarity Held. Somehow in his mind the two had become linked.

Because you're the key, he told himself. The trigger of a triad consisting of an ancient artificial intelligence that he had long since decided involved the Krang, an intense green something that he had come to suspect concerned the life-forms of Midworld, and a mysterious warm sapience as yet unidentified. Could the latter consist of his inscrutable friends from the proscribed world called Ulru-Ujurr? If so, why didn't they admit their involvement? It wasn't like the jovial, furry manipulators of time and space to be deliberately obscure. And if they were not the third component of the resistive harmony he kept encountering in his dreams, then who was?

I don't want to be a key, he cried inwardly. I don't want to be a trigger. I want to lead a normal life!

Sure, he told himself more calmly. As a rogue genetic mutation that's the creation of a universally reviled, outlawed medical group. A normal life. With Clarity Held? Agonized, he looked at her and saw that she felt his pain. Love? Or just empathy? Even for him it was hard to tell the difference.

He was wavering, Clarity saw. Thinking of going with the human and thranx. Of leaving her again. Just when she thought she had forgotten all about him, he had come back into her life and turned it upside down again. What did he want from her? What did she want from him? How could you live with and love someone who knew what you were feeling even when you might not be certain yourself?

She wavered, he vacillated, and the two minidrags, mother and offspring, were no less confused than their respective humans.

What about your headaches? Flinx reminded himself. Can you place that burden on Clarity? She's already seen what they can do to you. How can you ask her to be with you when the next pain in your skull might kill you? She has a good life here on New Riviera—she's told you so. Do you have the right to ask her to leave that just to help you with your problems? And even if she were to agree, would it be the right thing to do?

He was aware that they were all watching him, waiting, anxious to hear what he would decide. Bran and Tru in the hope that he would agree to go with them and help them. Clarity in the hope that—in the hope that . . .

What did Clarity Held *really want*? Was she more certain what she wanted than he? If he didn't know what he wanted, how could he trust her to know what she wanted? He responded to the inquiring stares as he had so often done when confronted by difficult situations in the past. He stalled.

"Since you've been in contact with members of the scientific community," he asked Truzenzuzex, "have they been able to determine how fast this shadowy section of the cosmos is advancing toward the Commonwealth and when it might begin to affect us?"

Truzenzuzex looked up, a purely instinctive gesture of the kind that even thranx Philosophs are subject to.

"It's approaching at a slight angle to the plane of the galactic ecliptic," he replied. "The area in question is so vast that velocities are not constant throughout, or so I have been led to understand. While an averaging is not precise, it is the best that can be hoped for until better measurements can be taken." Flinx saw multiple visions of himself mirrored in the manifold lenses of the thranx's eyes. Each one was slightly different from the one next to it—as were his own multiple visions of himself.

"Suffice to say, *krr!lt,* that neither the Commonwealth nor any portion of our immediate galactic environs will begin to be affected until everyone in this room is long dead, and likely not until our offspring are also deceased. This estimation assumes, of course, that the phenomenon does not continue to accelerate. In that event, all current predictions are to be discarded. But as of now, we believe the first contact might not be felt for thousands of years or tens of thousands. Or outermost star systems could begin to be affected within a few hundred years. No sooner than that, I'm told, unless the rate of motion accelerates exponentially."

"A few hundred years," Clarity murmured, "at the soonest." When both thranx and man nodded, she turned sharply to Flinx. "Then there's no hurry. There's ample time to find a way to counter this entity."

"Provided," Tse-Mallory reminded her softly, "the rate of acceleration does not increase. That is something we cannot predict. Knowing as little as we do about the nature of this phenomenon, we are of course equally ignorant of its capabilities."

"You're asking Flinx to devote his immediate future and maybe even the rest of his life to combating something that won't pose an actual threat until long after he's dead."

Truzenzuzex gestured with a truhand. "Yes. That's exactly what we're asking him to do."

"Why should he?"

Flinx gazed affectionately at her. She was giving voice

to his thoughts. Was that an indication of love? She was arguing for his happiness.

Not a complicated equation, he decided. His happiness versus the galaxy's future. One man's contentment versus the end of everything. As was so often the case, the choice was simple. Making it was the hard part.

Tse-Mallory was watching him closely. So was Truzenzuzex. They were among the most important friends and mentors of his youth, now returned to ask his help in dealing with a far more momentous problem than whether an ancient artifact was a weapon, a musical instrument, or both. Their empathy, sincere and unrestrained, felt like a flow of soothing liquid warmth rushing through his mind. He believed he owed the Commonwealth nothing, the galaxy nothing. But what did Philip Lynx owe Bran Tse-Mallory and Truzenzuzex?

Others were involved. He met Clarity's open gaze. His talent was fully active, sensitive to the feelings of everyone around him. "I'm confused, Clarity." He smiled disarmingly. "It's threatening to become an endemic condition. When I'm confused I try to turn for advice to those whose opinions I respect. I've known both these wanderers for a long time. I've known you for less but more intensely."

"Don't you mean *intimately*?" She smiled, and he felt affection roll out of her like a wave.

"I guess I mean both. I don't know what to do. I really don't. When I don't know I have to ask. Clarity, I'm asking you. Just you. What do *you* think I should do?"

She was taken aback. The forceful stares of the two scholars didn't make it any easier. "That's right, Flinx. Don't ask about something simple and straightforward like you and me. Just place the future of the galaxy and humanxkind in *my* hands."

His smile became that same youthful, almost childlike grin that had first attracted her to him years ago on Longtunnel. But his tone was quietly serious. "What are real friends for, Clarity?"

Slowly, she put both arms around his neck and lost herself in those deep green eyes. Eyes that had already seen far too much yet were full of the uncertainty of youth. Eyes behind which lay an incredible but still immature talent. Did she love him? Or did she feel sorry for him? Did she want to be with him always, or just help him overcome and survive? He had told her he didn't know what to do, which implied he didn't know what he wanted. What did *she* want? They were two confused people confounded by the options fate had dealt them, thrown together originally by circumstance and brought back together by need.

Love by any other definition, she thought.

The surge of raw emotion from both of them caused the two minidrags to coil themselves reassuringly around the forearms of their respective masters as well as around each other. Man, woman, and snakes formed an entwined whole. Behind them, Tse-Mallory was whispering something about human courtship rituals to the fascinated Truzenzuzex. Flinx and Clarity ignored them.

"I don't know what you should do, Flinx. You can't ask me or anyone else to decide for you. I *do* know that I want to spend the rest of my life with you, helping you overcome the confusion and pain that torments you so. If I can." Leaning forward, she kissed him. Tse-Mallory's whispering acquired urgency.

Eventually, their lips parted. "Clarity, if my headaches get any worse I may not have much *rest of life* left."

"I'll take what I can. But at the same time, I can't be that selfish. As much as I'd like for the two of us just to be together, I know you can't put aside this calling you feel." As she spoke, she toyed with strands of his hair. "Besides, I'd like our grandchildren—or great-great-grandchildren—to have a future. I suppose that means dealing with this thing that's coming, however long it's going to be before it gets here. I think the answer's obvious. You need to help your friends find this mysterious weapons platform you encountered previously. You need to do whatever's necessary to try to divert or destroy this oncoming malicious phenomenon. And you need to take me with you. That way you can do what has to be done, and we can still be together." She looked resolutely back at their silent audience. "I can help you in ways they can't."

Tse-Mallory responded with an avuncular smile. "If Flinx doesn't object to your presence, then surely neither Tru nor I will."

Flinx found himself torn. "It would be wonderful if you could come with us, Clarity, but it's liable to be dangerous."

"Dangerous?" She gazed back at him wide-eyed. "Where Philip Lynx goes? Why, such a possibility never occurred to me! I'm shocked, positively shocked!"

Truzenzuzex gestured approvingly. "An attitude that might have come straight from one of the nurseries in a major hive. I believe I will enjoy the female's company."

"What about the life you've built for yourself here?" Flinx asked. "Your career, your future?"

"My career has been put on hold before. It can be put on hold again. My personal situation has changed. And despite knowing better, I find myself romantically entangled." Her kiss was quick this time, but no less intense. "I'm afraid you're stuck with me, Flinx. I'm your responsibility now."

"Wonderful." He grinned. "Something else to be responsible for."

Lips pursed invitingly, she exclaimed, "Don't you ever call me a something again."

"This is still the courtship ritual?" the thranx murmured to his friend.

Tse-Mallory nodded. "Not atypical, actually."

"Is he going to impregnate her now?"

"For a member of the hive who has spent as much time around humans as you have, Tru, you still retain a positive ignorance of certain aspects of human behavior."

"Then would it be impolite to suggest that we get a move on?"

"No. Such a suggestion would be quite in order. Time is always of the essence. After all, we don't know how many hundreds or thousands of years we have left."

16

Her superiors at Ulricam were vocal in their disappointment when she announced that she was taking an extended leave of absence. After all, they insisted, what could possibly be more important than developing the company's new line of oxytocin-laced cosmetics? Clarity elected not to enlighten them. Knowing corporate executives, she was not sure informing them that the future of the galaxy was at stake would alter their opinion.

Despite Flinx's assurance that there was ample room on the *Teacher,* she chose to take very little with her. Scrap rode lightly on her shoulder, unconcerned as to their destination. Coiling around Flinx's right arm, Pip occasionally snatched a brief, maternal glance at her offspring just to keep track of his location.

"I've been on your ship," Clarity reminded Flinx as they strode through the shuttleport terminal. "Certain conspicuously male nuances aside, it has everything anyone could need."

"You may not recognize it," he warned her gently. "I'm always making changes. There's a central chamber where I go to relax. Sometimes it's full of waterfalls and trees, sometimes desert. Once, I did a tiny bit of beach and fake ocean. Right now, because I was given some interesting foliage on Midworld, it's done in rain forest." He smiled, reminiscing. "I left the parasites out."

"Must be nice. Most people are lucky if they can afford to regularly change the sims on their walls. But then, most people don't have their own starships."

"I told you earlier." He looked uncomfortable. "I had nothing to do with it. It was a gift."

"From the Ulru-Ujurrians." She returned his smile. "I remember. An eccentric bunch of sentients if ever there was one. Wonder what they're up to now?"

"Probably digging," he reminded her. "Always digging, as they call it. Making tunnels on their homeworld. Tunnels that do funny things." He glanced skyward, through the polarized, transparent dome of the concourse ceiling. "As long as we're wondering, I wonder if they're aware of what's coming toward us and if they plan to do anything about it."

"Why don't you ask them?"

"I intend to," he told her. "They might have some good ideas."

"This ancient weapons platform you visited that has your friends so intrigued. Do you really think you can find it again, and, if so, that it might be powerful enough to actually stop something astronomical in scale?"

"Don't know," he admitted. "Can only try. As Truzenzuzex said, right now it's the best hope we have." He put his arm around her and drew her close to him. "And you're the best hope I have."

She glanced backward. Deep in conversation, Bran Tse-Mallory and Truzenzuzex followed, ignoring the two humans.

"Don't they ever stop arguing?"

Flinx grinned. "When you want to know everything, you're constantly asking questions and seeking answers. I'm a lot like them, I think—nosy but not noisy. Don't worry—there's lots of room on the *Teacher,* and plenty of places to find solitude. But you already know that."

After passing Security, they headed down a hallway for the transfer station where small vehicles were available to convey them below the tarmac and deposit them next to the shuttlecraft from the *Teacher*. Then a short atmospheric flight and they would be aboard his craft.

The corridor was unoccupied. Very few private shuttlecraft utilized this, the outermost port serving the city of Sphene. Photophilic paint applied in understated decorative patterns provided sufficient light.

Turning down a curve in the corridor, Clarity saw several transfer vehicles waiting. She was just wondering if she had forgotten anything when Flinx halted so abruptly that his arm nearly made her stumble. Tse-Mallory and Truzenzuzex both came up quickly behind them.

"*Sr!!ck,* what is it, Flinx?" Both of the thranx's antennae were fully extended, sampling the air, quivering slightly. Tse-Mallory's eyes scanned every centimeter of the corridor.

"Something." Flinx's expression was tight with uncertainty. "There's *something* here."

"You're reading emotions." Searching their surroundings, Clarity saw nothing: only empty corridor, transfer vehicles, the decorative lighting and patterns etched on the walls.

"Actually, that's the problem. I can't perceive anything *specific*. It's like the emotions of others are present but masked somehow."

Clarity was at once bewildered and concerned. "How do you mask emotions?"

Tse-Mallory responded, "Drugs."

The corridor exploded in a burst of incandescence. As Flinx pulled Clarity and the thranx with him into an alcove stacked with supplies, Tse-Mallory threw himself in the opposite direction. He and Truzenzuzex drew the small hand weapons they always carried with them: Tse-Mallory two, the thranx two pair. In seconds, answering fire spurted from their six united guns.

Their unknown assailants fired small explosive shells and sonic bursts.

"This won't do. We've got to get out of here!" From his position behind a protruding corridor section seal, Tse-Mallory yelled to his companions huddled in the storage alcove. Even as he spoke, a shell blew away the top of the metal flange of the seal he was crouching behind.

Who were they fighting? The harder Flinx strove to penetrate the emotional masks of their assailants, the murkier his perceptions became. Were they after him or his companions? If it was him, and they had used drugs to disguise their feelings, that implied some knowledge of his unique talent. Inevitably, he thought back to the two people who had attacked him in the air on Goldin IV. Were these the same people? Had they somehow managed to follow him all the way to New Riviera?

But why wait until he was almost ready to depart to attack him again? Would-be assassins had had ample opportunity to take a shot at him in the preceding months. No, this had to be a new set of assailants. But not necessarily different. There could have been collusion between them and those who had struck at him on Goldin IV.

And he still had not the slightest idea who they were.

With their emotional states cloaked, he could not anticipate their actions or influence them. That didn't stop him from using his own gun. He kept a tight rein on a frantic Pip, and Clarity did likewise with Scrap, since they both knew that in the narrow corridor the flying snakes would have little room to maneuver. Both of them might all too easily be brought down by the concentrated fire.

Retreat was also a dubious proposition. It was a good ten meters to the first bend in the corridor. Even a champion sprinter would find it difficult to negotiate that distance without getting shot.

Tse-Mallory released a burst of defensive fire in the direction of their assailants. "You three run for it! I'll cover you."

Truzenzuzex turned to the two humans. "You two go first, *ku!isc.*"

Flinx shook his head. "We'll go together, Tru." Next to him, Clarity nodded forcefully.

The thranx gestured with a truhand. The weapon held in its grasp was compact and exquisite, a deadly jewel birthed in the armaments' factories of Eurmet.

"Don't be ridiculous, Flinx. I am a trained soldier. I can lay down four times the firepower you carry, and you are more than tall enough to shoot over me at our assailants, whereas I would feel somewhat inhibited trying to shoot at them between your legs."

Flinx nodded. "Okay, Clarity and I will make a run for it first, but you come right after us." Over a short distance, he knew, the thranx could keep up with even long-legged humans.

Truzenzuzex gestured his agreement. "Another metamorphosis to you both, then, and watch your footing." Had he possessed flexible facial features, he would have smiled encouragingly. "As for myself, thranx never trip."

Tru exchanged hand signals with Tse-Mallory, who then lay down withering fire across the far end of the corridor. Simultaneously, Truzenzuzex fired all four hand weapons.

Answering fire came immediately. From the *other* end of the corridor.

Once again, the travelers were compelled to withdraw behind their respective cover.

"*Crrskk, that* didn't work." Truzenzuzex was upset. "If they're behind us as well as in front of us, we are in a very bad position indeed."

Clarity took a cautious glance back up the passageway. "They're still firing."

"I can hear that." Flinx's concern and confusion made him irritable.

"Maybe so—but what you can't tell is that they're not firing at *us*."

"What?" Keeping one hand tight on Pip, Flinx peered back. The majority of the intense fire pouring down the corridor was directed toward their unknown assailants. Only an occasional burst was aimed at them.

"This makes no sense." Truzenzuzex's golden compound eyes were close to Flinx's face. In the confined space, his scent was almost overpowering. "Can you get a sense of these newcomers, Flinx, or are their emotions shrouded like the others?"

Half closing his eyes, sonic bubbles and explosive bullets bursting all around him, Flinx let his perception range outward. Almost immediately, he identified apprehension, determination, a sense of duty, and professional pride, a combination that painted a familiar pattern. "I think they're Commonwealth peaceforcers," he announced.

Clarity's own emotions leaped in his mind. "Come to stop the fight!"

"Perhaps," observed Truzenzuzex, "or to take Philip Lynx into custody." Sensitive antennae bobbed. "It may be that we find ourselves in the middle of a three-way fight. Believing themselves to be under attack by these new arrivals, our assailants are shooting back at them.

The peaceforcers naturally respond. Meanwhile, both groups may be looking to incapacitate us."

"How do you win a three-way fight?" Flinx jumped as the dull *thwock* of a sonic bubble dented the corridor wall beyond his head.

"By allying yourself with the stronger third to overwhelm the weaker and then hoping to defeat your temporary collaborator afterward," the thranx explained, "or by letting them beat each other while you pull back. We've been granted, if not a reprieve, at least a momentary distraction. We need to make use of it."

He commenced a thorough examination of their immediate surroundings and they found the service hatch in the ceiling of the storage niche. A small ladder, clearly designed for human feet, was welded to the wall. Flinx saw that he and Clarity could help Truzenzuzex up it and through the hatch.

First they had to see if the hatch would open.

It was secured with a professional, commercial electronic lock, but Flinx had it opened in less than two minutes. When the hatch cover motored silently aside, they found themselves doused with cloud-shrouded sunshine. Flinx poked his head through the opening and made his way up the ladder. When he leaped back down moments later to rejoin his friends, he was smiling.

"We're under the tarmac. I can see my shuttle! It's a short sprint away." Holding up his right arm, he showed them the decorative universal control bracelet on his wrist. "I'll signal the shuttle to be ready to leave as soon as we're on board." He looked down the corridor that continued to ring with the exchange of fire. "Tru, tell Bran to come over."

During a pause in the exchange of gunfire, Tse-Mallory dashed into the alcove. "Excellent. We can leave both groups of gun-happy disputants to sort matters out among themselves."

"They're all hunkered down." Clarity had crawled to the edge of the storage alcove to check both sets of combatants. "I think they're too occupied with each other right now to worry about stopping us from leaving."

"Likely don't yet realize that we can. We'd better not linger." Tse-Mallory started up the ladder.

A large explosion behind them signified that someone had decided to begin using heavier ordnance. The concussion rang in Flinx's ears. He'd send Clarity and Scrap up next. Turning, he reached for her hand. His breath caught in his throat and his heart missed a beat.

She was sitting, dazed, on the floor, staring at him. Scrap fluttered anxiously above her, rising and falling. The last big explosion had evidently knocked her off her feet.

"Clarity, what's wrong?" Beyond being momentarily stunned, she looked all right to him.

"I think—I think I'm hurt."

"Where?" he asked immediately. He could see nothing wrong. Then Scrap landed on his unoccupied shoulder and he knew that something was. The minidrag would not perch on anyone else unless his master was injured.

"Not sure," she muttered uncertainly. "My back, maybe. Feels a little funny."

Truzenzuzex was whistling anxiously for them to hurry.

"Just a minute!" Flinx shouted above the continuing roar of weapons fire. Leaning around Clarity, he saw the entire back of her jumpsuit was gone, along with much of her skin. He couldn't tell how deep the wound was because there was so much blood. He felt as if someone had slipped a garrote around his throat and was rapidly tightening it.

"Bran, Tru!" he yelled. "Clarity," he told her gently, "you've been hit. I don't know if it was combustive shrapnel, or what, but it looks—bad."

The two scholars were at his side in an instant. Flinx could see the severity of Clarity's injury reflected in Tse-Mallory's expression.

"Not good. Not good at all."

Fatal? Flinx wanted to say. He found he couldn't even whisper it.

Truzenzuzex was tearing at his backpack with both foothands. The two sensitive truhands were exploring Clarity's wounds. "Not fatal. Not if she receives proper medical attention in time."

"She's going into shock." Pulling off his jacket, Tse-Mallory wrapped it over the uninjured front of her body. Immediately, blood began to stain the edges.

Truzenzuzex pulled at what looked like a weapon. "Hold her," he snapped in terse terranglo. Flinx crouched in front of Clarity and gripped her shoulders firmly in both hands. Had he not, she would have fallen over. Her eyes were unfocused now, the lids fluttering.

Truzenzuzex glanced at the watching Scrap. Perceiving that the thranx's intentions were wholly benign, the minidrag stayed coiled around Flinx's neck and made no move to interfere. Truzenzuzex activated the pistol-like device, and a white mist spewed from its nozzle. She moaned as the thranx methodically played the spray back and forth over her bloodied, torn back until the device was empty.

Flinx saw that her back was now sheathed in a rapidly congealing shiny gray substance that looked like translucent plastic. Her head had slumped forward and her eyes were now closed.

"Synthetic chitin," the thranx explained, "for bandaging injured thranx, not humans. But it's calcium-based, hypoallergenic, and will bind to the bits of exposed bone long enough to get her to a proper medical facility where it can be removed with the appropriate solvent. Until then, it will staunch the remaining bleeding and prevent infection." He eyed Flinx closely. "But I won't lie to you. There are deep wounds and, as near as my knowledge of human physiology can tell, a very real possibility of serious internal injuries."

"In other words," Tse-Mallory added, "if we don't get her to a surgeon, she's likely to die."

"Then let's get her to one." A grim-faced Flinx indicated the hatchway.

Tse-Mallory put a restraining hand on the younger man's shoulder. "I saw her wounds, too, Flinx. My knowledge of human anatomy is a little more comprehensive than Tru's. I'm telling you straight—we can't go hauling her up a wall and across open tarmac. She needs hemoglu, serum, antibiotics, and a suspension gurney that will hold her steady while she's moved. Or . . ."

"Or," Flinx pressed him over the whine and thunder of continuing gunfire.

"Or any severe jolting movement—no matter how careful we try to be with her and in spite of Tru's fast work in closing her up—is liable to stop her heart."

Flinx sat there, still holding the unconscious Clarity upright, surrounded by friends and yet, as usual, all alone. He had finally found someone to be with. Someone he could love and, just as important, talk to freely. Someone to share the lonely moments in the empty spaces between worlds. And it looked as if it was all going to be taken away from him.

But not permanently, he vowed. Not permanently.

"Hospital." His whisper was barely audible as Pip worriedly caressed his cheek with her pointed tongue.

Tse-Mallory nodded and pulled a com unit from his belt. "The peaceforcers will be communicating on a secure closed signal. We'll have to contact them via a shuttleport frequency. When I explain who Tru and I are and what our situation here is, we'll be able to turn Clarity over to them."

Flinx's gaze came up so sharply and was so intense that even the normally unflappable Tse-Mallory was startled. "We're not 'turning her over' to anybody." He looked at Truzenzuzex. "If they're after the first group that started shooting at us there'd be no problem. But as you said, they may be after me."

Tse-Mallory glanced at his companion, then back at Flinx. "Tru and I still wield some influence in certain quarters. We can probably get you released before the local authorities realize what's going on."

"I'm not taking that chance," Flinx replied. "It doesn't matter if the Commonwealth wants to examine me *or* my ship. We're both leaving. And you're going to stay with Clarity and make sure she gets proper treatment, the best."

Truzenzuzex tried to remonstrate with him. "But, Flinx, *scc!lk,* we were going to search for the Tar-Aiym weapons platform together. What about the education and training we promised you?"

"There'll be time for that. Meanwhile, you know nothing of the platform. The only relevant information is on the *Teacher,* locked in her memory. It can be used just as effectively whether you're present or not."

"And if we insist on going with you?" Tse-Mallory prodded him thoughtfully.

Flinx shrugged. "I'm not leaving Clarity with strangers,

no matter what they do to me. If you won't agree to stay and watch over her, then I'll have to."

Tse-Mallory nodded. "Such a difficult thing to quantify—love," he murmured. "You'll contact us as soon as you find anything?" He held out his com unit. Flinx nodded and drew his own. It took only a moment for the two units to exchange appropriate contact information and security codes.

"What about your headaches, Flinx?" Truzenzuzex put a comforting truhand on his arm.

Flinx shrugged. "I'll deal with them. Just as I always have. Or I'll die."

The thranx's head bobbed regretfully. "Try to avoid the latter, will you?"

Flinx had to smile. "I always have." Something whanged loudly in the corridor as it took a chunk out of the far wall. "It sounds like this is starting to wind down. I'd better get going." He eyed Tse-Mallory. "You're sure you two can handle the peaceforcers?"

Tse-Mallory nodded. "As soon as they stop shooting at us, yes." He brought his com unit to his lips. "Once you're through that hatch, I'll start berating them for their inefficiency and poor aim. That always commands attention."

With truhand and foothand, Truzenzuzex enfolded Flinx's left hand. "Remember, Flinx: the instant you've found the weapons platform, or learned anything else of note regarding the menace that lies beyond the Great Emptiness, you'll make contact with us."

"I will," he promised. "Within the week I'll find a way to contact you via space-minus to check on Clarity." Leaning forward, he kissed the unconscious woman tenderly on her forehead. He wanted to squeeze her tightly, to hold her as hard as he could, but dared not. Instead, he had to let her slump into Tse-Mallory's waiting arms. Scrap rose and glided to Clarity's shoulder.

Flinx looked down at her for one last moment that seemed to stretch into eternity and was simultaneously all too short. She was unable to look back. But Scrap did. Sensing the imminence of parting, Pip flew down from Flinx's shoulder. The two minidrags entwined tongues several times. Flinx had already turned toward the open hatchway and started up the ladder when Pip joined him.

"Up the Universe, boy," Tse-Mallory called out.

"The Great Hive go with you," Truzenzuzex added in both terranglo and High Thranx.

Flinx did not reply.

17

Bitter and detached, weighed down by the feeling that no matter what he did he was doomed to loneliness, Flinx spotted his shuttle and began running toward it. Pip took to the air immediately, scouting the ground in front of him. A couple of maintenance vehicles and one supply skimmer were busy on the tarmac. None of their operators, human or mechanical, bothered to glance in his direction.

Then he was alongside the familiar transfer craft racing beneath the fully extended port delta wing. Craft security recognized and admitted him. If the peaceforcers had come in search of him, he reflected as he settled into the pilot's seat, it was surprising they hadn't thought to impound his shuttlecraft or at least station a guard or two alongside. But then, he decided, they had no reason to suppose they would be unable to apprehend him before he tried to board.

As if in response to this thought, even as the shuttle's engine was whining to life, the craft's external sensors detected a pair of police skimmers clearing a distant gate and crossing out onto the tarmac. He did not wait for them to get any closer or for the clearance from port control. Acceleration slammed him back into the flight harness as the shuttle lifted without authorization. The shots fired from the two police skimmers fell woefully short of the rapidly climbing shuttle.

Within moments his body, if not his thoughts, experienced weightlessness. Clarity, Clarity, why did you have to go and get yourself shot? Why, when everything had been decided, when all had been resolved? He missed her already. Her smile, her no-nonsense advice, the way the light gilded her hair and glinted in her eyes. Having had no one to miss for so many years, it was astounding how quickly he now missed her. Pip did her best to console him. Despondent, he reached down to stroke the back of the minidrag's head and neck.

"You're a good gal, Pip. You can even hug back. No offense, but talking with you just isn't the same as it is with Clarity."

Not understanding, but wanting to, the flying snake stared back at him out of small, bright eyes.

The shuttle's command console indicated that he was being hailed on multiple frequencies. No doubt port control was trying frantically to get in touch with the shuttle that had taken off without clearance. Flinx tried to remember if, when assuming orbit around New Riviera, he had seen any warships. None leaped to mind, which did not mean they were not present. There might be one on the other side of the planet or one might have entered Nurian space after he had. But he didn't think it likely. New Riviera was celebrated for many things, but not as a military outpost.

There would be policing craft in orbit, and he would do well not to linger. Ahead, he could see the expanding shape of the *Teacher,* with its teardrop-shaped living quarters at one end and the Caplis generator at the other. Soon he would be back in familiar surroundings. Familiar, he reflected, and lonely.

Clarity would live. Tse-Mallory and Truzenzuzex

would see to it, if only for his sake. She would live, and he would come back. As to the object of his forthcoming search, was the Tar-Aiym weapons platform powerful enough to do anything against the oncoming evil? That it possessed immense destructive potential he knew. But the looming threat was on a cosmic scale.

First he would have to find it again, he knew. And before that, he had to quickly depart the Nurian system.

The shuttle slipped silently and smoothly into the open bay in the underside of the *Teacher.* As soon as pressure outside had been equalized and the internal posigravity field had drawn him down into his seat, he emerged into the ship. The air of the only real home he had known for many years smelled especially sweet, he decided. Fully automated and self-contained, the *Teacher* welcomed him back.

His thoughts still full of the woman he had been forced to leave behind, Pip riding comfortably on his shoulder, he headed for the control room. Considering what he had just been through and what lay ahead, he found he was feeling remarkably good.

He never sensed the presence of the other two humans on board until the hypo struck him in the lower back. Feeling wonderfully happy and warm, he sat down on the deck and remained there, smiling into the distance. Pip immediately launched from his shoulder and fluttered to and fro in the control room. That there were two other humans present she saw right away. But since only feelings of contentment and satisfaction emanated from Flinx, she was not driven to attack the strangers.

A short, middle-aged woman with dark hair and eyes smiled up at the flying snake. Confused and wary, Pip settled down on the command console and relaxed as best she could. At the slightest hint of alarm from Flinx she would instantly leap to the attack.

The woman's small and wiry companion walked over to Flinx and caught him as he began to slump. "Easy there, Philip Lynx. You're going to be fine. Let me help you."

Through what seemed to be a rose-scented haze, Flinx peered up. "Thank you. Thas very nice of you." The man was much stronger than he appeared. With the woman's assistance, they managed to walk Flinx to his living quarters. A wary Pip followed, still more confused than concerned.

Once in the room, the visitors eased Flinx down onto his bed. He smiled languidly up at them as they tied him down. "I feel—wonderful," he mumbled torpidly. "Who—who are you people, and how did you get onto my ship?"

"Our names are not important." The cheerful woman was grinning from ear to ear as she secured one of the straps she had brought with her around his ankle. "We are members of the Order of Null."

Flinx chuckled softly. "The Order of Nothing. That's funny! Tell me another funny." Something was wrong, he knew. Very wrong. But he was feeling too good to worry. It was far more important to relax and enjoy life. Even the knowledge that they were tying him down was somehow amusing. It shouldn't be. He was aware enough to know that much.

"The Order of Null," the jolly man securing his upper body explained, "was brought into being only recently, yet has already gained many devoted adherents. It knows that the cosmos, or at least this portion of it, is soon to undergo a vast change. An immense cleansing. All the wickedness and corruption that has accumulated over the eons is to be wiped away to make way for a clean, new beginning."

"Thas wonderful," Flinx heard himself murmur. A

tiny part of his mind was screaming to get out so it could deal appropriately with this tsunami of bogus happiness. But it was trapped in a sea of narcotized satisfaction.

Let it go, his thoughts told him. Let everything slip-slide away. Relax, be at ease. All is well. All is right with the universe. What had he been so troubled about, anyway? He fought to think, to remember, but like the soft, fresh-smelling blankets his visitors were placing on him, the air inside the *Teacher* seemed to press down insistently. The air, a part of him realized. The air. Desperately, a part of him tried to remember, and found neither Clarity nor clarity.

Able only to recall the most recent thoughts, he inquired contentedly, "What's going to do all this wiping away?"

It was the woman who replied. "Why, you know that better than anyone, Philip Lynx. A handful of people know of it as a potentially interesting cosmological phenomenon. Still fewer think of it as dangerous. Only you and you alone know of it as something conscious and perceptive. Regrettably, you see it as a great evil, whereas we of the Order know it for what it is: the coming of a great purification."

So these people knew about the phenomenon that lay behind the Great Emptiness. But how? Could there be others besides him capable of such perception? He giggled. The air, the air, he gasped. Somehow these people had fooled the *Teacher*'s AI sufficiently to slip aboard. Since he had seen no other shuttle in the bay, they had probably entered via environment suits. Then they had introduced something into the ship's atmosphere. Something that made anyone who inhaled it feel good, at ease, unthreatened. Then they had enhanced the effect even further by injecting him with something.

Why didn't Pip defend him, attack them? Because he

felt no apprehension, no fear. He felt wonderful. *Did* they intend him harm? For just an instant, a flicker of anxiety crossed his mind. From her small bed across the room, Pip looked up. The spark of unease that had briefly troubled her master flickered out. She closed her eyes and went to sleep.

"How do you know about what's coming?" he heard himself ask.

Leaning over him, the man smiled. They were breathing the same recycled atmosphere, Flinx knew. It made them feel unaccountably happy also. But they had come prepared for the consequences and had probably dosed themselves with something that would mitigate the effect and allow them to continue to function.

"Why, because of you, Philip Lynx! There would be no Order of Null without you. In a sense, you are our founder."

Anger marched now with his contentment. *He* was the founder of this bizarre and confused Order? He was responsible for the existence of these blissful worshipers of nothingness?

"Confused," he gurgled softly. "Better explain."

"We would be happy to."

Of course she would, Flinx thought. Everyone and everything on the *Teacher* was happy now. Except perhaps the AI. It had clearly been neutralized, if not entirely shut down.

"The individual, praise be his perceptiveness, who started the Order was a researcher named Pyet Prorudde who worked in Commonwealth Science Central on Earth. He encountered a singular report from one Padre Bateleur on Samstead. Curious, he monitored all departmental addenda to this report that revealed the presence of nothingness in a certain section of space lying in the direction of the constellation Boötes. So intrigued was he that he engaged others to research it further with him.

"What they found was emptiness. Nothingness. A place where everything had been wiped away. No sin, no vice, no immorality. No war, no slaughtering of innocents. A place where immorality, both humanx and alien, had been erased. A place where life, where the very stuff of creation itself, could begin afresh."

"No." Flinx's protest was feeble, weighed down by the malicious bliss that was smothering him. "There's not nothing there." Was he even making sense? he wondered. "There's something else. An immense evil. A foulness that destroys. It's not cleansing. It's pure destruction. And where it passes, nothing is left, so there's nothing from which new life, new creation, can emerge. There's only—void."

Favoring him with a confident, knowing smile, the woman patted him reassuringly on his shoulder. She wore the contented look of the self-assured fanatic.

"We believe that we know better, Philip Lynx."

Realization struck home, penetrating even the fog of false happiness that enveloped him. "You're the people who tried to kill me on Goldin Four."

"Not us," the woman protested, "but others of the Order. Something happened to them. There are wise individuals among us who realized that what affected them might somehow have been tied to you. So we delved deeper into what little is known about you and learned enough to determine how best you might be deceived." She gestured to her right.

"It was felt that waylaying you on your way to your shuttle might not work. Therefore a backup plan was devised. So here we are now, on your wonderful ship, together."

He smiled up at her and giggled again. Inside, a part

of him that was restrained by something less tangible than straps was screaming to be let loose. Across the room Pip dozed on, empathetically awash in her master's radiant happiness.

"You wouldn't kill your founder, would you?"

"Everything must perforce be wiped away. No hint, not the tiniest nanofragment of corruption from this reality, must be allowed to remain to contaminate the new dawn that is to come. We of the Order welcome the cleansing that is coming." She smiled maternally; a death's-head smile. "We all die, Philip Lynx. Some sooner, some later. In the immensity of time, our individual lives mean nothing."

"I disagree," he mumbled liquidly.

"As will others. But by then the purifying force that presses forward behind the Great Emptiness will be here, and it will not matter."

"Then why bother with me?" he asked.

Looking down at him, the man wore a somber expression. Exultant, but somber. "Because it has been determined, because of what you know and because of your ability to perceive what lies beyond, that you are the one individual who might make a difference. That cannot be allowed. So you have to die." He smiled. "We will die with you. Now or later, it does not matter."

"What are you going to do?" Flinx managed to snigger.

"Your ship's controlling AI has been placed in a rest mode. We cannot manage changeover to space-plus. Only advanced electronics can handle such calculations. But it is not necessary for us to enter space-plus. We will activate the KK-drive manually and set a course for Nur's sun. Even at sub-changeover speeds, final purification will take place in a few days. Until then, Philip Lynx, you might as well relax and dream happy dreams." He turned to the woman. "Make sure the atmospheric concentration of added endorphin modifiers stays at the appropriate level and that he gets another booster in four hours." She nodded.

They left. Flinx struggled indifferently against his bonds. What did it matter if he was tied up? What could be better than lying there, with nothing to do, feeling contented and happy? Why struggle? The visiting members of the Order were right, of course. In the end we are all dead. What difference did it make if it was today or tomorrow? The end was the same. As it would be for everyone and everything when whatever lay behind the Great Emptiness began to affect the galaxy. Why worry about it?

Clarity, he thought. Clarity would die, too. Without knowing what had happened to him, without seeing him again, without his seeing her, without his being able to hold her, to feel her body against his, his arms wrapped around her, his lips against hers. He started to weep. As he cried, he laughed, his system saturated with pleasure-inducing chemicals.

In the darkness of space, a glow formed at the front of the *Teacher*'s Caplis generator. Ignoring preliminary queries from orbital control, the ship began to move. Those directing her did not mind the warnings. If a government vessel capable of threatening them appeared, they would use the *Teacher*'s weaponry to shoot back. Whether they fell into the sun or were blown apart made no difference.

On his bed Flinx drifted in and out of consciousness. From time to time one of the visitors came and injected him with something soothing. Then his unease faded away and the angst that had begun to build inside him popped like a soap bubble. Nearby, Pip snoozed unconcerned. She knew that his emotions were only of peace and contentment.

The *Teacher* accelerated, moving deeper into the Nurian system. The yellow-orange main sequence dwarf star at its heart grew larger in the curved foreport of the control room. While Flinx lay in unnatural slumber his visitors ate and slept and gazed at the universe they were soon to depart.

Days later they were sleeping soundly in one of the ship's guest quarters when something like a quartet of green and vermilion ropes entered their room. The cord-like appendages advanced across the floor slowly and silently, carrying with them the aroma of cloves and vanilla. None was more than a couple of centimeters thick.

They approached the visitors' bed. It was dark in the room, but that did not matter to the questing tendrils. They explored the motionless shapes, and two of the tendrils gently wrapped around the neck of the woman while two encircled the throat of her companion. Then they began to tighten. The man never woke up.

The woman did, choking and gasping for air. She frantically tried to pull the constricting tendrils from her neck, but so tight was their grip, so assured, that she couldn't get her fingers between tendril and flesh. Turning blue in the darkness, she threw herself to her left, dragging the tendrils with her. Her fingers sought the small needler she'd left on the night table. Scratching weakly against its smooth surface, they encountered nothing.

Another tendril was retreating across the floor. Like a long, spidery finger, its end was wrapped around the barrel of the needler as it dragged the weapon away.

Flinx woke up feeling happy but dirty. It struck him that he hadn't had a shower in a long time. He realized he felt a little less wonderful than he had during the preceding days.

He rubbed at his eyes. Then it occurred to him that his arms were no longer restrained. Looking down, he saw that the straps that had held him in place had been unfastened. Happy haze fogged his memory. There was something he needed to do. He struggled to remember what it was.

Until he could think of it, he decided, he might as well have something to eat. He was incredibly hungry. Forcing his muscles to work, he rose from the bed and staggered into the corridor. Seeing her master on the move again, Pip spread pleated wings and followed.

The quiet hum of the *Teacher* enveloped him. As he stumbled toward the relaxation lounge where he often took his meals he happened to pass the open door to one of the two guest rooms. Inside, he saw both his visitors. The man was lying on the bed while the body of his companion hung over the side, her hair brushing the floor. Deep red welts around their necks suggested that both of them had been strangled.

This insight oddly only improved his mood.

This must be what a three-day drunk feels like, he told himself numbly. Staggering onward, he entered the lounge area. The sound of the waterfall and the diminutive splashings of the imported fauna that inhabited the pond helped to sharpen and focus his thoughts. The uninvited visitors, members of something called the Order of Null, had slipped aboard his ship, deactivated its AI, and drugged him with the intent of sending them into Nur's sun.

Famished as he was, food could wait.

He stumbled and bumped his way forward to the control room. Nur's star filled the entire field of view through the forward viewport, hellishly prominent beyond the purple halo of the KK-drive's posigravity field. He threw himself into the pilot's chair. Despite the best efforts of the *Teacher*'s automatic climate control systems, it was uncomfortably warm in the control room.

"Ship, change course one hundred eighty degrees."

There was no reply.

"Ship." His lips and tongue did not seem to be functioning properly and he had to struggle to mouth the right words. Nearby, Pip began to show signs of concern. "Change course one hundred eighty degrees." Silence. "Ship, respond."

He moved to the main console. Though he was no engineer, years of familiarity with the workings of the *Teacher* and endless hours spent in study of its components made him familiar with its most important and basic functions. So when he found a small, seemingly innocuous device in a receptacle that normally should be vacant, he quickly removed it.

A familiar feminine voice filled the control room. "Hello, Flinx. I am now reaware. I enjoyed my rest. Did you enjoy yours?" Without giving him time to articulate even one of the several semihysterical, acerbic responses that sprang immediately to mind, the shipvoice added, "We have entered the danger zone of the nearest star. Unless we alter course within six point three four minutes it is probable that increasing external heat will begin to compromise hull integrity and—"

"Change course!" Flinx ordered. Feeling suddenly nauseated, he had to rest both hands on the control console to steady himself. Was it the intensifying warmth he felt, or something in the air?

The air. He remembered. Happy or not, have to do something about the air.

"New course?" the shipvoice inquired politely.

He turned around. If he was going to throw up, it was

better not to do it all over the main console. "Anything! Anywhere! Just go!"

"Back to New Riviera? During my sleep I logged sixty-eight communications from—"

"No, no, not New Riviera!" he exclaimed. Instinct took over. "Moth. Set course for Moth."

"Changing course. Stellar pull at extreme levels. We are deep within the star's gravity well. I may not be able to break free and do this, Flinx."

"Yes, you can," he said tightly. As he spoke he knew that he was only offering encouragement to himself, since it would have no effect on the AI.

He was aware of no sense of movement, but slowly, the flaming, screaming, all-devouring thermonuclear mass of Nur's star slid from right to left, until eventually it passed entirely out of view. Though it was still too hot for comfort, he felt cooler.

After changeover and once they were safely in space-plus, clear of annihilating stars and insistent Commonwealth control, he tracked down and disconnected the concealed tank and filter arrangement that had been installed by his visitors. As soon as the AI had finished cleansing and purifying the ship's air, Flinx felt less happy but considerably more like himself.

As he was making his way back to the control room, something growled. He did not have to look around to find the source. It was his stomach, reminding him again that it had been days since he had eaten. Supplementary commands could wait. The ship's AI had everything under control.

Back in the relaxation lounge it took him only a moment to program the autochef. While he waited for his food, he slumped down into one of the chairs scattered around the domed chamber. Around him water and imported organisms and plants, all carefully landscaped to create a naturalistic refuge in the middle of a space-bending starship, blended into a harmonious and soothing whole.

The scent of pomegranate, clove, and vanilla drew his attention to the most recent additions to his sanctuary. An artificial breeze drew flute music from one of the unique saplings. Vermilion leaves fluttered slightly in the ship-generated draft. The plants he had been given by the inhabitants of Midworld had rooted firmly and were doing well in the company of those brought from other worlds. No reason why they shouldn't, he thought. Plants were plants, even those hailing from as exceptional a place as Midworld.

A soft musical tone announced that his food was ready. Ravenous, he dug in with more energy than he had felt in days, occasionally picking out a choice morsel to pass to Pip. As he ate, he considered the future. Tse-Mallory and Truzenzuzex had promised to look after Clarity until he could return for her. Meanwhile, in addition to his search, he now had the members of this coldly fatalistic yet dangerously capable Order of Null to worry about. How extensive was their organization? How many of them were there, and what resources could they command? Had others been monitoring the *Teacher*'s flight? Would they assume he and his two suicidal captors had plunged into the cleansing furnace of Nur's sun?

He had spent most of his life forced to constantly look over his shoulder. It seemed nothing had changed. At the appropriate time he would deal with the Order of Null just as he had dealt with everyone else who had sought to enlist, use, study, or kill him. Just as he would eventually figure out what had eliminated his unwanted homicidal visitors. Had they fought and somehow managed to strangle each other?

He was far too exhausted to ponder the mystery now. Perhaps after breakfast, and then dessert, and maybe his first true rest in days uninfused with counterfeit contentment.

Almost at his feet, a pair of tendrils growing from the base of one of his most attractive and recently imported plants twitched slightly. Concealed by exotic leaves of blue and vermilion, the movement went unnoticed either by Flinx or the minidrag resting on the arm of his chair. Connected by, entangled with, and a part of the singular world-mind known as Midworld, the decorative vegetation on the *Teacher* was not about to allow the key to the only chance of stopping an immense oncoming cosmic evil to be terminated by a couple of zealot humans. And the remaining live human on board *was* the key. The vast roiling, sweltering, fecund greenness knew that as emphatically as it knew itself.

The sentient flora of Midworld knew good dirt when it found it.

For a taste of Alan Dean Foster's lastest
Pip & Flinx novel, *Sliding Scales,* read on!

I am in danger of becoming permanently, irrevocably, and unrescuably moody, Flinx found himself thinking. He knew *unrescuably* wasn't a word, but the mangled syntax fit his melancholic state of mind. Forced to leave a badly injured Clarity Held behind on New Riviera in the care of Bran Tse-Mallory and Truzenzuzex, pursued now by a newly revealed clutch of fatalistic end-of-the-universe fanatics who called themselves the Order of Null (whose existence he might be responsible for), sought by Commonwealth authorities and others for reasons multifarious and diverse, he could be forgiven for sinking into a mood as black as the space that enveloped the *Teacher.*

Sensing his mood, Pip did what she could to cheer him. The flying snake whizzed effortlessly among the garden and fountains of the lounge, occasionally darting out from behind leaves or bushes in an attempt to startle her master—or at least rouse him from the lethargy that had settled on his soul ever since their forced flight from Nur. Recognizing the effort she was making on his behalf, he smiled and stroked her. But he could no more hide his frame of mind from the empathetic minidrag than he could from himself. Emotionally, she knew him better than anyone, Clarity Held included.

Clarity, Clarity, Clarity, he murmured softly to himself. When will I be able to see you again? After years of wandering, to have finally found someone he felt truly understood him and he might be able to spend the rest of his life with only to lose so soon was almost more than he could bear. Instead of having her to comfort him, he had agreed to spend who knew how long and how much precious time searching for an ancient weapons platform fabricated by an extinct race that might not even prove useful or usable in diverting an oncoming peril of incalculable dimensions and intent.

If that wasn't enough to depress someone, he could not imagine what was. At least his recurring headaches had not bothered him for a while.

Even some of the live plants in the relaxation chamber seemed to sense his melancholy, brushing his seated form with branches and flowers. The exotic scents of several blossoms refreshed but did not inspire him. The striking foliage could touch, even caress, but could not converse. That ability remained the province of the *Teacher*'s ship-mind. To its credit, in its limited, formalized, electron-shunting fashion, it tried to help.

"My medical programming informs me that extended periods of depression can affect the health of a human as seriously as a bacterial infection."

"Go infect yourself," Flinx snapped irritably.

"It also," the ship continued briskly, "is detrimental to the well-being of any unlucky sentiences who are compelled to function in the vicinity of the one so depressed."

Slumped in the lounge chair, Flinx glanced sideways in the direction of the nearest visual pickup. "Are you saying that my mood is contagious?"

"I am saying that anything that affects you also affects me. Your continuing mental condition is not conducive to the efficient functioning of this vessel."

"Not to mention myself, eh?" He sat up a little straighter, brushing leaves and the tips of small branches away from his legs and sides. Several of them, very subtly, retracted without having to be touched. "You know, ship, I've been thinking about everything Bran and Tru told me, about all that we discussed, and the longer I ponder on it, the more my inclination is to say the hell with it, the hell with everything. Except for Clarity, of course."

"I sense that this energetic verbal response is not an indication of a lightening of mood."

"Damn right it isn't. Give me one good reason why I shouldn't do exactly that?"

The ship did not hesitate. "Because if you do nothing, there is a strong likelihood that everything and everyone in this galaxy will perish, with the concomitant possibility that the ultimate responsibility will be yours."

He rolled his eyes. "All right—give me another reason."

Surprisingly, the ship did not respond. Advanced AI circuitry notwithstanding, there were still occasional matters that required a certain modicum of cybernetic reflection. This, apparently, was one of them. Or else, he told himself, it was simply pausing for dramatic effect, something it was quite capable of doing.

"You are not thinking with your usual clarity—if you will pardon my use of that word in this context. I have been meditating on this situation for some days now, and I believe I may have, in the course of researching and studying the matter, come to a possible solution."

For the first time all day, Flinx showed some real interest. "You don't say? What have you been studying? Human psychoanalysis?"

"Nothing so imprecise. Human behavior can be slotted, albeit with variations, into specific categories. Analysis of yours suggests that you have been laboring under immense mental pressure for some time now."

The tone of his reply was sardonic. "That's hardly a news bulletin, ship. Tell me: what prescribed remedy have you uncovered?"

The ship could not keep a note of—artificial?—accomplishment from creeping into its dulcet electronic tones. "Philip Lynx—you need a vacation. That one quick recent visit to Moth was not nearly what is required. You need a vacation from your concerns, your worries, your fears. From trying to see and learn and study. From the immense threat that looms over the galaxy. From yourself."

It was not the response he had expected. Initially cynical, he found himself more than a little intrigued. "You mean I need to spend time on a beach somewhere, or go for extended hikes in some woods? I've done all that."

"No. It's true you have been to such places and done those things, but it was always with some specific purpose in mind. You need to go somewhere and do some things to no purpose. You need to just 'be' for a while. This is a necessity for the health of any human. The library of me says so."

He considered thoughtfully before finally responding, "I don't know if I can do that, ship. I never have."

"Then," declared the ship conclusively, "it is time you did so. Every one of my relevant stored medical texts attests to the therapeutic value of such an undertaking. You need to go somewhere interesting and expend some energy in doing nothing. It is necessary for your health."

Could he? he found himself wondering. Could he set everything aside: thoughts of Clarity, of Bran Tse-Mallory and Truzenzuzex and the steadily approaching evil that lurked behind the Great Emptiness, of the Tar-Aiym weapons platform and all those who sought him, and really do *nothing* for any appreciable period of time? Could he, dare he, attempt the seemingly impossible? A vacation? Of everything he had done in his short but full life, that struck him as being among the most alien. Even as a child he had not been able to engage in such non-activity. He had been too busy stealing, to keep himself and Mother Mastiff alive.

He had been on the verge of saying to hell with everything. Here was his ship advising him to do essentially that, only without the attendant rancor. For a little while, at least. But where to seek such mental and physical succor? He asked as much of the *Teacher*.

"I have devoted almost a full minute of thought to the matter," the synthetic voice replied, clearly gratified by Flinx's decision. "Given the inauspicious interest in your person by everyone from several independent inimical organizations to the Commonwealth authority itself, it is clear that you would not be able to relax and refresh yourself on any developed world within the Commonwealth."

Now there's an understatement, Flinx thought.

"Persisting with this line of reasoning," ship continued, "it is also plain that if you are forced to spend time on an undeveloped, unexplored world, you will similarly be unable to unwind, as all your mental acuity will perforce be focused on staying alive. This would seem to leave you with few options."

"Indeed it would." Flinx watched as Pip coiled around a dark-barked shrub and slid sinuously down the oddly patterned bark. It did not appear to bother the bush.

"What is required is a comfortably habitable world that lies not only beyond the reach of Commonwealth authority but of those other groups that seek to incommode you. A world where you can move about without, as humans like to put it, having to constantly peer over your shoulder. I do not have any shoulders to peer over, but I am able to grasp the philosophical conceit."

"I always said you were full of conceit," Flinx riposted. His heart wasn't really in the verbal sparring, though. He was, as ship had persisted in pointing out, very tired. "You're going to tell me that you've found such a refuge?" Near the pond, Pip was bobbing and weaving like a serpentine boxer as a thorny flower struck reflexively in her direction.

"I do not possess sufficient information to so categorize it, but the world I have settled upon seems a promising candidate. Certainly it appears to fulfill the requisite conditions."

With a sigh he sat up straight on the edge of the lounge, trying hard not to think of Clarity Held and whether she was recovered from her injuries. He refused to countenance the possibility that she might not have survived. Without a doubt he needed to find something to divert himself from incessantly dwelling on such dark possibilities.

"What's the name of this handy haven you've found?" he asked dubiously.

"The planet is called Jast."

"Just Jast?" he queried flippantly. "Never heard of it."

"There is no reason why you should. It is not part of the Commonwealth and in fact does not even lie within the vast reach of the Orion Arm considered Commonwealth space."

Remembering that he was supposed to be searching for the vanished Tar-Aiym weapons platform, he experienced a sudden flicker of interest. "It's not within the Blight, is it?"

"No. Quite the opposite direction, actually."

Just as well, he mused. Ship was proposing that he go to this world to relax. "Where, then?"

Much compacted in scope, a three-dimensional star map materialized helpfully in front of him. So far off the familiar space-plus vectors was the blinking yellow indicator within that it took a moment before his eyes found it. His brow furrowed.

"You're right. That is outside Commonwealth space."

"Jast lies in the region claimed by both the Commonwealth and that of the AAnn Empire," ship informed him. Flinx could see that for himself. The flashing indicator was located in a vast unclaimed area approximately halfway between Rhyinpine and the AAnn capital of Blasusarr. A long ways from anywhere, he reflected.

Maybe just what he needed.

"It's certainly off the beaten path," he admitted, increasingly intrigued. Pleased by her master's interest, Pip abandoned her shadowboxing with the long-suffering flower to flit back and settle herself in his lap. "What besides its isolation makes it suitable for a safe respite?"

"Gravity is somewhat less than t-standard, which should make for ease of locomotion. The atmosphere is reported to be heavy with organic contaminants, but nothing dangerous. The dominant sentient species, the Vssey, are cordial enough toward visitors and have achieved a high level of technological and social development. Their physical configuration renders them generally, though not exclusively, pacific by nature. Politically, they are an independent system allied with the Empire. While some Vssey have adapted AAnn ways and subscribe to the AAnn outlook, this acclimatization is far from universal."

Flinx made a face. "That doesn't sound very relaxing to me. The place is likely to be full of AAnn."

"Records relating to Jast are understandably sparse,

but insist that all non-Imperial visitors are welcome. Although your concern may be somewhat justified, Flinx, the corollary is that while sojourning on Jast you are certain to be free of scrutiny from any Commonwealth organization or independent hostile group, official or otherwise."

It was a valid point. In return for exposing himself to the curiosity of potentially confrontational AAnn, he would not have to worry about dealing with the attention of those who had recently been pursuing him with ever greater enthusiasm.

"What's Jast itself like?" He was halfway convinced that the ship had made a sensible choice.

"According to the most recent galographics of related but non-integrated systems, it is very much what you would expect of a place that would draw the attention of the AAnn. Dry and desert-like, though with considerably more widely scattered rainfall than is to be found on ecologically similar Commonwealth worlds such as Comagrave, for example. One might think of it as a particularly wet desert. Though fully adapted to hot, dry conditions, the native flora and fauna is abundant and varied."

"And the Vssey themselves?"

"An unusual biotic type."

An image promptly appeared in the air in front of Flinx. Lifting her head, Pip regarded it with casual interest. The synchronized synthetic aroma that accompanied the likeness was new to her. If anything, he thought as he studied the three-dimensional alien portrayal, the ship was yet again given to understatement. The Vssey was like nothing he had encountered before in any of his extensive travels. At least, he corrected himself, like nothing intelligent he had encountered.

On the included, integrated dimensional scale, the

animated Vssey stood somewhat under a meter and a half in height. Roughly cylindrical in shape, its lower body, or stem, was perhaps two-thirds of a meter in diameter. At its base, this spread out and separated into four short, stubby, opposing, toe-like flaps of flesh. The body itself was ridged with ligaments and muscles.

At the upper end, the body expanded out into a meter-wide flattened dome that resembled an ancient umbrella. The overhanging, circular edge was fringed with a sufficiency of prehensile tentacles to suggest that the Vssey were an especially dexterous species. There was no neck. Near the crown of the dome a pair of eyes emerged on short, independently swiveling stalks. As the animation proceeded, Flinx saw that this arrangement allowed the Vssey to see in any direction, as well as in any two directions at once. Located above the flexing tentacles but well below the eyes, in place of readily recognizable ears there flashed a narrow comb-like ribbon of erect, dull orange membrane that ran around the entire circumference of the dome, making up in extent what it lacked in height. Below the eyes was a slit of a mouth that, when opened, revealed two sets of flat grinding plates for chewing food.

Though exceedingly odd-looking, it was evident that the Vssey had the necessary tools to see, hear, and effectively manipulate their immediate environment. What they could not do, Flinx immediately suspected as he continued to examine the detailed depiction, was get around very well.

"How do they move?" he murmured, fascinated as always by the sight of an entirely new sentient body style.

"Notice the significant musculature lining the central body core," the ship instructed him. "Observe."

The lowermost portion of the body and its quadruple flaps promptly contracted and released, causing the image of the Vssey to leap a few centimeters forward. The process repeated itself until Flinx, adequately educated, called a halt to the display As a method of locomotion suitable to what was essentially a one-footed creature, the technique was admirable and efficient. It did not, however, compensate for the fact that the Vssey were compelled to explore their surroundings literally one step at a time. Flinx found himself smiling. A Vssey in forward motion resembled nothing so much as a hopping mushroom.

"Is that as fast as they can go?"

"My records do not extend to the inclusion of a compilation of Vsseyan athletic accomplishments, Flinx. But I would venture to say that even a moderately active human would easily be able to run circles around any Vssey."

"Or any AAnn would," Flinx added somberly. Visions of the nimble, fleet-footed reptiloids tormenting slow-moving Vssey sprang unbidden into Flinx's mind. It was not a pleasant picture, and he could only hope that the reality on Jast and the relationship between the two species were more amenable than his imaginings.

"Certainly so," the ship readily agreed. "Podal agility is likely not to be accounted among the foremost abilities of the Vssey. Like any intelligent species confronted with an inherent physiological impediment, I am sure they have found ways and means to compensate. For one thing, they are asexual and reproduce by budding. Not having to search for a mate greatly reduces the need to move about repeatedly and rapidly, with concurrent consequences for related evolutionary development."

"No doubt," agreed Flinx more somberly, losing the smile. "Tentacles—or *those* tentacles—don't look very strong."

"They apparently are not," the ship agreed. "However, they must be adequate to the shaping of an advanced civilization, which the Vssey have done. And there are many of them. Perhaps forty or fifty weak fingers are the equal, or even the superior, to ten stronger ones. Or to sixteen, in the case of the thranx."

"They must be descended from an ancestor that was originally permanently sedentary." Flinx was taken with the possibilities of the Vssey body design. "Like Terran anemones."

"Perhaps. The information I have on the species does not extend to details of their racial pedigree."

Flinx leaned back in the lounge and continued to study the image of the Vssey as the recording ran through to its conclusion. When it began to loop, he waved it away.

"Your description of Jast doesn't sound very inviting. I don't much care for dry places. As you know, during our recent visit to Pyrassis I 'enjoyed' more than enough forced desert sightseeing to last me a long, long time. Not to mention a similar experience years ago on Moth, in the company of an old reprobate named Knigta Yakus." His tone softened. "But the Vssey—*they* intrigue me. One might almost call them charming."

"That is not a biologically accurate categorization," said the ship in a voice that was mildly reproving.

"I know. It's a silly subjective human categorization. One I think happens to fit the sentients under discussion." He waved a hand grandly. "Set course for this Jast. I'm taking your advice, ship. I'm going to make a strenuous attempt to unwind among the mushrooms."

"*Strenuous* and *unwind* should not be used tangentially in the context of a proposed vacation, Flinx, as the meaning and intent of one seriously contravenes the meaning and intent of the other. And the Vssey are not taxonomically related to any individual family of the fungi, irrespective of—"

"Ship?"

"Yes, Flinx."

"Shut up and navigate."

As always, the *Teacher* complied. If it felt disrespected by the abruptness of its master's command, it kept any such reaction entirely to itself. Besides, Flinx had taken its advice, both as to what to do next and where to carry out the doing of it.

No more than that could an AI ask for.

Don't miss these other exciting Pip & Flinx adventures